BEYOND
Poetry

Paperback ISBN: 978-1-7362248-1-6

COVER DESIGN: Robin Johnson
INTERIOR: Ian Koviak & Alan Dino Hebel
PHOTOGRAPHY: C L Tyson Photography, LLC
EDITOR: Katie Zdybel

BEYOND
Poetry

NATHAN JARELLE

Washington, D.C.

Believers

The world appears different to believers.
Allow your dreams to ignite.
Drown away your sorrows.
Replace your worries
with determined wishes.
Hold your imagination upright.
Discover opportunity over opposition.
Through belief,
we can change the trajectory of our lives
and others around us.
Believe.

NATHAN JARELLE

Author's Preface

Dear Reader,

Walk with me on this journey entitled *Beyond Poetry*, a tale of urban literature which transpires in Brooke's Rowe, an imagined section of South Philadelphia in late 1995. Welcome to a world of nostalgic memories: cassette tapes, fly apparel, around-the-way discourse, and surviving the wild wave of high school. We watched R-rated flicks unaccompanied by an adult but still had to be in before dark. We had the hott sneakers and music. We debated who was the greatest betwee Biggie Smalls and 2pac and took it personally. We had yet unearth social media platforms like Facebook, Instagr TikTok, Twitter, etc. We barely had cell phones, at didn't. You learned shit through word of mouth from s folks hanging throughout the neighborhood. We r backseat of your mother's Chevy or yo   ly's unbuckled and unafraid. Th holes from cigarette burns. You had a bicycle, and everybody around your hometown knew you by that bicycle. I had one suit for special events and one pair of dress shoes that my mother made me keep boxed when not in use.

As I sit here and reminisce about 1995, for me, I can smell my mother's fried chicken from the doorstep on my way home from school. I can see my father out in front of the house washing his car during the summer and raising hell about kids back in those days. I can hear my brother's boombox blaring from his bedroom window. I can still hear artists such as A Tribe Called Quest, Nas, Queen Latifah, De La Soul, Das Efx, and other rap artists of that time. We've come a long way since then, you and me. Don't you remember?

Beyond Poetry, though a work of urban fiction and suspense, for me, is a personal journey. Albeit the characters are products of my imagination, for nearly three decades, I found myself trapped in yesteryear, hoping to escape the sights and sounds of a world that has since left. I must face the reality that 1995 is gone. There will never be another year ke it. I find it difficult to move on when the holidays come nd and I don't hear my brother's stereo or see my father le washing his Lincoln. My dearest friends are buried, the ground while others are buried backward in the ny life's story. It's a cutting reality of how quickly rns.

rteen years old when I discovered writing. But the world writing would gift me. en stroke could illustrate

Believers

The world appears different to believers.
Allow your dreams to ignite.
Drown away your sorrows.
Replace your worries
with determined wishes.
Hold your imagination upright.
Discover opportunity over opposition.
Through belief,
we can change the trajectory of our lives
and others around us.
Believe.

NATHAN JARELLE

a world inside an already existing world. Throughout the years, I became immersed in the craft of writing. I wrote in journals that eventually became my friends, never realizing what was taking place.

Like many young black men in the city, I believed my destiny was to play in some kind of sport like the NFL or NBA. I thought I had to be a rapper or a musician. I thought I needed to perform comedy on stage like Martin Lawrence or star in black television sitcom shows like *A Different World*, *Living Single*, or *Fresh Prince of Bel-Air*. I thought it was the only way out of the city. I believed it was the only road to true success. I'm here to tell you that is not true! You're perfect without a ball in your hand or some damn microphone in your face. You're beautiful just the way you are, sweetheart. Your story is your gift. Your talent is you. You do not need a basketball to make a difference in your community. You are *already* the difference. It was through writing that I defeated these misconceptions of what it meant to be accepted by first accepting myself.

I do not envy the life of Leonard Gerard Robinson Jr., (a.k.a. "Junior"), the story's main protagonist, a poetic scholar from Brooke's Rowe. Throughout the book, we see Junior struggle to balance his turbulent upbringing with ambitions to liberate himself from the systemic traps placed within his path. I didn't have a lot of the same traps as Junior, but I incurred some which qualify me to tell the story of *Beyond Poetry*. To many, it's a book. For me, I'm finally free and can move on.

In this novel, I weaponize writing to illustrate to the world that anything is possible.

So, why Philadelphia? The answer is simple. I wanted to tell a story where the characters felt comfortable and not me as the author. I'm not from Philly, but to be honest, there's a *Beyond Poetry* in every city across the world. Somewhere, there's a Junior in us all. My job is to convince you, the reader, to see the world through Junior's eyes, and to persuade you of the reality of Brooke's Rowe, where political hope is scarce and the opportunity for black equity is non-existent. I drew inspiration to write this novel from some of my own childhood experiences. However, this sort of nostalgic memoir, though relatable, is nothing more than a fictional depiction.

At the time of writing, it is March 2021 and the world is still recovering from the deadly COVID-19. Ahead of us looms a long road to recovery. Millions of Americans are hungry and out of work. Meanwhile, across the table, there's an empty chair at dinner in some of our households due to Coronavirus. As America's forty-sixth President, Joe Biden, and Vice President, Kamala Harris, scramble to stitch the gash left behind by past leadership, for once in the past four years, there appears to be hope in our country's future.

To you and yours, God bless your health and family, and thank you for reading *Beyond Poetry*.

Prologue

LAST SUMMER

Somewhere along Joseph Boulevard on a crammed North Philly residential street in August of 1994, a group of unsupervised and underaged children fired bottle rockets into the sky as the city's sun dipped westward. As whistling projectiles heaved into the air, leaving smoke trails in its path, little girls played Double Dutch near a spent fire hydrant. Looming in the background was the nightfall, every child's worst nightmare, a dark and starry sky followed by the flicker of dingy streetlamps posted at every block. Nighttime in the Crawford Section of North Philadelphia was an underworld of crime-ridden turf wars over drugs and sub-section territories. Junkies carried knives, ready to puncture their cohorts and rob them as they napped in shady alleyways. Meanwhile, addicts leaned on overturned crates, fried on dope. Up the

1

street, dirty white boys tied bootstrings around their fore-
arms, pumping infected needles into their veins. Across the
way, hordes of rotting debris junked the roadway alongside a
row of tagged buildings, jersey walls, and dilapidated houses.
School "Drug-Free Zones" became drug zones at night for
criminals to deal drugs, supplying the decrepit subsection
with filthy intention.

Beat cops, responsible for upholding the law, were just
as terrified as the faithful Samaritans that lived there. In
Crawford, people were robbed for their Air Jordan sneakers,
Starter brand jackets, jewelry, and whatever else could afford
dope. Happened all the time. Stone-cold addicts burglarized
homes on the block, pawning whatever they could carry for
money to buy drugs. Worse, the neighborhood had seen an
uptick in the number of homicides over the past three years,
prompting residents to take precautions.

Junior was always in before streetlight. Lawrence never
was. Together, they'd make it home just in time before their
daddy would flail a leather strap at the boys for being late.
Like most North Philly boys, Junior and Lawrence had to
be within earshot for "the call". On any given late evening
before the sky turned jet black, dozens of parents along
Joseph Boulevard stood on their stoops to yell out their
child's name. If you weren't in earshot of hearing your name,
then you better be within eyesight. Rulebreakers were not
permitted to play the following day.

Some kids, like Junior, thirteen, and Lawrence, ten,
had more to fear than staying indoors. In August of '94,

Crawford-North Philly was a whirlwind of raging violence after dark. Naked men on PCP roamed the streets, punching out car windows. Junkies with rotting teeth bummed for change, chasing bus riders as they waited for their ride. Prostitutes worked the avenues, sucking dick in exchange for a hit of crack. Cops assigned to the Crawford beat treated blacks with disregard, confident they could get away with it. The two brothers had no intention of being swept into the bowels of North Philly's nightlife or of tasting the strap of their daddy's leather belt.

Junior threw Lawrence onto the back of his bicycle and raced down Joseph Boulevard. Pedaling like mad, he nearly slammed into a car pulling out in front of him. Along the way, an ice cream truck turned on its siren, signaling to the boys to stop.

"Junior, look!" Lawrence pointed. "An ice cream truck."

"Man, fuck that truck!" Junior yelled back to his baby brother, summer winds whipping in their faces.

By the time Junior turned the corner, Senior, the boys' father, was headed down the walkway to his truck. With Lawrence hanging on for dear life, Junior popped the curb and hurried down the sidewalk toward his daddy's large figure. Noticing the boys, Senior stood on the sidewalk with his veiny arms folded, watching with disappointment as the boys rolled in fast. The night before, Lawrence had come home late and paid for it with his backside. He'd hollered for Jesus as Senior's belt tattooed the skin on the back of his bony legs.

Senior was a huge man, massive. He scowled at the boys

from the bottom of Joseph Boulevard, focusing his attention on Junior as his son jammed on the brakes to avoid crashing into him. Lucky for Junior, the handlebars of his bicycle just missed his father's crotch. Senior looked down at his family jewels and slowly back up at Junior.

"S-Sorry, Daddy," stuttered Junior with Lawrence ducking behind him.

Grunting, Senior glared at Junior. "If you'd a hit those," he threatened. "I would've used yours to make a set of dice!"

Senior then eyeballed the boys, interrogating them both before granting them a pass. At one point, Lawrence nudged Junior from behind and nodded at Senior's belt. Thankfully, it didn't move. The boys were safe – at least for that night.

As both boys entered the house, accompanied by Senior, Junior smelled pot roast pinching at his nostrils from the slow-cooker in the kitchen. A liner of ugly, World War II-era wall-paper decorated the living room walls. Near the fire chimney, was an old box TV set that had blown out the previous summer. On top of that TV was a working TV with its antenna extended toward the ceiling. On the wall next to the family's china cabinet was a giant wooden fork and spoon set once used by Goliath before being slain by David. Near the staircase was a family portrait of the Robinsons taken in '84 shortly after Lawrence had been born. Near the VCR was a collection of Senior's favorite western movies on VHS. Beside Senior's movies was a short cabinet with a variety of old vinyl hits he and Sandy had amassed from their younger years: Curtis Mayfield, Isaac Hayes, Al Green, Minnie Riperton, Sly & The Family

Stone, Jerry Butler, Bootsy Collins, Billy Paul, and more.

Resting on the dining room table was a batch full of buttery-soft cornbread and a bowl of fresh collard greens. A volcano of smoke was still whistling from every container. At the oven, Sandy, the boys' mother, was putting the finishing touches on some homemade chocolate chip cookies, the boys' favorite snack. Blaring from the kitchen window sill was an old portable radio with Teddy Pendergrass playing in the background.

Lawrence tried first, reaching with his germy hand for a taste of golden cornbread. As he reached in for a quick steal, Sandy bopped him on his head with a roll of paper towels.

"You little nasty dog, you!" she fussed. "Wash your hands! You too, Junior!"

Together the boys darted upstairs to the hallway bathroom to wash their hands. Hungry and impatient, Lawrence quickly splashed a drop of water onto his hands and dried his palms using his shirt. As he turned to leave, Junior pulled him back in front of the sink.

"*Damn* you nasty, man! Wash your hands!" he shouted under his breath.

"Man shut the fuck up!" Lawrence whispered. "I was trying to find more soap!"

"No, you wasn't! Man, you was about to go back downstairs with your nasty ass!"

"Shut up fool, you ain't my daddy!"

Moments later, Senior began pounding on the door like the police and ordered the boys out of the bathroom so that he could use it. Lawrence smirked at Junior on the way out.

At the dinner table, the boys and Sandy waited for Senior to finish upstairs. When Junior hinted to his mother that Lawrence hadn't finished washing his hands, she sent his brother over to the sink to rewash them. As Lawrence took his walk of shame, Junior smirked back at him and went to work on Sandy for his Saturday plans.

"So, uh, Ma," he began. "You know it's the last weekend down at the movies for *Sugar Hill*, right? Can you take me and Lawrence?"

"Sugar who?" she asked.

"*Sugar Hill!*" Junior respectfully raised his voice. "You know, Wesley Snipes. Don't you remember *New Jack City*? Mario Van Peebles? Ice-T?"

Sandy had always been on the fence about taking the boys to see R-rated movies. They were too violent and the short section of Crawford where they lived had enough violence to go around to make one hundred movies. Unlike your average parents, the Robinsons used the movies as a tool to teach the boys about the reality of the streets. Upstairs on Junior's bedroom wall was a poster of his favorite movie of all time: *House Party* starring Kid-N-Play.

Minutes later, Senior entered the kitchen and took a seat next to Sandy. That night, it was Junior's turn to say the blessing at dinner. He asked the Lord to watch over his family and to bless his mother's hands for preparing their meal. Beneath the table, Lawrence signaled to Junior, tapping on his leg. Somewhere in the back of Junior's mind, he thought it would be a good idea to include the hope of seeing *Sugar Hill* soon.

Junior then threw in a bonus for Lawrence.

"And Lord," he began, "please God, please…I know *Sugar Hill* has been out for a while now and uh…we'd love to go. Oh, and Lawrence needs a new bicycle. Thank you! Amen!"

When Junior cracked open his eyes, Senior was staring at him like a convicted serial killer eyeing down his latest victim. Junior then looked over at his mother who seemed unamused by his irrelevant call upon the Lord for a movie and a new bicycle for his brother.

"Boy, if you ever play with God like that again, you won't live to see *Sugar Hill*! Don't you play with the Lord's name like that, Junior," she barked.

"C'mon, Ma!" Junior bargained. "*Sugar Hill* been out five months – *five* months at the Dollar Theatre. It's the last weekend. Me and Lawrence won't ask for nothin' else for the rest of the year… or next year. Promise!"

"Why don't you ask your father?" she suggested. "I'm sure he'd just *love* to take y'all."

Junior looked across at Senior who was still glaring at him and changed his mind.

"I'll wait 'til it comes on TV."

"No, Junior!" said Lawrence. "Then they'll bleep out all the cuss words. Remember what they did to *Boyz In The Hood*?"

As Sandy started serving her tasty meal to her family, Senior began to speak. He was a man of few words, but when he spoke it meant something. "I wish niggas used their heads for more than just target practice – 'cause that's where they get it from, those movies y'all watch," he said, prompting the table to go silent. "You boys lucky me and your mother let y'all watch that junk in the first place."

"It ain't junk, Daddy," bargained Junior. "Even Mom said it was educational."

"And it is." Senior cut his eyes at both boys. "Teach you niggas how to shoot and kill each other. Teach y'all how to be exactly who *they* want you to be. Educational. You boys sure is silly. If it's so educational, then why so many of these young boys still shootin' up the goddamn neighborhood every other night? Educational my ass."

"It's just a movie," Lawrence mumbled under his breath.

"Th'hell it is!" Senior pounded the table, sending dishes into the air. "Everything is just a damn movie to y'all. Th'hell with *Sugar Hill*. The answer is no! You want to watch some dopehead shit, do you? Wait 'til the motherfucka come on TV! No! Now, eat your food before it gets cold!"

Dinner remained quiet for the rest of the night as Senior's words burned into Junior's mind. He sat across from his daddy, unable to stop trembling under his father's sudden anger and wrath. *Sugar Hill* was off the table and so was asking for anything else that night, tomorrow, or the next day. On the television in the living room, the news reported that police found a decomposed body in a boarded house on the street over. The body belonged to a young woman who had been shot in the head. Senior then turned to look over at the boys as Junior lowered his eyes down to his plate.

"Educational, you say?" asked Senior. "You feel any smarter, Junior?"

Don't get so lost looking up that
you forget to look down.
A stumble will make you humble.

—LEONARD G. ROBINSON JR.

One

"What'd you say there, Junior?" Leonard Sr. greeted his son, Leonard Jr., at his bedroom door on a school night in August of '95. Sprawled atop his mattress, Junior's headset blared as he wrote in his journal, unaware that his daddy was standing there. Playing in the deck of his Sony Walkman was "Escape" by Pete Rock & C.L. Smooth from their rap album, *The Main Ingredient*. The volume was so deafening, Senior could hear it from the door. On the wall next to Junior's bedside was a huge Michael Jackson poster, and a picture of Whitney Houston (his crush) performing "The Star-Spangled Banner" at Superbowl XXV. As part of Junior's nightly ritual, he'd resign to his room to write, play video games, or listen to his Walkman. When that got boring, he'd read a Stephen King book, a *Marvel* comic book, or stare out into the city.

Seeing no response, Senior greeted him again.

"What'd you say there, son?"

Junior wrote poetry most nights. Once in a while, a short story. Beneath his bed was an old suitcase where he kept his journals along with a *Playboy* magazine he'd bought from a kid at school for five dollars. If Junior's parents found his magazine, they'd give him the blues. But it was his collection of journals from last year that Junior most worried about his parents finding.

He began his career as a writer the year before and had a book for every month since then. In his journal, he philosophized life through poetry. At fourteen, Junior was different than most of the boys in Philly. He was soft-spoken, quiet, and charming with a handsome gap-toothed smile. Whereas most of the boys in his neighborhood were boasting about sex or the latest pair of Michael Jordan sneakers, Junior kept to his journal. He spoke only when spoken to and seldom made eye contact. The students at Benjamin Franklin High, where Junior attended as a freshman, gave him hell. They teased him about his homemade haircut and made fun of his clothes. Not to mention, the boys there were much bigger than he was.

As Junior continued to write, still unaware that his daddy was standing there hovering over him, Senior became agitated.

"Aye nigga!" Senior shouted. In one swoop, he ripped off Junior's Walkman and tossed it down onto the floor. Startled to see his father standing there, he began to tremor as Senior's hot breath felt like summer heat. On the floor next to his daddy's big boot was Junior's Walkman. As he went to reach for it, Senior placed his foot onto the device. Junior looked down at his headset and slowly made his way up into the clouds where his father stood. Senior was a large man – larger than life. At six-foot-five and nearly two-hundred-forty pounds, Junior's daddy was big enough to mean business. He had tree trunks for arms that seemed made for bending steel, with fists the size of hams. All the neighbors who lived on the Robinsons' street were terrified of Senior, including Junior. Vicious dogs around Brooke's Rowe turned white as a sheet when they passed by the Robinsons' house. With their tails curled and ears peeled backward, they tip-toed by the house as if Senior was a rolling thunderstorm. He'd scowl at the dogs, daring them to shit on his bald lawn. Downtown, white folks stepped into traffic, giving Senior the sidewalk. He had thick, dark hands like a silverback gorilla and could yell so loud that the bass from his voice rattled the furniture in the house. His scornful glare was like a boxer staring at his opponent during the ring instructions. His ripping physique reminded Junior of a villain in one of his *Marvel* comics.

"Goddammit, Junior," barked Senior. "You ain't hear me callin' for you?"

"I-I didn't hear you," stuttered Junior. "I-I ain't mean t-to ignore you, Daddy."

As Junior reached down for his Walkman again, Senior tightened his foot on the device, nearly clipping one of Junior's fingers. He fussed and cussed, pounding his ginormous fist onto Junior's nightstand so hard that a row of loose change did the macarena.

"You don't pay *no* bills in this house to be ignorin' me or your momma, boy! So, when I call, nigga, you better answer! I'll *bust* your ass in this house! Now, what the hell you doin'?"

"J-j-just, writing, Daddy…that's all."

"Writin' what?" asked Senior. "Give it here! Lemme see!"

As Junior went to hand over his journal, Senior snatched it from his hands. Fearful of what his father might find, Junior trembled again as Senior breezed through his sacred book. Days earlier, Junior had written that he had tried one of his daddy's cigarettes and spilled some of his whiskey onto the basement floor after a short taste. The week before, he wrote about killing the motor to Senior's lawnmower after accidentally pouring oil into the gas tank. If Senior were to find out, he'd murder Junior and toss his corpse into the Delaware River.

Page after page, Senior turned through Junior's book. Occasionally, he'd make a grunting noise or look up at Junior with contempt. Finding nothing, he tossed Junior's journal down onto the bed.

"Go'on to bed," he ordered. "Next time I call your name, you better answer. And don't be wastin' time readin' them little damn comics, writin' in those little diaries you buy or playin' them goddamn video games, either. Plenty for you to do 'round here, Junior. Plenty."

"Yeah, but Daddy…"

"Junior." Senior lifted his large hand to quiet him. "Why don't you try to learn a trade or something useful instead of sittin' in your room all day like some low-life, huh? Where your friends at? Don't you got any?"

Junior then lowered his head. "You know how these kids are around here," he said.

"Can't be no worse than sittin' in here all day. Little girls write in diaries, not boys!"

Tears welled inside of Junior's eyes. Upon noticing he had hurt Junior's feelings, Senior backpedaled, but by then it was too late. Less than a minute later, Sandy showed up at Junior's bedroom door. Her eyes were as red as two hot fireball candies.

"He likes to write before bed – been doin' it for a while now!" she growled at Senior, foaming at the mouth. "As long as you keep dumpin' on him, Junior won't have to worry about the other kids messin' with him because *you* already do it for them!"

Sandy then entered Junior's room, lifted his journal from the bed, placed it into her son's hand, and left. Senior followed his wife back across the hall and closed Junior's room door for the night, ending his tirade.

Across the hall, Junior's parents argued that night over money, living in Philadelphia, and Junior's trade as a writer. It was the only constant in their twenty-two-year marriage: disagreement. Senior and Sandy woke up fighting and went to bed fighting. "Fuck you," one of them would say. "No, *fuck you!*" the other would shoot back. One night, Junior listened to his parents argue for two hours over an empty can of roach spray left under the sink in the kitchen.

For what Junior's momma lacked in stature, she made up for it in rottweiler-like aggression. She was sweet, but not soft

– she had to be to spend her whole life in Philly. Sandy was a short, heavyset, dark-skinned woman with short, beautiful black hair. If not for her city accent, neighbors might have mistaken her for being raised in the South. She cooked a mean pot of chitterlings and was one of few neighbors who still used a clothesline in 1995. Together with Senior, their most remarkable feat was their two boys, Junior and Lawrence. Once upon a time, they had been the proud parents of two living boys. It cut a nerve whenever the subject of Lawrence was brought up and what had happened to him the summer before.

Unable to sleep, Junior gazed from his bedroom window out into the warm city night, admiring the rows of tiny lights off in the distance. With his headset on, he listened to an old Miles Davis cassette tape Sandy had loaned him. The soothing jazz echoed throughout his ears as he cranked up the volume to drown out the heavyweight prizefight taking place across the hall in his parents' bedroom. Outside his window was a dirty street lamp harassed by a stream of moths. Up above, a crescent moon sat gorgeously in the corner of the city's skyline. Before Junior knew what had hit him, he was sound asleep. In troubled dreams, images of Lawrence flickered through his mind…

Last Summer

The day before Lawrence died, the boys had gotten their tails whipped over eighty dollars that went walking from Senior's nightstand. It wasn't the money; it was the principle and the fact that either of them dared to steal from him. As the boys walked in from school, Senior and Sandy went at it over the money. Junior's daddy had lost all his mind that afternoon. Pissed off and geeked on alcohol, he punched a hole in the wall the size of a basketball. It was the angriest Junior or Lawrence had ever seen their daddy. Spit flew from his mouth as he yelled, and his eyes were hazy and yellow. Unbeknownst to the boys, the Robinsons' rent was due at the end of the week. They'd been late the last month and the month before that. Junior's parents started upstairs, tearing apart their bedroom before searching through a pile of dirty laundry on the floor. They moved downstairs, tearing apart the sofa and closet, tossing clothes and couch cushions over their heads like cops looking for evidence on a search warrant. Eventually, Senior made his way to the boys and asked if they'd seen the money. Junior answered no, assuredly, and Lawrence said the same. The two brothers then watched as their parents ripped the basement apart.

Later that night, when the missing money magically resurfaced on Senior's nightstand, he went ballistic. He kicked open the boys' bedroom door, picked up their fan, and slammed it to the floor. It sparked and sputtered, startling the boys as they backed into the wall as if Senior was a loose pit bull.

"So, y'all must think I'm a damn fool?" he asked. "Is your daddy dumb? Is he stupid?"

Petrified, Junior looked over at Lawrence, confused. Lawrence offered the same dumb look. When no one answered up, Sandy entered next.

"Who took the eighty off of your daddy's nightstand?!" she asked.

Junior looked at his brother. Lawrence looked back at him. Neither said a word. Sandy then rolled her eyes and left, closing the door behind her, leaving the boys to deal with their lunatic father on their own. Some nights, Sandy saved the boys from getting beat but not that night. Senior then removed his belt from his pants and popped his leather strap, offering the boys one last chance to come clean before he slaughtered them. They cried instantaneously.

"Little crumb-snatchers!" he fussed to hell. "I'm gonna whoop the shit out of both of y'all if somebody don't fess up! Now, who took the goddamn money?"

"I swear to God, Daddy!" Junior pleaded for his life. "I don't know!"

"Me neither!" Lawrence sobbed.

Senior whooped Junior first and the longest. He was the oldest and knew better. Lawrence went next but got off easy. He called out for the Lord as he always did when faced with his daddy's strap.

At the end of it, Senior asked again about the money. Junior looked over at Lawrence and his brother looked back at him. Neither said a word. Irritated, Senior promised to whoop the boys again the next day after school and every day thereafter if the culprit didn't confess. As Senior left for the night, Junior went to bed convinced that he and his brother would get beat again the next day.

During the walk home from school the next afternoon, Lawrence finally confessed to Junior the truth about the money. He didn't give a reason, however.

"I was going to put it back," he cried. "I just forgot, Junior."

"Are you crazy?! Why did you take it in the first place, Lawrence? Man, you *know* Daddy is out of his mind. You're dead when he finds out. You might as well bury yourself in the backyard – cause I'm gonna tell him!"

Lawrence nearly fainted. "No! Junior you can't!" he gasped. "I'll die! Please!

"Better you than me!" Junior yelled back. "I ain't gettin' whooped for you no more!"

When the boys arrived at the house, Junior noticed his parents' cars were not there. If only temporarily, the boys would get some relief. Lawrence used the free time to follow Junior around the house, pleading with his brother not to tell.

"Wait 'til I tell Daddy," said Junior. "You're gonna get it!"

"C'mon on, man, don't tell on me," Lawrence cried again. "Please, Junior! Don't!

"Nope! I hope he skins you alive!" teased Junior. "You're a dummy!"

Lawrence then began swiping at Junior.

"Don't call me that!" Lawrence flailed at him. "I ain't no dummy!"

"Yes, you are!" Junior shoved him to the floor. "You're a fuckin' idiot. I hope Daddy whoops you for two whole days! You stupid dummy!"

"Well, fine! I'll just leave!" Lawrence said.

Distraught, he emptied his school bag on the bed and packed it full of random clothes. Junior didn't take his brother's running away seriously. He laughed as he watched Lawrence stuff a pair of underwear and a winter coat into his bag. Junior then went trolling after his brother, mocking him as Lawrence stormed up Joseph Boulevard, pushing his bicycle, crying.

"Where you going now, dummy?" asked Junior. "Where you gonna eat? You still gotta go to school. You'll never make it in Philly! You might as well take your whoopin' like a man!"

Ignoring his brother, Lawrence hopped on his bicycle and pedaled off.

"Fine then! Go!" yelled Junior. "Stupid! You're just gonna make Daddy even madder when I tell him what you did and you ain't home! You dummy!"

"Don't call me that!" Lawrence's sobbing cries faded as he pedaled further up Joseph Boulevard and into the heart of Philly's ghetto as Junior watched. When Lawrence's scrawny figure disappeared into the city, Junior went back to the house to wait for Senior and Sandy.

Less than an hour later, his parents arrived home. Like the nobler sibling, he waited on the porch like an obedient dog. Senior bypassed his son's loyalty, ready to whoop him again if necessary. Junior looked at his daddy's waistband at the belt holding his pants together. He wanted no part of any sequel from last night's affair.

"I got something to tell y'all." Junior hesitated. "Lawrence… is uh…not home." He caught his breath. "He left his book at school. Doggone Lawrence! He's something else."

"I'll say," said Senior. "Now quit bullshittin' around. What happened to the money? And I want to hear it from you, Junior. You're the oldest! So, you ought to know better. Now, how did that eighty dollars find its way back on my nightstand? I was born at night – not last night."

Junior took a deep breath as he prepared to speak. Before he could, gunfire erupted near the top of Joseph Boulevard as if it was Vietnam.

"Great, another shooting," said Sandy. "Where the hell is Lawrence?"

Saying no more, Junior raced up Joseph Boulevard to where he'd last seen Lawrence. Both Senior and Sandy went running after him as residents along Joseph Boulevard hit the deck.

"Goddammit, *get* back here!" Senior shouted from behind, barely able to keep up. Age and years of cigarette smoking had depleted his tired lungs, reducing him to a coughing jog. Sandy, a mail carrier, used to carrying pepper spray and getting chased by wild dogs, had a bit more stamina to go around. At the top of Joseph Boulevard, a turf war was taking place between rival gangs. Opposing members traded rounds from automatic machine guns.

"Boy, get back here!" puffed Sandy as she started to slow. "Get back here, now!"

"Lawrence, Ma!" Junior yelled from a distance.

"*What?*" Both Sandy and Senior recuperated. "Lawrence?!"

Up ahead was Lawrence on his bicycle caught in the middle of it all. He laid on the ground, screaming and crying as bullets whisked above his head. Junior arrived behind a parked car about twenty yards from where Lawrence lay. The moment Lawrence saw him, Junior motioned for his brother to stay down, which Lawrence did. Both Sandy and Senior arrived next to Junior. Bullets crackled from one side of Joseph Boulevard to the other as neighbors young and old ducked behind cars or fled in terror. Lucille, the candy lady on their block, was struck when a round ricocheted from a fire hydrant, went through a car window, and pierced her right shoulder. Nearby houses and businesses alike were plastered with bullet holes the size of nickels as gang members fired their weapons empty and stopped to reload. But there was one particular round that changed the Robinsons' life forever. While ducked behind a car, a bullet penetrated a van window, sending a shard of glass into Sandy's face, cutting her. As she yelped involuntarily, Lawrence became concerned for his mother's safety and attempted to rescue her. He was hit immediately, struck in the back of his head.

Time slowed down as even the shooters noticed that among the dozens of shell casings covering the asphalt was a ten-year-old boy with a hole in the back of his head. One of the shooters, a man later identified as Gregory Johnson, nineteen, was vomiting blood after being hit with a twelve-gauge shotgun in the stomach. But that didn't get nearly the attention as Lawrence, lying dead in the middle of the road with his bicycle over top of him. He jerked with shock as his soul departed. Sirens sounded from the distance as every city squad car rushed onto Joseph Boulevard; the hoodlums vanished in smoke. The shootout lasted less than two minutes.

On the scene, Junior watched alongside his parents as EMTs worked to save Lawrence's life. Bystanders shared in the Robinsons' grief, as paramedics covered his small face with oxygen, attempting to pump life into Lawrence's frail body. Junior's world went blank. He could barely hear Sandy crying out in agony asking God why. Junior looked down at the shell that once held his brother's soul, unable to make sense of what had just occurred. Lawrence was gone.

But when the cops started asking questions, suddenly, no one saw a thing. The more questions the officers asked, the more the size of the crowd of onlookers began to diminish. For Sandy, it was the ultimate betrayal. She had lived in Crawford since she was a little girl and at one point was Vice President of Neighborhood Affairs long before Junior and Lawrence had come along. She had also been a mentor to black boys and girls who lived there. That day, Thursday, August 25, 1994, the city of Philadelphia turned its back on Junior's family. Over the next year, he'd grow a callus over his severed heart.

"So, that's it?! Y'all just gonna walk off?" Junior watched as his mother howled to the crowd of onlookers as Senior attempted to cart her away. "Y'all saw my ten-year-old son get shot, and y'all ain't gonna do nothin'? Fuck y'all! I babysat your kids!" Her voice hoarsened as she cried. "Gave away my last to y'all when I was Vice President! You motherfuckers!"

Whatever faith Junior had in his city that day was left on the street next to Lawrence. He would never forgive Philadelphia for what it had done to his family.

On the day of Lawrence's funeral, family and close mourners of the Robinsons crammed into 116th Street Baptist Church on Greenbelt Parkway to celebrate the life of Lawrence Robinson. Junior sat in the back of the church in his black suit and tie, refusing to see Lawrence asleep in his western-oak coffin. Just feet away from where his brother lay, Senior and Sandy wore their best masks for the occasion. Surrounded by arms, they thanked relatives for coming and shook hands with folks they hadn't seen in years. Unmoved by the fakery and fluff of well-wishers, Junior kept his distance. At one point, Junior noticed his mother turn to whisper something into his daddy's ear. Shortly thereafter, Senior got up from his chair and joined Junior at the rear of the church. He hadn't said much since the shooting, which puzzled Junior. Senior was a complicated man to get to know. Most often, he spared his feelings in exchange for his riotous and ruthless behavior. During the service, however, Senior was all jokes – which was nothing like him.

At the back of the church where Junior sat, Senior scooted beside his surviving son and placed his long arm around

Junior, pulling him in close. Junior looked over at his daddy to see if he was crying or not – he wasn't. He had never seen Senior cry, not even for Lawrence.

As Senior glanced down into his son's watery eyes, Junior stared straight ahead at a fixture of Christ on the cross near the front of the church, not blinking. Once in a while, a tear ran off Junior's chin and dripped down onto his suit. To cheer him up, Senior reached into his breast pocket for an old handkerchief to wipe his son's face as Junior weaved out of reach.

"I'm good," said Junior.

Shrugging, Senior returned his handkerchief back in his suit.

"Never thought I'd see the day we'd be burying one of y'all," said Senior. "Fucked up."

When Junior didn't answer back, Senior switched gears to a new topic, trying his best to keep his awkward conversation afloat as Junior stared lifelessly ahead. As Senior carried on endlessly, Junior couldn't wait for his daddy to shut up.

"I forgot Sandy had such a big damn family. Look at all this," he said. "You see Ellis's boys? Man, those suckas got big since the other year. Almost as tall as you, Junior."

Still, Junior didn't answer back. Although, he did peep over at his cousins near the front row and could tell they'd put on some size since he last saw them. Figuring he got Junior's attention, Senior continued.

"Maaaaann, Carter's daughter. Shit, she 'bout as big as a house. Baby ought to be here any minute now. Look over there," pointed Senior. "You know who that is? That's Uncle Duke – y'all used to call him 'Dookie'. Hmph. Nigga ain't been to the house in almost six months. Duke said he'd drop by later after the service. He better, shit."

"What for?" asked Junior. "Seems like the only time we get together with family is when somebody die. This time it just happened to be Lawrence," he said. "Duke ain't coming by, Daddy. Ain't none of these folks coming by – not until it's one of us lying in a box next."

Senior didn't talk for the rest of the service. As the reverend began his eulogy, he kissed Junior on his forehead and slipped back to the front of the church next to Sandy. Later, as the service concluded and Lawrence's coffin made its way down the aisle, Junior darted from his seat at the back of the church and into the nearest restroom. He wanted no part of remembering Lawrence in that way. A cousin later came to get him after his brother's body was moved. Unable to afford a full burial, Lawrence was buried in an unmarked grave next to Sandy's mother at Hyatt Park Cemetery on Rhode Island Avenue.

At the repast, Junior sat out on the stoop of 116th Baptist Church overlooking Philadelphia. Twice, Sandy came to offer him food. The first plate he rejected and, on the second, Junior accepted – not because he was hungry – but so he could be left alone. After Sandy went back inside, he offered his meatballs and macaroni salad to a row of starving pigeons in front of the church.

Back at home, Junior exited his mother's '85 Buick Skylark and stood next to Sandy as she looked down Joseph Boulevard. To everyone else, it was just another day. Snaggle-toothed old-timers sat on their porches skipping checkers and drinking Colt 45 malt liquor as they reminisced about the good old days. Across the way, young girls skipped rope in the street as boys tossed around a football, pretending to be Randall Cunningham or Warren Moon. A week earlier, everything had been normal. Junior looked over at his peers playing carelessly in the street, wondering which kid would be next.

For days after the funeral, Junior noticed his mother would spend hours by the windowsill waiting for Lawrence to show up on his bicycle while Senior busied himself with work. Late in the evening, she'd return upstairs to her room where she'd moan for much of the night. Weeks went by. A month. Two months. Just as Junior had predicted back at the church, not a single family member had stopped by to check on the Robinsons. Early into Lawrence's investigation, detectives warned Sandy that without any leads, her son's case would go cold. It did, and so did Sandy.

In the two months following Lawrence's death, Junior's mother barely ate or left the house. When Junior left for school in the mornings, she was asleep. And when he returned home, she would still be asleep. Except to munch on a light snack, Sandy seldom left the bedroom – not even to bathe.

The first month was the hardest for Junior's mother. She laid in bed helplessly, unkempt, her fingernails and toenails dirty and long like Freddy Kruger's. On the weekends, when Junior was home, he'd help Senior cart his mother into the hallway bathroom where they bathed and returned her to bed. By the time Junior and his daddy had finished bathing Sandy, a ring of grimy crud slithered down into the drain.

Junior was no better during those first two months. His parents didn't know it, but he had stopped going to school to hang out at Hyatt Park next to the patch of humped dirt where Lawrence rested. He got found out when the groundskeeper began noticing he was the same boy from the day before and the day before that. Fearing he had run away, the cops were called and Junior was taken to his house back on Joseph Boulevard.

Then one day, two months later, it happened. Junior came home from school to see Sandy sitting at the kitchen table rummaging through a newspaper with a cup of coffee. Her hair was curly and wet as if she'd just got out of the shower. Her nails were neatly trimmed and painted.

"We're movin' to South Philly," she said to him, her face still buried in the *Philadelphia Weekly*. She barely looked up to acknowledge him as he entered the house. A few weeks later, the Robinsons relocated from Crawford in North Philly to Brook's Rowe on the south side of town.

Brooke's Rowe, in a lot of ways, was no different than Crawford. Shootouts happened. Drugs. Homicides. Prostitution. Police Brutality. Fights. Stabbings. Bodies found in abandoned houses long after rigor mortis and decomposition set in. But Brooke's Rowe was a thirty-six minute drive south of

Crawford, which was better than nothing. For the Robinsons, it was an opportunity to start over. They left Crawford without a goodbye, leaving in the middle of the night to avoid the drudgery of neighbors swarming over them.

1401 Kennedy Street became Junior's new address the evening he moved into his Brooke's Rowe home on the south side of Philadelphia. Once there, Junior's parents encouraged him to get around and socialize – although the same rules from Crawford applied in Brooke's Rowe. Junior still had to be in before streetlight or at least within earshot of hearing his name get called.

The change of scenery had worked wonders for his family – all but him. Sandy was able to transfer from the northern postal district to the southern, and the change added more clientele to Senior's handyman business. To aid Junior in his recovery, Sandy encouraged him to take up a new hobby. By that time, Junior couldn't fathom something as complex and misunderstood as poetry. So, he tried his hand at several sports, hoping to fit in with his peers throughout Brooke's Rowe.

Down at the rec center, a short walk from the house, he tried to make new friends by trading some of his video games but got cheated. He had a bicycle that he chained to a parking sign that got stolen when some savage popped the chain with bolt cutters. In basketball, the boys outran Junior on the court, which didn't endear him to get picked in a second or third game. In football, the boys were much bigger, stronger, and ran twice as fast as him. They'd offer Junior a spot on the team but played too rough for a kid as fragile as he was. They'd hit Junior so hard, knocking the wind out of him until he cried. Of course, the boys all teased him. They taunted Junior, calling him names like "faggot", "fruitcake", and "dummy" when he dropped a pass. All were names he used to call Lawrence. One day, during his tour of the neighborhood, Junior stumbled into a local boxing gym. The manager there, a guy known around South Philly as "Uncle Skeeter", allowed Junior to tap on the bag. Impressed, the man offered Junior a chance to spar with another amateur boxer there. Junior took one look at the blood-stained ring apron and politely declined.

Unable to compete athletically, Junior took notice of his associates' clothes down at the rec and decided he'd found his way to fit in. The kids around Brooke's Rowe wore nothing but the finest in Reebok, Guess, Nike, Adidas, and other top-flight apparel. Hoping to win them over, he petitioned Senior for $140 to buy a pair of Bo Jackson sneakers. Junior's daddy looked at him like he had six heads.

"$140?" asked Senior. "For some goddamn tennis shoes?" he laughed. "Tell you what, Junior. Work with me on Saturday. I got a couple of water heaters to put in out in Camden. You do good, I'll get you a pair. But let me tell something," said Senior. "Them folks down at that rec center ain't gonna like you no better. Trust me."

So, on a Saturday, in the dead of morning, Junior went to work with Senior out in Camden, New Jersey to install the water heaters. From 6 a.m. until 4 p.m., he hustled tools from his daddy's truck up to the house where they worked until the job was finished. Senior put him to the test, making him complete some of the smaller tasks, hoping to make a protégé of him. For Junior, working with his daddy was strictly about the shoes.

For their last job of the day, Senior coached Junior into changing the oil in an Oldsmobile Delta Eighty-Eight. Afterward, as promised, he awarded Junior a wad of crisp twenty-dollar bills and gave him a hearty handshake. Junior noticed his hand fit completely inside his daddy's wide palm.

"Mmmhmm." Senior half-smiled. "Very good, Junior," he said to him out in the parking lot of the strip mall in front of Footlocker shoe store. "Go'on, get your Bo Johnsons."

"It's Bo Jackson," laughed Junior. "The football player?"

"Boy, I don't give a damn about no Bo Jackson-Johnson or nothin'," said Senior. "Just hurry up, I'm tired. Go!"

Junior exited his daddy's truck, walked into Footlocker, and returned twenty minutes later with the beautiful pair of silver and black Nike sneakers. He opened the box and took a whiff of his brand-new shoes, waiting for Senior's approval.

"Why would you buy some bullshit like this?" Senior held up one of Junior's shoes. "Ain't nothin' special about 'em, Junior. Ugly-ass damn shoes."

"They ain't ugly!" said Junior. "These are better than Deion's!"

"Who the hell is Deion?" asked Senior.

"Just forget it, Daddy." Junior placed his shoe back in the box.

When Junior got home after working next to his daddy, he showered, threw on his new Bo Jackson sneakers, and headed down to the rec center. Just as Senior had predicted, the boys there mocked and laughed at Junior's chicken legs and big feet. The moment Junior entered the gymnasium, the kids all stopped dribbling and surrounded him.

"Goddamn! Big ass feet!" One kid pointed and laughed.

"Word to my mother! Man, where'd you get those?" another kid asked.

"I bought 'em," said Junior. "I got a job working with my pops."

"A job?" asked another kid. "Nigga, you ain't got no job. Broke-ass bum. Take your brother's shoes back home, bitch!"

The entire gym erupted, including some of the adults who were there. Junior stood in the center of the gym, watching as his peers scoffed at him. Shortly thereafter, he turned and left.

He cried for most of the walk back to Kennedy Street feeling sorry for himself, without a friend in the world. Not wanting his daddy to see him crying, he used his t-shirt to dry his eyes before passing by Senior as he fixed on his truck.

"So, what'd your friends say?" asked Senior. "Are you Bo Jackson or not?"

"I ain't got no friends," mumbled Junior as he walked by. "Man, I ain't shit."

Senior threw down his oily rag and charged after Junior, snatching him up by the arm.

"What the fuck did you say?" he growled. "You ain't *what*?"

"...I said, I miss Lawrence," he began to cry. "Don't you, Daddy?"

Senior then loosened his grip on Junior and exhaled.

"Damn it, Junior." He shook his head. "You know I miss your brother. Now, why'd you have to take it there? Huh?"

Senior then took his big, greasy hand and wiped away Junior's tears.

"Don't ever let me hear you talkin' about you ain't shit. You hear me?" Senior held Junior by his chin. "You say you ain't shit – next thing you know – you won't *be* shit. Just like your father. I told you last week about those stupid shoes. It ain't the shoes that make who the man is – it's the man that's in 'em. Remember that."

After his daily lesson, Junior returned to his bedroom, boxed up his Bo Jackson sneakers, and pushed the box far under his bed. He then reached inside his closet for an older pair of sneakers he owned. They were weathered and dull, but comfortable. Afterward, Junior went into the bathroom across the hall from his room to wash his face. He stared at his reflection before overhearing Sandy call him down to the basement. When he arrived, Sandy asked him to lift an old cardboard box loaded with books from off the floor. Without surveying its weight, Junior went to lift his mother's box from the floor, and it split completely in half. Sandy rolled her eyes as she walked over to give Junior a hand.

Down at Junior's feet, he sifted through a collection of his mother's old school books before finding a journal made out in his mother's full name, Lonnie Sandra Woods, dated back in 1969. Without permission, Junior picked up one of his mother's composition journals and began to read aloud. She snatched her journal from his nosy paws and bopped Junior over the head for good measure.

"Boy, gimmie that book! Get your own!" she laughed.

"You never told me you wrote poetry," he said. "Can I finish that last part?"

"Hell no! You cannot!" She chuckled at his audacity. "But if you wanna write, I'll take you down to the drugstore and you can get your *own* journal. You got any money, sucka?"

Junior zipped off to his bedroom and grabbed his Bo Jackson sneakers from beneath his bed and returned down to the basement.

"What? I thought you wanted those?" asked Sandy.

"I did," said Junior. "But…they make my feet look too big."

Down at the strip mall, the clerk looked over Junior's sneakers with a magnifying eye and asked him the reason for the return.

"They hurt my feet," Junior lied to the man.

Eyeing both Junior and Sandy suspiciously, the clerk who sold Junior the sneakers earlier that afternoon went into the register and handed him back his $140.

Money in hand, Junior ran out of Footlocker and into the drugstore a couple of doors down and purchased a journal, a set of ballpoint ink pens, a can of Arizona Iced Tea, and the biggest bag of Skittles he could find. He even tipped Sandy a few bucks for driving him down to the store. Adoring his cute gesture, she handed Junior back his three dollars.

On the way back to Kennedy Street, he asked his mother for tips on what to write. Sandy offered him the same advice a writer once gave her.

"Just say… something," she told him, "but say it from the heart."

So, while most of Junior's peers around Brooke's Rowe were out playing ball or chasing young girls down at the rec, Junior wrote. Between Lawrence, girls, and feeling like the pariah of his new neighborhood, he had a lot to say and carefully crafted his thoughts inside his journal before moving onto poetry. At first, Junior wrote corny, cookie-cutter poems that he crumbled and tossed into the bin inside his bedroom. Disappointed, he opted to quit, but Sandy made him continue. Junior resented when Sandy wouldn't allow him to quit things the way he wanted. It took him days to come up with something decent to show his mother. Then one day, it happened. Junior strung together his first poem, ever. He titled it "Waters" and dated it in the upper-righthand corner of his journal for November of '94.

As streams run and rivers rush,
lakes remain on hold like phone calls
from oceans that don't call back from the shoreline.

LEONARD G. ROBINSON JR.

After reading "Waters", Sandy shoved Junior into her car, drove him down to the nearest library, and got him a membership card. On the weekends when she was off, she'd run

Junior down to the public library where she introduced him to the most brilliant minds of African-American literature: Langston Hughes, Maya Angelou, Claude McKay, Carter G. Woodson, Zora Neale Hurston, and a host of others.

"Why'd you bring me here?" he asked.

"I brought you here because I *know* I could've written better if I had someone to encourage me when I was your age," she said. "You can go places as a good writer, beyond Philly or anywhere else in this crazy ghetto we're trying to survive in. So, keep on writing, Junior. Whatever you do, no matter what happens, don't stop!"

Sandy handed Junior his library card with his name written neatly in cursive on the back: Leonard Gerard Robinson Jr. He spent over an hour looking up books beside his mother until he happened across two or three authors that resonated with him. Sandy couldn't help but smile as Junior breezed through his set of books while waiting in line at the register.

"Got everything?" she asked.

"Think so," said Junior. "You think I could be a good writer?" he asked.

Sandy kissed him on the cheek.

"I think you could be anything you want to be, Junior. You don't have to be a Michael Jordan, Bo Jackson, or Randall Cunningham. I want you to use your head for something else besides a target for someone to throw a ball at. Knowledge can't be deflated, but a football or a basketball can. Do you understand?"

"Yes ma'am." Junior nodded. "Yes ma'am, I do."

I break my own heart.
And sometimes you do it for me.

—LEONARD G. ROBINSON JR.

Two

The morning after Junior got into trouble over his Walkman, he rode the bus to school, angry and embittered. Senior's words had cut him deeply, depriving Junior of his vigor throughout the day at school.

By the time Junior began his freshman year at Benjamin Franklin High in September of 1995, poetry was second nature to him. Since Lawrence's passing, he had amassed over four thousand poems. In fact, Junior had filled so many journals that Sandy bought a large shipping box just for him to store his thoughts in. And since the Robinsons didn't own a computer, Junior wrote all of his entries by hand. When storing his work became a chore, Sandy bought Junior an extra dresser to house his works. After every journal Junior finished, he laced it with a whipping signature and added the date, time, and place where he was. Some journals Junior finished in his bedroom, down at the library, or on the back porch.

Standing at his locker inside Franklin High, Junior

fingered the combination slowly, still depleted of all enthusiasm from the night before. Inside was a row of poems he'd taped to the walls and ceiling. Poetry, it seemed, was his only escape. Before the bell sounded to start his day, he took down the old poems and replaced them with new ones from the previous night.

Junior hated Franklin High. The teachers there didn't give a damn and neither did the kids. He had earned the name "Little Poet", as he was always seen with a journal in his hands. In conversation, he was bashful but genuine, sweet, and had an innocent smile. Although the girls found Junior cute, he lacked the confidence to keep their interest for long. He looked down when he talked and avoided the social cliques. It was hard for Junior to talk to anyone. After the strife following Lawrence's death, he remained leery of everyone around him.

Franklin High wasn't the same drug or gang-infested warzone as Crawford, but it was still a warzone. Tatted on the side of an old automotive shop across from Junior's school was a picture of the devil and the caption "Hell Zone". And that's what it was. Weeks earlier, police had found a man with his thoughts blown out from a double-barreled shotgun. Out in front of the school, embroidered in the sidewalk, was a memorial for the deceased man police found by the auto shop. Hanging above the shop on a weak phone line was a cluster of mismatched sneakers, some of which had fallen over the years. Junior was hoping to graduate from Franklin without becoming a memorial.

Adjusting to high school for Junior was stressful. Like the rec center back at home, the boys were much bigger and taller than him. They'd walk by Junior in a crowded hallway, snickering at his homemade haircut, harping on his clothes. The girls there were mostly pretty –– pretty far out of Junior's league. Some wore large hoop earrings with vibrant hair and flashy jewelry. Not to mention, the teachers there taught at a much faster pace than what Junior remembered in middle school the year before. The popular kids at Franklin excelled in sports, sold dope, or bootleg tapes, CDs, and VHSs. The rest were comedic like Martin Lawrence, had natural beauty like Halle Berry or Denzel Washington, or could rap lyrics like Biggie Smalls. Junior was none of these things. He was awkward and didn't talk much, wore clothes Sandy bought for him down at the thrift store and had a homemade haircut to save Senior money.

The few standout athletes at Franklin High were all on the football team and received special treatment. One kid, who was a senior, was awful at reading but had the best grades because he was a star receiver who garnered collegiate attention. Another kid got to park in the staff lot because his father once played ball for the Philadelphia Eagles. Few teachers gave a damn about the kids' futures. The kids with star appeal were treated better than everyone else, while the regular blue-collar kids like Junior found themselves at the back of the line.

Fights happened at Franklin like anywhere else. At freshman orientation, Junior saw a kid get a jailhouse beatdown for accidentally bumping into another kid. The victim ended up with a broken nose and concussion. Later that same day, a fight happened in the lunchroom—three girls against one. At the end of it, hunks of braided hair and blood were scattered across the cafeteria floor. Supposedly, it was over a boy who wasn't even a student there.

Down on the first-floor near the freight elevators, kids gathered in a tight circle with their spliffs and performed freestyle rap battles. Each day, students brought an arsenal of lyrics to perform in what was known as the "cipher". The champion was a guy named "Spider Da Chief", a twenty-year-old repeat sophomore who was rumored to have once done a verse with a rapper named "Big L" out of Harlem, New York. And every freestyle battle Spider participated in, he brought his own personal human beatbox with him. The Doug E. Fresh wannabe was a freshman known as Hamm. Using his mouth as a mixing machine, Hamm could drum any rap song past or present to the delight of the cipher.

Junior went to the cipher once, but the stench of heavy weed was too much for him. He passed on smoking after watching his fellow classmates cough stitches into their scalps as though they had the flu. During a break, a kid named "Jokey" hustled bootlegged movies that hadn't yet made it to VHS. For the right price, students could get their hair cornrowed by a girl named Sasha during third-period gym. Weekends were for house parties. Somebody, some-where, knew some kid whose parents were out of town and there would be a party with alcohol. Someone always came looking for a fight. Eventually, the cops would show up and shut everything down.

For lunch, students could eat either inside or outside on the school's campus. To dodge his peers and avoid conversation, Junior ate on the bleachers near the ballfields. Afterward, he'd read or write inside of his journal until the bell sounded, ending lunch. But despite going out of his way to avoid confrontation, trouble found Junior.

Midway through his dreaded day, a kid, known around school as "Big Warren", ran behind Junior as he walked to class, snatched his journal from out of his hand, and darted down the hallway, goading Junior to chase him. During the run, Big Warren began ripping pages out of Junior's book, taunting him, daring him to fight. The chase lasted from the third-floor beyond Junior's locker, down to the first-floor and back to the main level. Winded and gassed, Junior panted like a dog as he stood bent over at the waist with his hands glued to both knees. Meanwhile, Big Warren continued to tear into Junior's journal, inciting a crowd. Leaking testosterone, he egged Junior to a fight, calling him names and claiming to have slept with Junior's mother as the crowd oohed.

Ticked off, Junior rushed at Big Warren and paid for it with a body slam to the floor. Outweighed by more than a hundred pounds and under-matched, Junior was no threat to the Franklin High superstar linebacker. He scooped Junior off his feet, bouncing him from locker to locker before pinning him to the floor. As Junior flopped around, writhing in pain, Big Warren smacked him across the ear and head until the side of Junior's face turned red. Then, as Junior tried to cover himself, Big Warren gave him a final shot to the stomach, folding Junior in half like a cheap lawn chair.

"Welcome to Franklin, bitch." Big Warren stood over him.

He then opened Junior's journal, gagged, and spat in the center.

"Write that, faggot!"

Afterward, he strolled off, leaving Junior in a pile of severed poetry.

Hurt and embarrassed, Junior crawled across the floor, clutching his head and body with one hand as he collected the torn poems from his journal with the other. As most laughed at his misery, a couple of students helped him to his feet. Wobbling on fidgety legs, he scrounged the rest of his belongings and went in the opposite direction, using a row of lockers for support.

Later that afternoon, Junior discovered that he had been the victim of a brutal hazing. Each year, members of Franklin High's football team would scope out a freshman for demolition. Junior was an easy target, or so they thought. He was a bony, soft-spoken kid that appeared easy to punk or push over and would offer little resistance. What no one knew, except for Junior, was that contrary to his "safe" demeanor, he was tired of life kicking him around.

When Junior's day ended, he spied on Big Warren, following his adversary as he returned to his locker to tell his girlfriend goodbye. In the few minutes Junior spent tailing

Big Warren from a distance, he began hating his adversary even more. Not only was Big Warren the star linebacker, he was also quite the smooth-talking pretty boy – which Junior envied. On his way to his bus in front of the school, Junior observed as Big Warren high-fived students and teachers alike. The school's principal, Dr. Stanley, adored Big Warren, calling him a "living legend" and praised him as his favorite in all of Franklin. Junior looked down at his severed journal from earlier and growled. As he continued to follow Big Warren out to the bus, he thought of how helpless he had been to protect Lawrence and became agitated. At that moment, whatever punk was inside Junior left his fragile body. He became surly and vengeful, like Senior, wanting to do nothing more than destroy Big Warren and end his dreams of someday playing professional football.

As Big Warren boarded his bus, Junior bypassed his own. Next to the main entrance in the garbage bin was an empty glass bottle of Lipton Iced Tea. Junior armed himself with the glass bottle and climbed onto Big Warren's bus and followed him to the back. The moment Big Warren turned to take his seat, Junior readied himself with his weapon.

"Remember me, bitch?" said Junior.

In one arcing motion, he cracked Big Warren across the face, breaking the bottle in half as glass scattered throughout the bus. As his adversary fell onto all fours, Junior mounted Big Warren from behind, grinding the spiky bottle into his adversary's ear as Big Warren wailed like a wounded pig. Junior then looped his arm around the kid's neck, riding him like a wild bull as Big Warren gasped for air.

"You tore up my journal! I'm gonna make sure you never play football again!"

Junior reached into his pocket for an ink pen and jammed it into Big Warren's arm, dropping him flat against the bus floor. Junior then mounted him and began pounding Big Warren's face with punches as he begged for mercy. As he reached to move Junior off of him, Junior bit him across the hand as other riders cheered on the melee. The bus driver, a retired Vietnam veteran, took his time getting to the back, allowing Junior to carry on as he choked Big Warren until he turned blue. No student interfered in the savagery. It felt good to Junior, releasing his demons from the past year around his enemy's throat until the blood vessels in Big Warren's eyes burst, and he gagged for air. It was more than just the journal. It was his Walkman from last night. Not getting by with the kids in Brooke's Rowe. It was Lawrence from the previous summer and everything else that had gone wrong for him since the move over the past year. It was the first and only time in Junior's life that he had come close to killing someone. He was a kid overtaken by the devil.

By the time the bus driver had cleared a path of hooting high schoolers, Junior's shirt was covered in blood. Junior looked up to notice the kids were all looking at him as if he was some sort of rabid animal; he was. Back to reality, he dismounted Big Warren and apologized to his peers as the bus driver escorted him back into Franklin High to the principal's office. When staff learned about the damage done to Big

Warren, the police were called, and Junior was taken down to the Juvenile Justice Center down in Center City.

Sandy was at work when she got the call from JJC about what had happened. The aide there told her that Junior had been arrested for aggravated assault and battery of a student on school grounds. Junior was huddled on a lone bench inside the detective's office when Sandy arrived to pick him up. Fire was in her eyes as she showed up still donning her carrier uniform, scowling at him. When Junior noticed it was his mother there to get him as opposed to Senior, he exhaled; Sandy – although she was strict – was much easier to explain things to than Senior.

At an officer's desk, Junior waited as his mother signed his release form and read the narrative concerning his incident at school.

"I-I didn't start that fight!" he began explaining. "I was headed to lunch and then…"

Before he could finish, Sandy buttoned him up. "Quiet!" she snapped. "Can't you see I'm trying to read, Junior?"

As Sandy read and continued filling out his release forms, she eventually asked Junior if he was alright.

"You OK?"

"I'm alright," he said. "Man, I swear on a stack of bibles! I was minding my business on my way to lunch when…"

"I didn't ask you what happened yet," she interrupted. "I asked if you were OK. Are you hurt or anything?"

"I'm good," he assured. "But I'm telling you, it wasn't my

fault. I know I might've lost it a little bit, Ma, but it was Big Warren, he kept on..."

Sandy then yoked Junior by his collar. She was angrier than she had been when she first arrived to pick him up. Talking through her teeth, she demanded Junior stop talking.

"We're inside a goddamn police station," she snarled at him. "You wanna incriminate yourself in front of all these cops? Now, stop talking! You can tell me on the way home!"

Junior got the message.

On the way home, Junior told his story to Sandy on repeat as she listened without saying a word. Fearful of what awaited him when he got home, Junior re-told his story again with a higher pitch than the first, second, and third time he told his story. According to the paperwork filed by his school, he was suspended indefinitely until his expulsion hearing the following week. Sandy about flipped when she read that Junior would miss at least ten days of school and that he could face expulsion.

"Fuck!" she cussed. "Fuck me!"

Sandy didn't say the word "fuck" a lot. So, when she fucked, she meant it. Junior didn't say it, but in his head, he thought the same. *Fuck*, was his mother upset. During the drive, Sandy raised holy hell at the possibility of him getting expelled. He was supposed to be the first male Robinson *ever* to graduate from anything. Senior dropped out young. Junior's grandfather never went. Meanwhile, Lawrence was buried in an unmarked grave with a bullet in the back of his head next to Sandy's mother who quit after the eighth grade.

As they entered their tiny row house on Kennedy Street,

Sandy removed her jacket and laid it across the sofa cushion before rendering her final verdict.

"Believe it or not, I'm not mad at you," she said. "I can't be."

"You're not?" Junior asked, surprised.

"It's been a lot on us lately with Lawrence being gone and everything," Sandy empathized. "I haven't been myself either over the past year. So, how in the world can I expect you to be any better, right? For God's sake. You're only fourteen."

Junior looked on as Sandy lifted up a picture of Lawrence and him from the coffee table.

"I just don't want you to go around using last summer as an excuse to fight, Junior. Like your daddy said, these niggas out here don't give a damn about nothin' and certainly not you. It was my dream for you and Lawrence to graduate high school, and it still is. Regardless of how any of this turns out – do you understand?"

"Yes, ma'am," answered Junior. "So…I'm not in trouble?" he asked.

"I don't know yet," she told him. "I haven't made up my mind. We'll see how this all turns out. Now go away before I change my mind. Let me talk things over with your daddy."

Quickly, before Sandy changed her mind, Junior hurried up the staircase, down the hall, and into his bedroom. Careful to stay out of his parents' sight, he kept inside his room except for when Sandy called him for dinner.

That night, through the floorboards of his bedroom, Junior overheard his parents arguing over the incident as he wrote inside his journal. He hadn't realized it until then, but his parents had fallen behind on the bills. A picture of him together with Lawrence on his dresser rattled with great fury as Senior's voice ricocheted from the walls. There were talks of the family splitting up and him moving to New Jersey. Next was Delaware and then Maryland which was funny to him considering Junior hadn't been as far as an hour away from Philly. But whenever his parents brought up the notion of divorce, it broke him down. Distracted by the rhetoric of being separated, he blurred his parents' talks of leaving with his Walkman. Junior's parents had been married for twenty-two years. If not for him and his brother, Senior and Sandy would've split ages ago. Junior also learned that night that on the day Lawrence was killed, his parents had gone down to the courthouse to file for divorce. Together, they'd punked out at the commissioner's office, promising to give things one last try just to arrive home to their ten-year-old son shot dead in the middle of Joseph Boulevard. Sadly, losing Lawrence was the band-aid their marriage needed to stand on its last leg for the time being. The irony in his parents' marital woes prompted Junior to write a new poem.

Sadly, there's a comfort in hurt called familiarity.
Nobody wants new pain.
An old, achy broken heart is better than a new one.

LEONARD G. ROBINSON JR.

Notice of Expulsion

In the days following Junior's suspension from Franklin High, the Robinsons received a notice in the mail from the school's principal, Dr. Stanley, certifying that Junior would be expelled. In bright, bold letters, the words "Notice of Expulsion" were printed near the top of the page and solidified in his signature. Attached was a summons for Junior's expulsion hearing scheduled for later that week. In the document was Junior's full name along with a synopsis of the incident. Warren Grant (a.k.a. Big Warren,) was also summoned to appear. The letter was co-signed by the chair of the Philadelphia City School Board.

Junior could feel Senior's voice vibrating through the floor when Sandy told him he had to miss a day of work to attend the hearing. He had just booked a job for a transmission repair on the west side for $800. It was his biggest job all month. Fuming, Senior slammed the backdoor so hard that the handle broke off. Junior waited for his daddy to come upstairs raising hell for costing him money. Thankfully, Senior never came.

On the morning of Junior's hearing, he wore the same suit and tie he had worn to Lawrence's funeral the summer before. Sandy got him a haircut down at the mall, convinced that a professional trim would make a difference. She wore a pretty, summer-green flowery dress with a matching hat, and Senior wore a dark brown suit and tie with polished dressed shoes.

The hearing was scheduled for 8:30 a.m. in downtown Philadelphia at the John F. Kennedy Center for Wellness and Education. Junior entered next to Sandy with Senior following behind, sucking on a Jolly Rancher candy to kill off his cigarette breath. The panel deciding Junior's fate at Franklin High was a mixture of six members including members of the city's school board along with the chair. Four of the persons hearing Junior's case that morning were white and the other two were black. The moment Senior walked in, he surveyed the panel, shook his head at Junior, and nudged Sandy's arm as he took a seat.

"This ain't gonna go well," Senior whispered to her. "I think they're gonna fuck Junior."

Sandy, ever the optimist, had a different idea.

"Oh, stop!" she whispered back. "We ain't been here but five minutes and you already checked out. Why don't you have a little faith sometime?"

"Faith don't mean nothin' with four crackers sittin' up there," he said. "I'm tellin' you, it's a setup! They're gonna kick Junior out of school. Mark my words!"

"Shhhh!" Junior intervened, quieting his folks. "It's about to begin!"

The board treated Junior's expulsion hearing like a criminal trial. A copy of the bus driver's written statement was the most damning evidence throughout the hearing. Witnesses present during the fight were called in to testify against Junior. When asked whether they believed Junior had a propensity for violence, eight out of nine answered "yes". With each board's witness, Junior drooped further into the bench, believing his future at Franklin High was over. At one point, Sandy leaned across Senior to scorn him for his slouchy etiquette. "Sit up!" she barked quietly, careful not to draw attention to him. When Big Warren entered last to testify against Junior regarding their fight, Junior pointed him out to Sandy. Throughout Warren's testimony, she rolled her eyes and whispered into Senior's ear.

There was nothing "big" about Big Warren, Junior discovered at the hearing. To save his promising football scholarship, he painted Junior as a homicidal maniac with a dark spirit. Twice, he showed the panel the marks from his scuffle with Junior. Reaching for a row of tissues at the center of the table, he began to cry as he recounted his nightmare.

"Forgive me y'all," he choked. "It's just difficult for me to talk about what Junior – I'm sorry – what Leonard did to me ten days ago."

The more Big Warren talked, the more Junior hated him. He sat, listening to Warren's filtered testimony as the panel tuned in. Big Warren said that he and Junior had a "disagreement" earlier in the day before the massacre had taken place. With his face in his hands, he fake-cried again. By then, Senior had had all he could take as he leaned over to whisper into Junior's ear.

"What a shithead," said Senior. "I ain't ever seen such a tall, strong punk in my life."

When it was Junior's turn to approach the podium, the tide of the board was against him. Junior said that his thrashing of Big Warren was precipitated when Big Warren attempted to haze him during the break by destroying his journal. He did just as he and Sandy had rehearsed the night before, using the exact language Big Warren had said to him during their first fight.

"And then he called me a 'bitch' and said 'welcome to Franklin' and walked off – after he'd already torn up my journal," Junior explained to the panel. "I don't know Warren – he's not a friend of mine. I was upset, but I accept responsibility for what happened. Please give me a second chance at Franklin High."

The chair of the panel then began to cross-examine Junior.

"Soooo," the woman began. "You're saying that Mr. Grant physically provoked you first? Is that correct?"

Junior looked over at his parents before answering.

"Yes, that's correct," he nodded.

"Well, if that's the case, how come you didn't report it to a staff member?"

"Because…" Junior glanced over at Sandy. "Look, I was wrong for hitting Warren with that glass bottle, but I was only trying to defend myself. I didn't report it because I didn't think anybody would care. I'm sorry. Please, just give me another chance."

"Chance?" the woman asked. "Why should *anyone* give you a chance, Mr. Robinson? Surely, it would be another thing if what you said happened first was documented. But there's no documentation nor evidence that Mr. Grant attacked you. Meanwhile, I've got a bus driver and eight other students claiming *you* were the aggressor in this confrontation. Catch my drift?"

The panel did more than just fuck Junior; they crucified him.

There to testify on Junior's behalf was none other than his mother, Sandy Robinson. Like any good mother, she went to bat for her son, presenting copies of Junior's transcripts from previous years. It shocked Junior to learn that his mother had saved his report cards from as far back as the second grade. He sat in his chair like a swollen lump as Sandy read aloud a signed letter dated from 1991 from the City Coordinator with Boys Scouts of America.

"'Thank you, Mrs. Robinson, for gifting us with your son, Leonard Robinson Jr. He's been a true pleasure to work with throughout the summer and will go on to do great things for his community in years to come.'" Sandy carefully folded the letter and placed it back into her bag. Acting on her son's behalf as his lawyer, Sandy questioned Big Warren, calling bluff to his fake tears and cross-examining his holey story. She was good and better than Junior anticipated. In her closing arguments, Sandy told the panel about the family's tragic loss the summer before, losing Lawrence, and how difficult it had been for Junior since the move.

"It's been hard on us as a family, especially Junior. His brother was his best friend."

Sandy then called on to Junior to speak, encouraging him to read a short selection from his journal. His masterful writing was well-received by the panel. Junior then went on to say that it was his goal to be the first man in his family to graduate from high school. Before long, the panel called for a short recess to deliberate on a decision on whether to expel Junior.

Out in the hallway, the Robinsons came together at the end of the hall.

"Geez, Ma, you sounded like a lawyer!" said Junior. "You sure you never practiced?"

Feeling herself, Sandy glowed.

"I thought about it once – but who knows. The most important thing is that we get you back into that school. Don't worry; your father and I got your back. Everything will be alright."

Senior was less enthused about the awaiting decision.

"Hmph," he grumbled. "If I know one thing, I know white folks," said Senior. "There ain't but two blacks on that panel and they're just as white if not whiter than the white folks already up there. Can't trust 'em. Nope! I'll believe it when I see it."

Junior's daddy was always skeptical. He was suspicious of everyone but particularly when it came to white people. As Senior stepped away to use the bathroom, Sandy told Junior that his grandfather, Senior's daddy, had been chased down and beaten to death by racist cops in North Carolina for failing to use a turn signal at a stop sign. Before she could finish the story, Senior exited the men's bathroom.

"C'mon, let's get this over with," Senior urged his family back to the courtroom.

The Decision

When Junior and his family returned to the hearing, they were surprised to be greeted by a representative from the Department of Human Health. The woman, named Eliza Simmons, had been summoned by the panel much earlier but arrived late to the hearing. She came in befuddled, dropping a stack of manila folders on the floor with her glasses tilted to the side like Damon Wayans in *Blankman*. She was sloppy, unprepared, and unorganized. Junior looked over at his mother and could tell she was not impressed by the woman. Senior looked at Eliza Simmons and leaned across Junior to get at Sandy.

"Yup. Here comes the horse shit," he whispered to Sandy.

Miss Simmons, summoned on behalf of the panel, alleged she had reviewed Junior's incident and concluded (without interviewing him) that Junior needed psychological counseling. In front of the panel, she questioned Sandy about Junior's upbringing, accusing her of not providing a stable home for her child. Sandy took offense, to say the least, but was on her best behavior for Junior. She answered every erratic question posed by Miss Simmons, still hopeful that Junior would be given the green light.

"Yes, we lived in North Philly for a time," Sandy begrudgingly answered. "Yes, I am aware that a child's home environment can dictate how they function at school."

Question after question, Sandy answered everything Miss Simmons had for her. In the end, the panel returned with a unanimous vote to expel Junior for the remainder of the 1995-96 school year. Once officiated, Junior would not be eligible to attend any regular public school across Philadelphia. As soon as the decision was called, Junior bolted from the room and out into the hallway as Senior went after him. From the hall, Junior could hear Sandy giving the panel a piece of her mind.

"Y'all got this wrong!" she said. "Y'all expelled the wrong kid! My son is not a criminal and that's how exactly how y'all treated him today, like a damn criminal!"

Out in the car, Junior listened as his parents debated over what had happened.

"I can't believe it!" said Sandy. "I can't believe they did that to Junior!"

"I can," said Senior. "I told y'all it was some bullshit afoot. Always is."

As Senior fired up the engine, Junior rode in the backseat of his mother's Buick Skylark speechless, staring back at his reflection in the window. Upfront, Sandy carried on in her diatribe that the school system had failed her son. She called the two blacks on the panel "alternate negroes" for voting unanimously to expel Junior and declared there was a bias against him due to Big Warren being a football star. Junior's expulsion was another loss inside the Robinson household. Lately, it seemed all his family was good for was accepting losses.

At a gas station near the house, Senior stopped in to buy cigarettes and play his favorite lottery numbers. As soon as

Senior exited the car and walked inside and Junior began to whimper, Sandy turned around to rebuke him.

"Sit up straight! Wipe those eyes! Pick your damn head up," she ordered. "Now, Junior! Do you want your daddy to come back and see you acting like this? Fix your face."

Using his suit sleeve, Junior wiped his nose and took a deep breath as he tried to stomach the idea of repeating the ninth grade next school year.

"Can't keep cryin' every time something bad happens," she explained. "Now, I know you're upset about what they did to you back there. I know you're pissed off, and I am too – and so is your daddy. But you have to hold your head up!"

"What for?" he asked. "It's over. I'm finished. I'll be a freshman again next year. You heard what they said. I'm expelled," he complained. "That means I'm out for the year."

"You're not *out* of anything, Junior," she corrected him. "There's other options. We'll just have to find you an alternative school in the meantime, that's all. I told you before, I'm in your corner. I'm not gonna let you fall behind – not on my watch. And for God's sake, hold your head up! If people keep seeing you with your head down, they're gonna *keep* it down! Do you understand?"

"Yes, ma'am."

Sandy then turned back around in her seat.

"Good. 'Cause, everything ain't worth losing your cool over, you know. You have to learn to move forward, that's all. There's always a way."

Seconds later, Senior ripped open the car door, threw his

stuff in the back next to Junior, and slammed the door so hard that Sandy's car rattled from side-to-side.

"Shit!" he banged on the wheel. "Shit-shit-*shit*!"

"Th'hell is wrong with you, slamming my door like a damn gorilla?" asked Sandy.

"I missed the number by one point," Senior complained. "I wrote 3-7-2. The motherfucka hit for 3-7-9. We could've won five hundred dollars! Ain't this a bitch?"

Junior always found Senior's lottery challenges comical. He broke into a small grin as Senior carried on up the road, cursing and pounding on the wheel. Sure, five hundred dollars wasn't life-changing money, but for Junior and his family, it was a start. Sandy couldn't believe Senior, especially not after the conversation she'd had with Junior about controlling his emotions. Junior's expulsion worries had subsided in exchange for a crumbled lottery ticket and Senior raising hell on the way back to Brooke's Rowe.

In the backseat, Junior was thinking to himself that attending an alternative institution in Philly wasn't the same as attending public school, but it was better than no school at all.

Pain is in all things. Can you see it?
There is a misfortune to being fortunate.
Sickness to being lovesick
and misery to wealth
No road is perfect. Not even close.

—LEONARD G. ROBINSON JR.

Three

After his hearing, Junior sat dejected inside his bedroom at home, sulking over the panel's decision to oust him for the remainder of the school year. To keep him sharp in case an alternative school came along sooner than expected, Sandy loaned Junior two books for him to read. At the top of the pile was *Miseducation of the Negro* by Carter G. Woodson, one of Sandy's old books. When Junior finished, Sandy gave him one of Lawrence's old books, *Sounder*, written by William Armstrong. After each chapter, Junior's mother would ask him questions, testing his understanding of both books. If anything, books offered Junior a temporary escape from the disappointment resulting in the outcome of the hearing.

Despite his support at home, anger burned inside his

young heart. The kids in or around Brooke's Rowe still rejected him, eventually turning Junior into a hermit. They nicknamed him "bum" and "scrub" whenever he came around. They questioned his heart and his testicular fortitude, and they accused him of being homosexual.

"So, what book did you bring with you today, bum?" a kid asked him.

"Tony Browder," said Junior.

"Who the fuck is that?" another boy laughed. "Man, don't you do anything besides read?"

"Word to my mother," a third kid chimed in, laughing. "That's some faggot-shit right there. Like, who the fuck comes down to the park to read?"

Enraged, Junior grabbed his drink and book and headed back to Kennedy Street as his hecklers mocked him. Despite what had happened with Big Warren, Junior wasn't the fighting type. The few skirmishes he'd encountered back in North Philly were when someone had picked on Lawrence or pushed Junior into a corner. Before his fight with Big Warren, the last fight he got in was on the way home from school when a junkie tried to accost him and his brother for five dollars to buy crack rock. Junior leveled the man with a brick to the face before running off with Lawrence.

When Junior returned home after being ousted from the park again, he'd had it with trying to get along with the boys around Brooke's Rowe, life's injustices, and the recent chain of traumatic events over the past year. Fed up with being the fall guy, he swiped at his journal atop his dresser, knocking it down to the floor, and punched a dent into his nightstand. Later, when Junior's mother opened his room door to find that he had torpedoed his bedroom, she knew exactly what went wrong.

"So…what'd they say this time?" she asked.

"Man, what didn't they say?" Junior scowled at the TV screen as he watched an old re-run of *Good Times*.

Sandy entered and took a seat next to him.

"You know, Junior," she said. "I don't think these boys around here hate you. I think they're just jealous of you."

Junior looked at Sandy as if she was a fool.

"Jealous?" he laughed. "Of me? What for? I get ten dollars a week for my allowance. I still own a Nintendo when all the other kids around here have Sega Genesis, Super Nintendo, or the new PlayStation. My father cuts my hair. I don't even have a girlfriend!"

"At least your daddy *cuts* your hair. At least you get that ten dollars. Most of these kids around here in Brooke's Rowe don't know what it's like to have a father *or* a family."

Still, Junior continued to complain about the torment he received. Before long, Sandy left him alone to cool off. Instead, he drowned in his misery, feeling sorry for himself. On the TV, a documentary of the ex-boxer, Philly's own "Smokin" Joe Frazier, appeared on the set. Junior studied the entire one-hour feature presentation, admiring the ex-champion's tenacity and menacing glower, and decided he'd adopt Frazier's mean look. Whether at school, down at the store, or elsewhere in Philly, he'd sport a sinister scowl on his innocent mug to scare off would-be troublemakers from picking on him. Later at dinner, Junior showed up to his mother's table looking like a pitiful mixture of Joe Frazier and Carlton Banks from *Fresh Prince of Bel-Air*. The fakery was spotted immediately by Senior.

"Boy, don't come to my table with that negative energy," Senior glared.

Junior's fake stare diminished immediately, but he decided he wasn't yet done with his new look. After dinner, he went back to the bathroom mirror to work on his face.

One day, while at the grocery store with Sandy, an old friend of hers from Crawford spotted them in the lot and ran over for a chat. Junior decided to put his new face to the test. He gave the elderly woman the gloomiest look he could, eye-balling her the way Joe Frazier would his opponents before the start of the bell. For all of his hard work on his new look, the woman was hardly phased by him. She reached through the window of Sandy's car for Junior's face and gave him a quick tickle to his neck. Junior broke character instantly, breaking into the cheesiest Jell-O Pudding smile, ever.

The Robinsons' ex-neighbor, Mrs. O'Neal, said that another shooting had happened on Joseph Boulevard where the Robinsons used to live. A girl, fifteen-years-old, was hit in the neck but expected to survive. Another ex-neighbor, Mrs. Walters, was in the hospital with a concussion after getting mugged for her purse after coming from the liquor store. The vandals knocked her to the ground, robbed her of her wedding ring, gold watch, and ripped the earrings from both ears.

"It's good y'all got out when y'all did," said Mrs. O'Neal. "Child, I'm tellin' ya. Nothin' but them little bad-ass nig-gas 'round there. Make no sense! Robbin' folks in broad daylight."

As Mrs. O'Neal carried on, Junior looked over at Sandy and could see the wheels inside his mother's head-turning. He knew she was wondering if the precinct near Crawford had ever built any leads around Lawrence's case.

On a hunch, Junior and his mother rode to Philly's Eleventh District Precinct to inquire about Lawrence's case. A full year had passed since the shooting. Riding through his old neighborhood, Junior reminisced about the aftermath of his brother's death. Detectives treated Lawrence's case as just another black person senselessly gunned down over gang ties, drugs, or being in the wrong place at the wrong time. Yet, when Karen or Susanne is robbed at a gas station in Marlborough or Prescott Hill, it made news all week.

When Junior and Sandy walked into the police station, the desk sergeant made them both wait on a stiff wooden bench for nearly two hours. The stench inside the police station was a mix of foggy cigarette air and brewing coffee beans. Officers bypassed Junior and his mother as though they were no different than the deceased mouse lying next to the water machine in the hallway. Meanwhile, a blonde-haired woman named Emma came in howling after her dog was mowed down by a cab and was offered fresh coffee and expedited to the nearest lieutenant's office.

After fidgeting in their chairs with sore bums, an investigator finally approached Junior and Sandy carrying a clipboard in his hand. He was a young black detective, no older than thirty.

"Robinson?" the man said without fully introducing himself.

"Detective?" Sandy sassed back before following him into the nearest interrogation room.

In the room on the table was a huge white box with Lawrence's full name written on the side. The top of the box was caved in as if it was used for a footstool or a table. Next to Lawrence's name, the date of his death was written: August 25, 1994. Flashes of the grim day rewound in Junior's head like a cassette tape. The detective thumbed through a folder inside Lawrence's box. On the side of his brother's box was a large hole, big enough for Junior to see the stained shirt paramedics had removed from his brother's body the day he was killed. With his hand, Junior turned the side with the hole toward the detective.

"You OK with all this?" Sandy asked him. "It's OK if you don't want to be in here, Junior."

"I'm good," replied Junior. "Let's just get it over with."

After watching the detective thumb through Lawrence's file and mumbling to himself, he'd found what he was looking for.

"Ah, here it is!" said the detective. "So, we matched the bullet found in your boy's neck to a gun found in a separate shooting that happened earlier this year. One of our guys from the vice unit thinks we were on the verge of tracking your son's killer, but he died in Baltimore before we could bring in him for questioning. So, the investigator assigned to your son's case closed it out. Sorry for keeping y'all waiting. We've been busy."

Then, like it was no big deal, the detective placed Lawrence's file back into the box.

"Well, from what I remember," said Sandy, "there were a few boys out there shooting that day, Detective. Any leads on them?"

Irritated, the detective pulled out Lawrence's file and whisked through his folder again, shaking his head.

"Nope," he closed the folder, placing it back into the box. "Unfortunately, these kinds of cases are hard to solve. I'm sure you understand."

"No, I *don't* understand. Why are these cases harder than any other?" asked Sandy.

"C'mon, you know how it is, Mrs. Robinson; black people don't speak up when shootings like this occur. Nobody sees anything. That's the way it usually goes – it's the code of the streets. Folks get amnesia. Frustrating for me as a detective. As soon as black people start caring about their community, we can get more of these kinds of cases solved faster. Is there anything else I can help you with today?"

Annoyed, Sandy cut her eyes at the detective.

"Well, seems to me y'all solve whatever cases y'all *want* to solve," she said. "Anytime a damn dog can get more justice than my son, I think that's a problem, sir."

"Well, I'm sorry," the detective claimed.

"For what?" Sandy shot back. "The dog gettin' more justice or that piece-of-shit statement you said about black people not caring about their community?"

"Look, Mrs. Robinson…"

"Mrs. Robinson my ass," Sandy cut in. "Let me tell you something, young man. You can be as blue as you wanna be, black man. But after your shift, you can take that stupid uniform off – but you can't take the black off of your coon ass! Let's go, Junior, we're leaving!"

Without hesitation, Junior and his mother stormed out of the Eleventh District Station.

On the way back to Brooke's Rowe, Junior went off in the car about the treatment his mother had received over at the station. He fussed enough for both he and Sandy as his mother sat, soaking it all in, barely saying a word.

In front of the house, Junior carried on about everything from institutional racism to being tired of being the fall guy around Brooke's Rowe. Sandy unbuckled her seatbelt, listening to everything Junior said about police, crime, being black, and how he planned to live his life going forward. Tired of being victimized by the city and its drudgery, Junior vowed to take matters into his own hands.

"Is that so?" Sandy said to him, unmoved by his rebelliousness.

"I'm serious, Ma!" he claimed. "That's why as soon as I get older, I'm buying myself a gun! Ain't nobody gonna mess with us anymore! If other people can shoot, so can I!"

Sandy coiled her head toward Junior and slapped him across his juvenile mouth.

"Look here, dammit! Don't you be goin' 'round talkin' stupid like that! I lost one son already, and I ain't gonna lose another! You are *not* some goddamn hoodlum in the street. I raised y'all better than that! You hear me?"

Junior didn't answer Sandy, but his eyes did.

"Now, what happened back there was just...I'm mad, too," said Sandy. "I'm pissed off. But you can't be stupid out here, Junior. You judge a person by what's in their heart, not what uniform they're in. Otherwise, you ain't no better than everyone else! Character first. Then take it from there. Do you understand me?"

"Yeah, but the cops around here are messed up," argued Junior. "You saw how the detective treated Lawrence, Ma. Like it wasn't any big deal at all – it never is to them when it comes to *our* people! What good are they if we can't rely on them to help us out?"

"A lot of cops are bad, but not all of them," Sandy told him. "And that goes to say, if you get stopped by one – you are to be respectful. Nothing else! If something goes wrong, we'll deal with it later, Junior. Now, I don't want to hear this... filth coming from your mouth about 'taking matters into your own hands'. We are *not* street people! Is that clear, Leonard Gerard Robinson, Jr.?"

"Yeah, but Ma..."

"JUNIOR!" Sandy interrupted, raising her voice loud enough for the world to hear. "Boy, I am *not* playing with you right now!" She jabbed him in the chest. "Th'fuck you think you're gonna tell me about some raggedy-ass police

65

that I don't already know? I was born in 1954 – not in 1995. I know what goes on out here in the street because I *lived* it! And your daddy *lived* it." She mushed his face twice. "Now, *get out* of my car before I break your fuckin' neck! Go!"

Careful not to further anger his mother, Junior climbed out of Sandy's Buick and slowly walked into the house. Once inside, Senior greeted him in the living room.

"Where's your mother?" he asked.

"She's uh… out in the car," said Junior. "She'll be in soon."

Senior lowered his eyes at Junior as he went out the door.

From the bedroom window, Junior watched as his six-foot-five daddy lowered his head to climb into Sandy's car. He couldn't hear what was being said but could see his daddy put his arm around his mother and thought to himself: Lawrence. Ashamed that he had scared his mother by his "by any means necessary" rhetoric, he reclused to his journal to stay out of his parents' way. Inside his numbered journal, he completed a poem entitled, "Zip Code".

> *Reside in Heart*
> *and not on some secluded island*
> *inside the fortress of your mind.*
> *Live for others.*
> *Drink harmony. Smoke tranquility.*
> *Become a fertile soul capable of birthing peace,*
> *prosperity, and positivity.*
>
> LEONARD G. ROBINSON JR.

Afterward, he penned "Freedom", concerning his discussion with Sandy from earlier.

I am free but not dom.

LEONARD G. ROBINSON JR.

Later, as Junior opened his bedroom door to go brush his teeth for the night, he was surprised to see Sandy on the other side of his door. She stood against the wall as if she was contemplating saying goodnight or leaving Junior to marinate on her slap from earlier.

Junior backed onto his bed without greeting her as he lowered his eyes down to the floor. Sandy took a seat next to him. As she stared at him, Junior kept his eyes on the floor. On his bed next to him was his journal, still turned to his latest poem, "Freedom". A light grin grew on Sandy's face as she looked down at the number in Junior's book to see that he'd nearly reached the 4,000 mark. Junior looked up at his mother, and back down at the floor.

"Sorry," she apologized. "But dammit, Junior, you scare me when you talk stupid the way you did earlier. I'm still serious about what I said. I'm *not* having no bullshit happen to you out here. I need you to use your head to think your way out of problems – not create 'em. You're our little investment, OK? I'm countin' on you."

Sandy then held Junior by his soft face, attempting to force him to look at her. He tried to hide the fact that he was smiling behind his failed mask. As he looked away, fake angry, Sandy stuck her finger into Junior's ear, causing him to jerk away. Even upset, he was still a cute kid.

"I'm sorry, too," he laughed. "You're right, I shouldn't talk like that. I feel bad."

"Don't." She held his face. "I know your heart. I know you're not mean or malicious. I know you didn't mean those things. You were just angry. I get it, Junior. I do."

As Sandy got up to leave her son's room. She turned back to face him.

"I talked to your daddy earlier. We both think it'd be a good idea for you to help out with his handyman business. Just for a little while. Until a school comes along."

"Oh God!" said Junior as his mother laughed. "Ma, no! Daddy is gonna go postal! Remember the last time I helped him change Mr. Lewis's radiator? He tried to kill me."

Sandy chuckled again.

"Well, you ain't stayin' home doin' nothin'. Besides, it'll be fun. You can learn a lot from him out there in the field. I know he can be surly at times, but he's a brilliant man *and* he's still your daddy. Just stay out of his way and you'll be fine."

"How in the world do I do that if I have to work next to him all day?"

"You'll think of something. Now, you may want to get to bed. Leonard gets up at 4 a.m. just about every morning. So, I'd turn that lamp off and put away that journal if I was you."

As Junior's door closed for the night, he plopped down onto his bed and watched as the blades of his ceiling fan circled his bedroom. Tomorrow would be a new day filled with much uncertainty.

Fathers, let your world revolve around the son.

LEONARD G. ROBINSON JR.

The Grind

As expected, at 4 a.m. sharp, Junior awoke to the bright UFO light blinding him from his ceiling and Senior barking down orders like an army sergeant. His eyes slowly adjusted to the large, almighty figure hovering over him. Leonard Robinson Sr. was already fully dressed and equipped with his list of clientele for the workday. Without warning, he ripped the covers off Junior and tossed his pillow down onto the floor.

"Let's go, Junior. Get on up from there!" he said. "C'mon, I wanna leave by 4:30."

Junior was always a slow mover in the morning. He did everything slowly, from putting on his clothes to washing his face and brushing his teeth. In the bathroom, he stood in front of his reflection like a zombie, tossing a palm-full of ice-cold water in his face. Across the hall in his parents' bedroom, Sandy was still sound asleep while Senior loudly organized his work tools for the day down in the living room. With ten minutes left to spare, he hollered at Junior from the bottom staircase up to the bathroom.

"Junior?" he shouted, "Boy, hurry the hell up! We're late!"

Not a single person in Philly was late at 4 a.m. except for Senior. Out in his truck, he laid on the horn, nonchalant of the neighbors on Kennedy Street; he had a business to run.

Without as much as a piece of scrapple or a cup of orange juice to start his day, Junior scaled into his daddy's shabby '81 Ford truck at 4:36 a.m. Already, Junior had committed his first mistake. Once inside, he turned to look over at Senior, noticing his daddy was fed up with him already.

"I said I wanted to leave well ahead of five o'clock, not at nig-o-clock," he said.

"It's 4:36!" said Junior.

"I *said* 4:30! Next time, I'm gonna leave without you!"

Junior caught himself before sassing off at his daddy. When Senior threatened to leave him the next time he was late, "good!" nearly slipped off his tongue. Had he said that Senior would've knocked him into a new school year.

For the next two weeks, or until Sandy could find Junior a suitable school, he'd work next to his daddy hustling tool-boxes throughout Philly and New Jersey. On the center console of Senior's truck was an account ledger with phone numbers, oddly shaped drawings, and a plethora of misspelled client names. It looked like something a first-grader had written while sleepwalking across the Sahara Desert. Without his daddy's permission, Junior reached for his father's ledger and nearly became an amputee.

"Can I at least see where we're going and what we're doing for today?" asked Junior.

Eyeballing him with distrust, Senior allowed Junior to look into his ledger.

Despite being a mediocre speller, the ledger which Senior owned turned out to be a complex spreadsheet of old and existing clients. Next to their names were the dates, times, and costs for Senior's labor. A closer look revealed that, when it came to spelling, Senior had barely finished grade school. For instance, the name Elizabeth was spelled "Elsibet", Harry was spelled "Hary," and they lived in "Nuarc, No Jursay". The page thereafter was a diagram for the braking system of an eighteen-wheeler. Though the nomenclature was difficult for Junior to digest, the drawing was illustrated perfectly.

In one immaculate concept, Junior's daddy had secured a concrete job. Detailed in the diagram were rows of trees, lamp posts, fire hydrants, and every other inanimate object found on a city street. Within the illustration, the sidewalk which Senior would pour the concrete contained detailed measurements with mathematical formulas used to calculate the value amount of concrete mix needed to complete the job. Senior had also taken the initiative to illustrate objects near the street zone where he worked and the distance from his working site. Then, almost as a gaffe, in the top corner of his works was a colorful sun along with a stream of clouds or whatever precipitation made it to his work that day: rain, sleet, snow or ice. For windy pictures, Senior's drawings were leaned in the direction of the wind that day. As Junior awed over his daddy's artistic talents, Senior took back his ledger and placed it in the visor above him.

"Man, you never told me you could draw, Daddy!" said Junior. "Yo, that's dope! Does Mom know you draw like that?"

"Nope, and don't you go shootin' your mouth off, neither. Besides, who gives a shit about an old man that can draw, anyway? As long as the work gets done."

"I give a shit – I mean – I care, Daddy." Junior straightened. "I ain't never seen nothin' like this. It's incredible! You can't just sit on your talent like this. Man, do you know what kind of work you could find drawing pictures like that?"

"Mmmhmm," Senior grunted as he sparked a cigarette and fanned away the smoke.

"*Mmmhmm?*" Junior mocked him. "I can take this down to the library where I get my books. I'm sure they could post it up. It's a part of Philly! Have you ever thought about going into business as an artist? A lot of money in that."

Senior took a drag of his cigarette and placed it in his ashtray.

"With a talent like that, Junior, it comes down to politics, and your daddy ain't the savviest at talkin' to people or handling them kind of affairs." He blew out of a cloud of smoke. "That's why I drive this old truck here. I'm comfortable where I'm at, right here in my little box. You got me?"

Disappointed, Junior turned back in his seat.

"Yeah," he said. "I got it, alright."

Senior then glanced over at Junior and realized his seatbelt was off.

"Nigga, you crazy?" he said. "Put your seatbelt on. Save a life why don't you, Junior."

Making his daddy angry was not at all in Junior's

best interest. On the way to their first assignment, Senior stopped in at a gas station to get a pack of cigarettes before remembering he'd forgotten to sketch for a job later in the week. To save time, he sent Junior in to pick up his favorite brand of Newport cigarettes. When Junior returned without the cigarettes and told his daddy the attendant wouldn't sell them to him, Senior told him to go back inside and have the attendant look over at his truck. When the attendant looked over, Senior put up his middle finger, and the attendant gave Junior two packs of Newports and a free honeybun for himself. Back in the car, Junior looked over at his daddy as if he was God.

"You know him or something?"

"Know him?" asked Senior. "Bastard owes me ten bucks."

For their first assignment together since the expulsion, Junior and his father drove down to Tom's River, New Jersey. In the back of Senior's raggedy pickup was a grey toolbox with an assortment of his tools. He was always picky and snappy when it came to his tools and gave them each special names, Junior noticed. He had an old worn wrench he called "Betty Mae" since it was rusty but reliable. In his pocket was a folding-knife he nicknamed "Cut Ya" since it was razor-sharp. All of his tools were wiped down before and after every job he worked. And despite his coldness at times, Senior was quite the prankster. Before beginning their job, Junior's daddy asked him to grab his grey toolbox from out the back. When Junior went to lift it, he went down fast to the ground as Senior laughed at him.

"Here, let me get that for you." Senior flexed as he hoisted the box into the air and tossed it onto one shoulder. "Stick with me, Junior." He winked. "I'll show you how to work."

The boat in Tom's River didn't have shit on Senior's toolbox. With his hat cocked down to the side, he whistled and hummed old-school R&B hymns as he repaired the motor on a small boat. He was also friendlier than he usually was at home during the evening hours when Junior came in from school. Not only was Senior brilliant at restoring small engines and a variety of other things most couldn't fathom, but he was also quite the teacher. With the engine fully apart and disassembled, he called Junior in to watch as he carefully reassembled the motor to the boat, showing his son each working part. He guided Junior's small hands as he carefully reunited the engine with the boat's blade. Senior then reattached the motor to the boat.

"Go'on," he said. "Give her a tug. Let's pray this works."

Junior cranked on the motor cord as the boat fired up instantly. The blade then powered on, kicking up suds from beneath as Senior high-fived Junior.

"Goddammit, Junior!" he shouted. "Now that's what I'm talkin' bout! Gimme some!"

Junior gave it all to his daddy. He slapped his father's huge hand and cheesed from ear-to-ear as Senior celebrated with a stumped cigarette he found inside his pants pocket.

Despite being off to a good start, Junior was hardly the handyman. Later, at a job on the northside of Philly, Junior dropped Betty Mae down into the sewer. He didn't say that he'd lost his daddy's favorite wrench, but it put Senior into a mood when his tools suddenly went missing. While fixing the brakes on a Cadillac Coup de Ville, Senior asked if he could bring him a 5/16 size wrench, and Junior bought a ¾ size instead. Senior looked down at the wrench and back up Junior.

"Something wrong?" asked Junior.

Senior then flipped over the wrench so Junior could see it was the wrong size.

"We wouldn't have this problem if you hadn't dropped good ol' Betty Mae down the damn sewer, now would we?"

Junior was stunned.

Days later, while the two were on a landscaping job in Cherry Hill, Senior sent Junior up the ladder to unclog a client's gutters. Somehow, Junior forgot to tell his father that he was afraid of heights. As the ladder swayed amidst the summer winds, his chicken legs fluttered nervously as he looked down at Senior for validation.

"Th'hell you lookin' at me for?" he said. "Pay attention to what you're doin'."

After a few minutes, Senior left Junior up on the ladder to get his cigarettes from the car. Worried, Junior wrapped one arm around the ladder and used his free arm to remove a section of cluttered leaves from the top of the downspout. As he went to remove a patch, a wasp whisked by his head, scaring him. He dropped the patch of leaves back into the gutter and hurried down the ladder, shaking.

"Lord have mercy. What is it now?" asked Senior.

"Man, it's bees up there!" Junior complained.

"Bees gotta eat, right? Go'on! Finish up."

It took Junior nearly half the day to finish the client's gutters with Senior glaring at him most of the day. But, by the end of that week, Junior had earned his share of eighty dollars. Junior reflected that it was the same amount that had gone missing from Senior's nightstand the summer before. Junior looked down at the cash in his hand and thought of Lawrence as Senior counted his money next to Sandy downstairs in the kitchen. Junior looked over at his nightstand at a picture of him and his brother taken outside of Veterans Stadium in September of 1992. That year, Sandy had taken the boys to watch Randall Cunningham and the Philadelphia Eagles beat the Phoenix Cardinals 31 to 14. Junior remembered then that five dollars had gone missing from Sandy's wallet the night before. She never questioned the boys, believing they both knew better than to steal. Afterward, he remembered Lawrence showing up at the park with the biggest candy bar and slice of pizza he'd ever seen. Suddenly, it dawned on him. Junior then took the eighty dollars he received from his daddy for a week's worth of work and headed downstairs to return the money. Senior looked at him as if he was a brand new fool.

"So, what's this?" Senior looked down at the money on the table. "Oh, I get it," he laughed, jabbing Junior on the shoulder. "All of a sudden, you too good for eighty bucks, now?"

Senior laughed, but Junior didn't.

"Maybe you ought to keep it, Daddy," said Junior. "Use it for bills or something."

Senior then scooped the money from the table and placed it back into Junior's hand.

"I said you did good for the week," he said. "Now, scram. I ain't takin' it back, Junior."

Disregarding Senior, Junior then offered the money to his mother which angered Senior. He threw his money down onto the table and stepped into Junior's face.

"Hey!" he barked. "Did you hear what I just said? Now, put the goddamn money away!"

"I don't want it!" Junior threw it onto the floor. "You keep it!"

"Th'hell has gotten into you, Junior?" Senior picked up the cash.

"Ain't nothin' got into me! I just don't want it!" Junior raised his voice before bolting to the door. "Why can't you just listen to me sometime when I tell you stuff, man? I said I don't want it!"

Slamming the door behind him, Junior jetted from the house and raced down Kennedy Street, crying. Behind him, he turned to see Senior fire up his truck and come flying up Kennedy after him. As Junior tried to run, Senior pressed on the gas, eventually cutting his son off in a neighbor's driveway. Sandy was in the passenger seat and jumped out to take hold of her son as Senior raised holy hell at Junior from the inside.

"Sh-sh-sh," Sandy comforted her son. "Tell me what's wrong. What's wrong with the money your daddy gave you, Junior? Now, eighty dollars is good money. You ought to be thankful you got that."

Gathering himself, Junior took a deep breath. "I *am* thankful," he said. "It's plenty, Ma."

"Well, then what's the problem?" she asked.

Scowling from the driver's seat with his truck still blocking the neighbor's driveway, Senior looked on at Junior, waiting for an answer. Instead, Junior took a seat on the curb as Sandy sat next to him. Senior then parked his truck and stood beside Sandy as Junior began to talk.

"Lawrence had said something about taking the eighty last summer before he did it, I just didn't say nothin'. I wasn't sure if he would. Now he's dead and it's my fault."

As Junior began to cry, Sandy draped over him.

"You're right. You should have told us," Sandy said with a tear in her eye. "But it's not your fault Lawrence is dead. That was due to senselessness, Junior. You didn't pull the trigger on Lawrence. None of us did. It was a mistake."

As Sandy consoled Junior out in the middle of Kennedy Street, Senior placed his hands on both hips and paced back and forth as he relived the nightmare from the previous summer. Before long, Senior took a seat next to him along the curb and issued his son a full pardon. In Senior's hand was the crumbled up money Junior had earned throughout the week, with interest. As Junior attempted to turn down the money, Senior hushed him.

"It ain't eighty," he said. "I stuck a lil' bit extra in there for you...take it."

Looking over at his mother, Sandy nodded as Junior accepted the money.

Later that evening, back at the house, Junior counted the hundred dollars he received from Senior. Before bed, he kept twenty from his stash and wrote "For Lawrence" and placed the rest behind a picture frame of him and his brother on top of his dresser.

Can I drink from your fountain?
Your waters are nourishing and fulfilling.
I can feel myself heal at a taste of your eloquence.

LEONARD G. ROBINSON JR.

New School

Finding Junior an alternative school in the middle of September was a burden itself after he had been expelled from Franklin High. After a long workday beside his daddy, Junior would return home to Sandy waiting on him. From there, they'd cruise around Philly looking at both private and alternative schools. Douglas MacArthur Military Academy, an all-boys school on the west side, wanted $5,600 per semester with $2,000 upfront. Richardson Baptist wanted double that, and Eisenhower High said that Junior had missed the enrollment deadline by a week. Every other privately run institution was either out of the Robinsons' budget or too far away. Frustrated, Junior overheard his mother complaining over the phone to his Aunt Tonique about his dilemma. By then, he had missed two weeks of school and Sandy was desperate.

Together, he and Sandy had visited a total of eighteen schools across Philadelphia.

While down at the post office, a colleague of Sandy's encouraged her to visit Medgar Evers Secondary School, located on Sunnyside Avenue. On a windy Friday afternoon, Junior and his mother visited the campus with the hope of having him start by Monday.

The principal was a man named Thomas Levy, a stumpy, sloppy, fat white man with a potbelly that protruded above his belt. He had a wide, porky neck and gray, crusty hands riddled with eczema. He greeted Junior and Sandy in the parking lot as they arrived late that Friday afternoon. As Sandy drove up beside his shiny Nissan Sentra parked at the head of the lot, he waddled over to the passenger window like a duck.

"Sure, we take boys like Junior all the time." He winked down at Junior. He had foul dragon breath and rotting coffee teeth on his gumline. "I'm headed home, but if you bring him back Monday morning, I'll get you guys enrolled."

Junior didn't like Mr. Levy the second he met him, nor did he think much of Medgar. From the outside, the building looked like an asylum for the criminally insane. The glass windows on the first-floor were covered in iron grating and a brown film as if they hadn't been washed since the Great Depression. At the front of the school was a fractured mural of the school's namesake. Junior surveyed the surrounding neighborhood and looked up to the sky. A dark cloud loomed over his proposed new school, and he felt his anxiety spiking out of control. On the way back to Kennedy Street, Junior voiced his concerns.

"Did you see what I saw?" he said to Sandy. "Something ain't right about that school."

Desperate to get him back into school, Sandy shrugged him off.

"Yeah, well, there aren't too many other options available, Junior," she said. "What am I supposed to do? Keep you out until next year?"

Junior kept his mouth shut. Sandy was right. For the past two weeks, she had driven him all over Philadelphia, hoping to find him a new school. He was on the verge of missing the mandatory enrollment date set by the Philadelphia School Board.

Back at home, Sandy told Senior she had found Junior a new school for him to attend, but Senior was preoccupied with changing the oil inside his truck. "Mmmhmm," he grunted as Sandy went on about their son's new school. Meanwhile, inside, Junior fretted at the idea of attending Medgar as he recalled Mr. Levy's golden teeth and peeling hands. Mr. Levy looked like a child's nightmare come to life with some relevance to a character in *Tales from The Crypt*. To take his mind off Medgar, he turned to his journal to write. When that didn't work, Junior went to his Nintendo for a quick video game before Sandy called him to the table for dinner. Senior, however, beat Sandy to the punch.

"Take a run with me down to the store, I need to grab somethin'," he said. "And hurry up, I want to get back here before it gets dark. You know how these niggas are around here, Junior."

> *"Why do I need permission to be black?"*
> *asked the boy whose black parents told him to behave*
> *when it came to racism.*
>
> LEONARD G. ROBINSON JR.

A Race Down the Road

As Junior and his daddy readied to leave the store's parking lot later that evening, Senior patted his breast pocket for his Newports. Slapping the lighter to his dashboard, he took a long drag of his cigarette and exhaled as he turned from the parking lot of Trak Auto. In the backseat on the floorboard of his pickup was a can of rags, an air filter for his truck, a Sunkist soda for Junior, and an ice-cold Budweiser beer to go with Sandy's fish-and-collard-greens dinner.

Pushing his pickup faster than he'd normally drive, Junior thought of saying something but didn't. Senior always hated backseat drivers, especially when Sandy got on him. Instead, Junior kept his thoughts to himself as he glanced over at the dashboard and noticed Senior was approaching fifty-five miles per hour in a thirty zone.

Near the intersection of 19th and Bogdan Street, the traffic signal switched from steady green to yellow. Rather than slowing down, Senior pushed his truck past seventy to make the light and flew by a marked police car idling on the next block over. From the passenger side mirror, Junior saw the patrol cruiser zip onto Bogdan and slip behind his daddy's truck. Suddenly, the flash of blue and red illuminated them as Senior pulled to the side of the road. The truck was overcast with two spotlights. A voice appeared on the loudspeaker.

"Driver! Turn off your vehicle!"

Afterward, a second, third, and fourth police car appeared next to the initiating cruiser.

Shaking, Junior turned to look back and saw nothing but blue and red lights behind them as Senior shut off the motor.

"Driver, place your keys on the roof of your vehicle!"

Junior saw the look on Senior's face and could tell his daddy was irritated. Removing his keys from the ignition, Senior complied with the voice coming from the loudspeaker.

"Now, driver and passenger, place both of your hands on the dashboard!"

"Y'all want to tell me what this is all about?" Senior yelled.

"Just do it, man!" a second officer yelled.

Junior glanced in the passenger side mirror and saw two police officers with their guns drawn, moving soundly toward his daddy's truck. Nervous, he trembled as he recalled the story of Rodney King that had taken place in Los Angeles several years earlier. On Sunday, March 3, 1991, officers from the Los Angeles Police Department were filmed beating Rodney King mercilessly. In the video, officers battered Rodney King during a traffic stop, leaving him a bloody mess. The story made headlines across the world.

For Junior, it was one of many stops he'd experience. The first time, Senior's truck was impounded for expired tags and Junior ended up calling Sandy from a parking lot payphone. During the second stop, the summer before, Sandy was behind the wheel when an officer gave her shit over a burnt brake light. Unfortunately, for the officer, Senior was in the car. Bad temper and all, he threw the officer's ticket book (and threatened to toss the cop) over Benjamin Franklin Bridge. Senior spent three nights in the city jail and was ordered to pay a fine of $250.

With their hands on the dashboard, five police officers encircled Senior's Ford truck, four on the driver's side, and one where Junior was sitting. They shined their flashlights throughout the truck, asking Senior all kinds of questions about where he had come from and the bag with Senior's unopened Budweiser in it.

"You're not supposed to have alcohol in the vehicle," one cop said.

"Why? It ain't open," said Senior. "How else am I supposed to get it home?"

"Shut your mouth! We're asking the questions here!"

Quivering, Junior nudged Senior to stop talking, which he did. But knowing his daddy, Junior wondered if he hadn't been in the car if Senior would've ended up dead that night. He was quiet and peaceful most days but had a violent temper when provoked that led him to not give a damn about anything.

Gripping onto his steering wheel, Senior stared ahead as officers asked him for his license and registration. Without warning, he leaned backward to reach down into his pocket as officers placed their hands on top of their service weapons.

"You just asked for my license," he said. "Now, do you want the motherfucka or not?"

"Take it easy, pal," the cop said.

"Fuck you," Senior shot back. "*You* take it easy. This is bullshit."

"C'mon Daddy, stop!" said Junior. "Just give 'em the license so we can go home. Mom is waitin' on us."

Exhaling, Senior reached into his wallet and handed the officer his driver's license.

"Be right back," the cop said as he and his co-workers disappeared between the sea of blue and red lights.

Looking back, Junior watched as his daddy puffed on a cigarette and waited for them to return with a citation for speeding, unmoved by the event. Five minutes later, the officer returned and issued Senior $200 worth of tickets. Quoting every scripture in the Pennsylvania State Traffic Law, the officer explained the citations to Senior and handed over his ticket book and a pen for him to sign with. Scanning, looking, Junior noticed the words seemed foreign to Senior as he attempted to read the fine print. The cop became a smartass, telling Senior that he didn't have all night and demanding him to sign the citation or face arrest.

Panicking, Junior offered to help.

"Here Daddy, let me help. I think here it's saying that—"

"Dammit, Junior!" Senior interrupted. "Let me do this!" he hollered.

Pitifully, Junior watched as his father struggled to interpret the issued citation. He watched a side-eye as Senior traced the ticket word for word using his index finger. The rookie cop raised his eyebrow at Senior before looking over at Junior. The cop then looked over at his squadron of oppressors as they covered their pompous smirks and looked at one another, realizing what they had in front of him. It then became immediately apparent to Junior: Senior, for all his handyman, tough-guy talk, was illiterate. Sweat trickled from his forehead as he stared down at the citation helplessly, his eyes scrambling across the printed ticket looking for a miracle. Impatient, the officers began patronizing Senior, treating him like a runaway slave desperate to find his way north.

"Uh…you sure you don't need an interpreter or something?" the cop asked.

The officers standing around Senior's truck all laughed. Ignoring his outburst from earlier, Junior intervened to spare his father further embarrassment.

"Just sign right there on the line." Junior pointed. "It's saying you were speeding. We'll take it back to Mom; she can talk to you about it later."

With the officer's pen, Senior quickly scribbled his signature on the line and handed the officer's ticket book back to him, relieved. The officer, still attempting to contain himself amongst his colleagues, removed Senior's copy and placed it onto his dashboard.

"Have a good night." He grinned before eventually driving off along with his buddies.

After the stop, Junior sat looking over at Senior as he reached for his car keys from the roof of his truck and cranked the engine. He couldn't believe that his father was illiterate, not after seeing his beautiful illustrations earlier in the week. Anger brewed inside his daddy as the feeling of embarrassment and inadequacy overtook him. As Junior tried consoling his father, Senior lashed out, burying Junior for interfering in the stop.

"You should've let me handle it!" he barked. "You had no business gettin' in the middle of that. Th'fuck is your problem, Junior? Huh?"

"I was just trying to help, Daddy," he apologized. "Sorry. I didn't mean nothin' by it."

"I don't need your help! I can sign my own goddamn ticket!"

For the remainder of the ride back to Kennedy Street, Junior sat in silence.

> *They enslaved us for 400 years. Gave us new names.*
> *Raped our mothers. Raped our fathers.*
> *Whipped us for running. Whipped us for dreaming.*
> *Whipped us for reading.*
> *Then sold us away.*
> *Whipped us for running. Whipped us for dreaming.*
> *Whipped us for reading.*
> *Stole our dreams. Stole our opportunities. Stole our future.*
> *And then called us ignorant niggers.*

LEONARD G. ROBINSON

Never Seen a Man Cry

Ashamed of his illiteracy, Senior escaped down to the basement where he remained for the night. Junior, believing he was at fault, summoned Sandy to his bedroom for advice.

"I didn't mean it, Ma," he said. "I was just trying to help. If I thought Daddy would've got angry, I wouldn't have said anything. I didn't know."

Sandy looked down at the citation issued to Senior earlier that evening and sat next to Junior on his bed.

"It's not your fault," she said. "It's my fault. I should've told you."

Sitting on his bed, Junior heard a sound coming from the vent on the floor. He sat closer to the vent, listening: it was his daddy, crying in the basement.

As Sandy headed down to check on Senior, Junior waited a few minutes to pass before tip-toeing to the top of the basement stairway to hear his mother smoothing things over with Senior. It was the first time Junior had ever seen a man cry, and the first time he'd seen his father succumb to anything in fourteen years. Before his cover was blown, he headed back upstairs to his bedroom to write and allow for Sandy to work her magic on Senior. Unlike most nights when Junior's parents cussed and traded insults, that night they put on the show of a quality marriage of two partners who understood one another. Later, when the dust settled, Sandy returned to Junior's bedroom to allow Senior time to recoup from earlier.

"Everything OK?" asked Junior, concerned.

Sandy rolled her eyes.

"So, what'd you write tonight?" she asked, switching topics. "Anything good?"

Junior switched expressions. "What?" he laughed. "Man, *all* my stuff is good!"

He handed his journal over for Sandy to read.

I no a lot of people so that I won't know a lot of people.

LEONARD G. ROBINSON JR.

"Whew! Too deep!" she applauded him. "I'd be careful with that one!"

"For what? So far, everyone I've run across in Brooke's Rowe has been against me."

Sandy then handed Junior back his journal.

"Everyone?" she asked. "As I said, I'd be careful with that one. We all need somebody in this world, Junior. Everybody. Including you."

Sandy left, allowing Junior to marinate on her wisdom.

Plant a seed, water it, and birth a tree.
But some young seeds
don't get the nutrients they need.
Instead, they get forgotten
by other forgotten seeds.

—LEONARD G. ROBINSON JR.

Four

The brakes on Sandy's Buick Skylark whined as her car came to a stop, alerting the world that Junior had arrived for his first day of school. With his loaded backpack over his shoulder, Junior stepped out of his mother's car and looked over at the tatted brick outside of Medgar Evers Secondary School for his first day. Next to the school's namesake was the weathered mural of the prominent Civil Rights Activist. Stenciled beneath the iconic hero were his eternal words, "You can kill a man, but you can't kill an idea." When Junior had first gotten his library card the year before, he had happened upon an article about Medgar Evers, left on the computer by a visitor. Junior stared at the dilapidated building as he trudged toward the entrance behind Sandy, anxiously. He wondered how the city could allow a school named after such a powerful man to go to hell in the two decades since the school had been built.

That day in the library, Junior had learned about Evers: born Medgar Wiley Evers on July 2, 1925, in Decatur, Mississippi, Evers rose to prominence as the First State Field Representative for the NAACP (National Association for the Advancement of Colored People). Before his untimely death, he had fought for the equal rights of African-Americans and, like his contemporaries, became a target for white supremacists. On June 12, 1963, upon returning to his Jackson, Mississippi home, Evers was assassinated in his driveway after returning from an NAACP meeting.

The closer to the building Junior got, the more nervous he became. His stomach filled with the same butterflies as when he and his family had first moved to Brooke's Rowe last fall. He walked with his head pointed down at the ground. Occasionally, Junior would look up to acknowledge the mural of Medgar Evers painted on the wall with other contemporary trailblazers Rosa Parks, Dr. Martin Luther King Jr., Malcolm X, Muhammad Ali, as well as a picture of Jesus Christ with his arms around Emmitt Till. Beneath the mural on the sidewalk, however, was an unfortunate picture: a group of truants skipping dice across the asphalt.

As Sandy led the way, Junior lagged behind her embarrassed. Near the door, he peeked at the boys shooting craps and quickly turned away before they could make eye contact with him. By then, it was too late. They sized Junior up immediately, taking shots at him as he followed behind Sandy like a sheltered puppy trying to keep up with its owner. Intimidated, Junior raised the hood to his thrift store windbreaker over his head and stuffed his hands inside his pockets. As Sandy approached the door to Medgar, she looked back to see her son slouching along and scolded him for his defeatist manner.

"Hey!" she whispered to him. "Pick your head up! Take those hands out of your pockets and walk like you come from someplace. You ain't no damn bum!"

As the boys continued their tomfoolery, Sandy turned to survey the boys picking on her son. Unimpressed, she stood there looking at them.

"Man, let's just go inside," said Junior. "C'mon, Ma."

Sandy didn't budge as the jokes from the dice shooters continued. They went from picking on Junior to ribbing on Sandy. They got on her postal service outfit and beatdown Buick Skylark parked at the bottom of the lot. One of the boys took it a step further. Disrespectful, he claimed to be Junior's biological daddy. It triggered Junior, but not enough to take on four boys all twice his size, if not bigger. But Sandy, who'd lived the better part of forty years on Philly's north side, could give a damn about a group of young punks tumbling dice and their corner-store criticism. Unafraid, she pushed the door to Medgar closed and walked over to the group, and stood in the middle of their dice game.

"Yeah, real cute." Sandy kicked at the dice. "Now, which one of y'all can tell me something about those people over there on that mural, and fast – 'cause I got to work, and I ain't got time to be out here bullshittin' with a bunch of low-life niggas like y'all."

Disoriented by her boldness, the boys looked at each other, fumbling for words as they deliberated, mixing up their ancestors' names and accomplishments. Junior was stunned at Sandy, but at the same time, not surprised. She was fearless, and in her years as a mail carrier had fought off dogs and once leveled a man who had tried to rob her. She was old school and built differently than most of the so-called troublemakers lurking around their hometown.

As the boys fished for answers, Junior's mother turned to look back at him, shaking her head in disgust at the uninformed miscreants as they struggled for clarity.

"My, my, my," Sandy sang. "So, what do we have here? Are you serious? Y'all should be ashamed of yourselves. Ignorance for black history is the fruit of white supremacy. That's why y'all killin' each other now! And y'all gonna keep on killin' each other, too! And that's why twenty-five years from now, y'all kids are gonna keep getting killed by racist white cops and you ain't gonna do a goddamn thing about it," she continued as Junior stood at the door to Medgar chewing anxiously on the string to his jacket. Embarrassed, one of the boys reached into his jacket as if he was gonna pull out a gun or a knife, and Sandy called his bluff.

"Go 'head, shoot! Go'on! Kill me!" She threw her arms out to the side. "That's all you niggas good for anyway. Or, what you *can* do, is pick those dice up off my sidewalk and take your asses inside that school – cause I'm payin' for it. Where your mommas at? Y'all need one!"

The boys each looked at each other and over at Junior. Three of the boys did as Sandy ordered, and one walked off. Sandy then returned to Junior at the door to Medgar, disgust painted on her face, hidden behind a smirk of victory as she continued inside. Once in the foyer next to the main office, Junior's momma grabbed him by the arm, jacking him next to the wall.

"Do you know the people on that mural out there, Junior?" she asked.

"Yes," he exerted.

"Good. You better."

Inside the main office, Junior and Sandy saw Medgar's principal, Mr. Thomas Levy. His collared shirt was fastened together with a cheap, red clip-on tie around his wide neck as he waddled around his office like an intoxicated duck. His protruding belly hung over his shirt and the sleeves to his suit extended down to his fingertips. He was the tackiest principal Junior had ever seen. On the outside, he resembled the look of a pedophile or chronic porn user who'd struggled all his life with dating. As both Junior and Sandy waited for him to make copies of his paperwork, he slithered throughout the office like a crooked salesman. At one point during the meeting, he reached across the table to shake Junior's hand. Junior looked down into the dry, scabby palm of Mr. Levy's hand and hesitantly shook it. The principal's dehydrated hand felt like open sores and sandpaper; Junior gagged. Not to mention, Mr. Levy gave a flaccid shake. Junior then remembered what Senior had once told him about a man with a weak handshake. "If a man ever gives you a weak handshake, watch 'em!" said Senior, "He's probably fixin' to kill you later." Mr. Levy then smiled into Junior's face, showing the top row of coffee-colored teeth, with pastry plaque wedged around his gumline. As Mr. Levy went to shake Sandy's hand, she returned a fist bump.

Despite his sleaziness and cheap clip-on tie, Mr. Levy, for what it was worth, appeared to be quite the accomplished scholar, Junior noticed. On the wall inside of his office was his Master's and Bachelor's Degree from Berkeley College along with several commendations of service from the mayor's office in Philadelphia. He had also been featured in a March of 1980 *New York Times* article for developing a mentorship program for disadvantaged youths in Queens, New York. In the picture, Mr. Levy looked nothing like he did in the present day. He was slim, had a head full of hair and pearly white teeth.

Mr. Levy took Junior and Sandy on a brief tour of Medgar which ended on the fourth-floor. As was the case outside, the interior of the building was subpar at best, with graffiti on every floor and scattered patches of mold or smog near the ceiling and around some windows. Some of the windows were so badly rusted that they creaked as Mr. Levy opened them to let a passing breeze of Philly air into the school.

Back inside his office, he blew through Junior's file in a

cheap pair of bifocal reading glasses attached to a bootstring that wrapped behind his ears and meaty head. Meanwhile, as Junior waited on a verdict, he continued to look around the man's office. He took notice of Mr. Levy's artifacts, eyeing pictures on his wall of the principal's past life. According to the photos, Mr. Levy had always had a bubbly neck. Once upon a time, he was a happily married man with two kids – a boy and a girl. As Junior's eyes continued around the room, the pictures of Mr. Levy's perfect life were replaced with pictures of just him with his children. Down on Mr. Levy's desk in front of him was a framed photo of a young boy that resembled him. Beneath the picture was the gold-plated inscription: "Catonsville Boys and Girls Club, 2nd place at Top Batter Award – Elliot "Ellie" Levy. September 1985." Junior peered into the grainy photo on Mr. Levy's desk and lifted the frame before Sandy could scold him.

"Is this a picture of your son, sir?" Junior held up the photo.

Mr. Levy looked down at the photo and back up at Junior. In his bi-focal glasses, his eyes were as big as two tennis balls.

"*Was* my son, yes," he said. "Some damn drunk driver hit him on his way home from practice a few years ago. They never found the scumbag who did that."

Sandy ripped the photo from Junior's hands and returned it to Mr. Levy's desk.

"Well, he's still your son." She mugged at Junior. "Nothin' will ever change that."

Nodding in agreement, Mr. Levy took down Sandy's contact information and filed it away with Junior's application.

Shortly thereafter, Sandy left for work, leaving Junior in the hands of his new principal and the staff at Medgar.

Black is the skin I reside in.
Love is the language I speak.
Poetry is my air. God is my sun.
Music is my Holy Water.
I am who I am. That's just how it be.
Let the rest just hate on me.

LEONARD G. ROBINSON JR.

Getting to Know Medgar

Junior's first day at Medgar was nothing like any first day of school he'd ever had. After Sandy left him, Mr. Levy pointed Junior to an empty cubicle outside of his office. According to Mr. Levy, more than half, it not all, of the school was on a field trip down at the zoo for the day. With few teachers lurking throughout the building, he promised to assign Junior to a staff member.

Around 9 a.m., Junior followed Mr. Levy up to Miss Wallace's class on the fourth-floor. When they got there, however, the room was pitch black. Next was Mr. Madison in 234, but he requested leave to take his pregnant wife to the doctor. The music teacher, Mrs. Patterson, preferred to use her free day to develop lesson plans and had no intention of being a sit-in for Junior. With the door shut to her room and

Junior waiting on the opposite side, she was concerned with more than just developing lesson plans.

"Jesus Christ, Levy!" Junior listened in. "Haven't you given me enough black students here at Medgar, already?" Junior couldn't tell which was more disturbing, the fact that Mr. Levy didn't fire Mrs. Patterson on the spot or that Medgar's music teacher was darker than him. P.E. teacher Mr. Reid had volunteered to watch Junior but then had a family emergency. Out of options, Junior returned to the empty cubicle outside of Mr. Levy's office.

"Sit here at Miss Haughton's desk, Leonard," he said. "She should be in soon."

"Actually, it's 'Junior,' sir," Junior corrected. "Everyone calls me Junior."

Mr. Levy gave him a dirty look.

"Fine. Junior, it is," he conceded. "Just hang out here. She'll be in. She's my secretary."

While seated at Miss Haughton's cubicle, Junior went back to his inquisitive nature, finger-fucking the artifacts atop the secretary's desk. He lifted the woman's nameplate and fancied the pictures on her desk, admiring her exquisiteness. Dark skin with long hair. If Junior and Mr. Levy couldn't agree on much else, they at least had the same taste in women.

By ten o'clock, Junior was still trapped at Miss Haughton's cubicle. To pass the time, he switched between his latest book rental and writing inside his journal. Another staff member entered the office at that time and saw Junior sitting at Miss

Haughton's desk and began asking him questions. Junior kept his answers shorter than his poems, not sure who else would hear his words. Later, a school resource officer, a black man named Darcy, passed by the main office and introduced himself to Junior. As they exchanged words, the man looked down at Miss Haughton's desk, over at Junior and rubbed at the skin on the back of his wrist.

"Stay alert, young blood!" he warned before shaking his head and walking off.

Junior knew exactly what the gesture meant. It meant that the photographs of the black beauty he'd been admiring on Miss Haughton's desk was not Miss Haughton. The butterflies from earlier that morning returned to Junior's stomach as he pictured a prissy, blonde-haired, blue-eyed white woman. Junior spent the next hour reminiscing about the cop who pulled over his daddy Friday night.

Well past eleven o'clock, then noon, and still no sign of Mr. Levy's secretary, Miss Haughton. After waiting around for nearly two and a half hours, Junior took her absence personally. He lifted her name plaque and dropped it onto her desk before removing his gum and lodging it beneath Miss Haughton's chair to teach her a lesson. When Mr. Levy came out of his office for lunch and saw Junior still sitting at Miss Haughton's cubicle at 12:04 p.m., he flipped out, raising hell inside of his office. Minutes later, his secretary showed up to work.

Miss Haughton entered the building in a pair of phony movie-style shades with loose curls in her orange hair. She was whiter than white and about as pale as a junkie recovering from heroin addiction. She looked nothing like the photo of black excellence on her desk. Moderately obese with heavyset chunky legs, she had small, puffy hands like a newborn. She entered the main office, bypassing Junior with a quick "Yo!" as she rushed into Mr. Levy's office and closed the door, bags dripping from her cattle arms.

With the door to Mr. Levy's office closed, Junior listened as the two went back and forth, shouting at each other. It was nothing to Junior, who for the past fourteen years had been listening to Senior and Sandy fuss every day.

As the door to the principal's office flung open, Miss Haughton went over to Junior, who was still seated at her desk.

"C'mon kid, we're going to 206." She rolled her green eyes, annoyed. On the way to the second-floor, Miss Haughton went off on Mr. Levy in front of Junior, calling him every name in the book from a pervert to a slob. She then apologized to Junior for being late.

At the door of 206, Miss Haughton reached into her purse for the room key, realized it was missing, and sent Junior back to Mr. Levy's office to pick up a spare key. That fast, she'd lost the key. When Junior got back to the main office, however, Mr. Levy had left for lunch, forcing him to hunt down a janitor to unlock room 206. The janitor was all too familiar with Mr. Levy's often unprepared secretary.

"Let me guess: Miss Haughton?" the man said before handing Junior one of his backups. "Man, I can't tell you how many times she's done that shit to me. Here. Take it."

Key in hand, Junior returned to room 206, letting them both inside. Afterward, he took a seat at the back of the room as far away from her as he could.

For nearly a half-hour, Miss Haughton bloviated about Philly history, boring Junior to the brink of death. She went on from everything to Sir William Penn and the origin of their city's name to "Smokin" Joe Frazier, Teddy Pendergrass, and other notable figures. She asked Junior all kinds of weird questions from his favorite color and food to his favorite subject at school. Hoping to deter her, Junior kept his answers short. "Blue. Pizza. I don't know. I don't like school," he answered. Eventually, Miss Haughton got the message and left Junior to write inside his journal.

Less than a minute into his latest works, he noticed a pair of feet beneath his desk and looked up to see Miss Haughton standing there in his face. She was as commanding a person as Sandy was, looming over top of Junior as he wrote. If nothing else up close, she had sharp, pretty green eyes with dotted pink freckles around her face.

"Yo man, can I help you?" Junior asked, irritated. "I'm kind of busy."

"So, what are you writing?" she asked him. "Ooh, pretty handwriting! Can I see?"

Junior wasn't the type to willingly surrender his journal to anyone. After all, it was the reason he had got himself expelled from Franklin High in the first place. He didn't trust Miss Haughton further than he could throw her. If not for her jade eyes, Junior might have thought of saying something mean or cutting, the way his father would. To get her off of his back, he handed over his journal to Miss Haughton as she pulled a chair beside Junior's desk and took a seat.

She kept a poker face as she read Junior's journal, flipping through his creation of works. Junior looked up at the clock on the wall, counting down a full minute before he decided to take back his journal from Miss Haughton. With each passing poem, Miss Haughton's expression softened. Eventually, she landed a poem Junior had written that morning in her absence, "Silhouette".

> *Foolishly, I fell in love with a silhouette*
> *and waited for its owner to show.*
>
> LEONARD G. ROBINSON JR.

"Silhouette" made Miss Haughton do a double-take at him, Junior noticed, which softened his expression toward the bumbling secretary. Her face then straightened to a look of seriousness. She asked Junior how old he was. "Fourteen," he mumbled, before asking for his journal back. Miss Haughton obliged him.

"You write *very* beautifully, Leonard," the woman complimented him. "That was impressive. I've never read anything quite like that in my life."

Junior softened some more, cheesing at her from ear-to-ear.

"Actually, it's 'Junior', and thank you, ma'am," he laughed.

"Junior, huh?" she asked. "All right then, Junior, I'm Casey – everyone calls me by my first name." She extended her hand for a shake.

Casey's hand felt nothing like Mr. Levy's bear claw from earlier. The inside of her palm was an improvement, moist to the touch, soft and welcoming.

"Well, I must say, Junior," she complimented again, "I was thoroughly impressed. So, how long have you been writing?"

"About a year...one long year," he laughed.

You look nothing like what you've been through.

LEONARD G. ROBINSON

Casey

Casey's energy was inviting to Junior. She had a serious, but cute Jersey-girl accent and wore a nose ring. As they conversed throughout the afternoon, he looked into her freckled face with admiration, laughing at her corny jokes and childish humor. Unlike Mr. Levy, she had a smile that lit up the walls of room 206. Her gutty laugh was infectious to Junior, making him laugh like mad whenever she did. Hanging on her every word, he gazed at Casey often and read her poetry from inside his journal, seeking more of her approval. Together, they spent the afternoon discussing life in Philly

103

and reminiscing about lines from their favorite songs and movies. For Junior, it was the first time in nearly a year that he had had a real conversation with someone besides his parents. Casey said that she had just turned twenty-nine and lived in an apartment building just outside of Brooke's Rowe.

Junior couldn't believe a woman as ghostly white as Casey favored some of the same stuff as he and Lawrence once had or that she lived near Brooke's Rowe. Surprisingly, Casey knew more about black family sit-coms than any white girl Junior had met. She named every character on *A Different World, Martin, Fresh Prince, Good Times, Living Single, Family Matters,* and *Hangin' with Mr. Cooper.* She challenged Junior line-for-line in *Harlem Nights, Menace II Society, Boyz in the Hood,* and *Above the Rim.* She told Junior she loved rap music and had a bigger crush on 2pac than Junior had on Whitney Houston. Junior didn't believe Casey at first until she showed him the inside of her bag. Down at the bottom was nothing but the finest in cassette tapes: Biggie Smalls, 2pac, Wu-Tang Clan, Nas, Geto Boys, The Roots, A Tribe Called Quest, and every other artist Junior listened to. Junior then popped open the tape deck of his Walkman and showed Casey 2pac's latest album, *Me Against the World.* Casey nearly fainted.

"Yo! You *gotta* let me dub that, Junior! I'll bring it back tomorrow, I swear to God!"

Laughing, Junior handed Casey his 2pac tape and asked to check out some of the cassettes in her bag. Reaching toward the bottom, Junior pulled out 2Pac's '93 album *Strictly 4 My N.I.G.G.A.S.* He then raised his eyebrow at Casey.

"What's that look for?" she asked. "I told you I was a 2pac-head."

"Yeah, but what are you doin' with *this* in your bag?" Junior chuckled. "I'm still surprised I haven't pulled out a Garth Brooks album or some other country shit. I know there's one in here and I'm gonna find it, Casey. You can't hide it from me!"

Offended, Casey glared at him. "Wait a second, man. What's that supposed to mean, Junior?" she asked.

"C'mon Casey, not too many white girls *I* know, know every line to *Harlem Nights*."

"What makes you think I'm white, Junior?" she asked.

"Well, aren't you?" he asked. "It's nothing wrong with being white. I mean, some white people are racist – not all of 'em – but I'm just sayin'. You're not like most white girls from Philly I've seen around. That's all. Nothin' bad, you know?"

Smiling back at him, Casey gave Junior a dose of his own medicine. "That's OK, you're not like most young black men I've run across in Philly, either," she laughed. "But look kid, I'm not like *any* white girl at all. First of all, I'm not white. I'm albino. It's when there's a defect during the birth process that causes an absence of melanin in the skin. So, I'm black just like you."

Realizing the gaffe, Junior apologized. "My bad, Casey," he apologized. "I guess I got too comfortable."

"It's all good, J.," she told him. "So, what's up man? Are you gonna let me dub that 2pac tape or what? What'd you bring to eat today, anyway?"

"Not much. Couple peanut-butter-and-jelly sandwiches."

Casey looked into Junior's paper bag lunch and laughed at him. "No wonder you're skinny!" she said. "C'mon, there's a Domino's not far from here."

"What about Mr. Levy?" asked Junior.

"Th'hell with Levy," said Casey. "Let 'em get his own. C'mon, let's ride!"

Pizza was Junior's love language – and the only language he spoke when it came to meals. In the freezer at home, Sandy kept a handy supply of microwavable pizzas. Nothing compared to Domino's, though. Occasionally, she'd order Junior a large box to last him through the weekend. It didn't make it through Saturday.

Out in the lot, Casey led Junior to her blue '87 Toyota Camry station wagon. On the passenger side, he stood there contemplating whether to go.

"Man, c'mon!" said Casey, waving him on. "I thought you wanted Domino's?"

"What about Levy?"

"What *about* him? Are you coming or not?"

Junior looked around in Casey's car, hoping to find something credible to turn down her invitation to leave campus. Finding nothing but strewed junk throughout, he shrugged and opened the car door, and threw on his seatbelt. As Casey's car left the lot, he prayed that he didn't run into his parents somewhere in the city.

Leaving Medgar was treacherous for Junior. His mother was assigned to the south Philly mail-carrying route, and

Senior's handyman career meant he was often around these neighborhoods. Not to mention, Junior's daddy was well-known in and around Philadelphia. If someone saw Leonard Sr.'s boy lurking around town during school hours, Junior would be on punishment. With pizza on the line, however, Junior took the risk.

On the way to Dominos, Casey spoke freely and candidly to Junior as if they'd known each other ten years. She talked about her struggles growing up as an albino girl in New Jersey and shot the shit with him as Junior ducked down into his seat at every tan Ford truck or gray Buick Skylark that passed. While at a light, Casey told him the story of how she'd got jumped after school in the sixth grade for being mistaken as a white girl saying the word "nigga".

"Man, I got my *ass* beat, J.!" she laughed. "They took my coat *and* my shoes. And when they found out I was black; I *still* didn't get back my things or an apology! Can you believe that? Kids are cruel, man – it's crazy."

"I know," Junior exhaled.

When they got to Domino's, Casey parked her car in front of a fire hydrant, darted out with the motor still running, and asked Junior to move her car if necessary. Junior looked down the street and saw a parking enforcement officer making his way up. As he ticketed cars along the way, Junior freaked out.

"Yo man, I don't have a license. I'm only fourteen! What do I say?" he asked.

"Neither do I! I'm suspended!" she said. "I don't know,

just…drive around the block or something. I'll be right back. Don't let 'em ticket us, J.! Please! I can't afford a tow right now."

With his eyes wide, Junior watched as the parking enforcement guy made his way up the block towards Casey's car. As the man got three cars away, he slid over into the driver's seat of Casey's Toyota, threw on her hazard lights, and got out to pretend as if the car had broken down. The guy gave him a nod and ticketed the car behind him.

Junior had known Casey for barely two hours and was already breaking the law. Not to mention, he had access to her car, pocketbook, and whatever else the bizarre, orange-haired woman had left behind in her vehicle. In the center console were Casey's apartment keys. Above him in the visor was a check stub from the previous pay cycle. Based on the stub, Casey netted around $826 bi-weekly. In the glovebox was her Motorola cell phone and an empty bottle of Escitalopram – also known as "Lexapro". Junior knew it was for treating anxiety, as Sandy also took the medication. The glovebox nearly exploded when Junior opened it: parking tickets, receipts, check stubs, doctors' notes, lease agreements, and scraps of paper.

As Junior spotted Casey walking back from the side mirror, he repacked her glovebox and moved back into the passenger seat. Casey then slid into the driver's seat and placed a large box of Domino's pizza onto Junior's lap. The heat from the box burned through his pants and onto his leg.

"Did they get us?" she asked. "You didn't let 'em get me, did you?"

"Not even close," said Junior. "I saw the guy coming up the street, so I got out and acted like I was checking on the car. So, he kept going."

"Aha, that's straight – I saw that. I was wondering what the hell you were doing! I was watching from the window like, 'fuck man, is this kid gonna steal my car?' Thanks for helping me avoid that ticket."

"Thanks for getting the pizza."

Back at Medgar, Casey stole a television cart from the school's library and with Junior's help, rolled it down to room 206. Over pizza and a 2-liter Pepsi Casey stole from the teacher's lounge, the two cackled with cheesy mouths at an episode of the *Fresh Prince of Bel-Air*. Their party was interrupted when Mr. Levy walked down to check on the two and saw the television cart and Junior with a slice of Domino's pizza on his desk. He went right after Casey.

"May I see you out in the hallway, Miss Haughton?"

Out in the hallway, Levy gave his secretary the blues. Casey returned afterward with a disgusted expression, rolling her eyes at Junior.

"He said we gotta get rid of the TV," she groaned. "What a dick!"

Junior helped Casey return it to the library, they finished up their lunch, then spent the rest of their afternoon inside Junior's journal.

When the day ended, Casey wrapped the remaining slices of pizza with foil from the teacher's lounge and placed the 2-liter Pepsi into Junior's hand. Written on the plastic was the name "Mr. Washington." When Junior showed Casey the name written on the side, she made sure the lid was tight and gave him a row of cups to go with his drink.

"Never did like that guy," she winked. "Look, have a great evening, J. Come see me tomorrow morning when you get in. We'll talk some more."

Casey hugged Junior, as he hugged her back with one arm loaded. Afterward, she went into her pocketbook and handed him one crisp five-dollar bill.

"What's the extra bread for?" asked Junior. "You've done enough already."

"I'm an investor," she grinned. "I'd love to read some more of your work, J. You think you can make that happen?"

"Yeah, for sure," he said. "I'll bring one of my other journals in. Shit, I'll bring two!"

"OK then, Junior!" she chuckled. "Bring me two!"

As Junior pushed through the doors of Medgar Evers Secondary School and out into Philly, he skipped down the staircase to his mother's car with a pep in his step, unlike anything Sandy had seen before. Friendship was on his mind, and love in his heart. It was the first time Junior had felt the euphoria of genuine friendship since Lawrence had died the previous summer. With five extra dollars inside his pocket, he thought of bringing Casey his entire collection of poetry. At the door to his mother's Buick, with his arms full, he smiled and nodded at Casey as she waved back. Suddenly, the dark cloud atop Medgar dispersed and the City of Brotherly Love felt like a new world.

From the car window, Junior stared back at Casey, forgetting to greet his mother. Sandy looked over at Casey standing on the staircase and back at Junior.

"Earth to Junior. Are you in there?" she laughed.

"Sorry Ma," he said before leaning over to kiss her on the cheek. The last kiss Sandy got from her son was on his twelfth birthday. "OK?!" she laughed, looking down at the pizza and bottle of Coca-Cola in his lap. "So, what's all this? And who's the white girl? Where'd you get the pizza? Is she your girlfriend?"

"No, Ma!" He felt himself blush. "That's Mr. Levy's secretary, Casey. She's…just a friend."

"Mmmhmm," Sandy teased playfully. "Well, she must be some kind of friend to know that you love Domino's, Junior. Ooh, wait until I tell Leonard what I saw today! Junior got a girlfriend!"

"Maaaan," Junior pulled his hoodie onto his head. "Just drive the car, Ma. *Dang*."

I don't know yet if it's love I feel,
But when I think of you,
you're the sun that lights my little dark world.

—LEONARD G. ROBINSON JR.

Five

When Junior arrived at Medgar the next day, his energy from the day before shriveled. He fell back into a shell of himself. When Sandy dropped him off that morning, suddenly there were school buses, cars, and sidewalks loaded with students and faculty unlike the day before. With his shoulders slumped forward, he trudged out of Sandy's car with his head down, prompting her to roll down the window and yell at him.

"Pick your head up!" she barked. "Act like you got a good momma and daddy!"

As Junior ascended the staircase up to Medgar, he passed by the colorful mural of the school's namesake, Medgar Evers, and saw the dice shooters his mother had tormented the day before. Junior passed by the group of boys using his arm to shield his face.

Once inside, Junior stopped by the main office and spotted Casey and Mr. Levy's silhouettes arguing through the

112

office blinds. They cussed at one another the way Junior's parents fought at home, raising their voices at each other. Mr. Levy called Casey immature and fat, and Casey made fun of his eczema, suggesting he buy new hands. Soon after, she emerged into the hallway to see Junior standing there and her expression softened to him.

"Junior! Hey!" she snickered. "You didn't hear any of that, right?"

"Well, I uh…" he began. "Nah, I didn't hear anything. I got the journals, though."

"Great," Casey said. Reaching into her bag, she handed Junior back his tape. "Here's your 2pac tape back. Thanks for letting me borrow it. Man, I listened to it all night."

Junior followed Casey into the nearest stairwell. Along the way, she praised him for his poetic genius from the other day and asked to read more of his work. Junior obliged her with two of his oldest journals from the previous year. Together, the two sat on the staircase in the corner, ignoring the army of rushing feet passing beside them. As Casey turned each page, Junior gave his state of mind with each writing.

It's your own fault. You hurt you.

LEONARD G. ROBINSON JR.

"Man, I was fuck – messed up when I wrote that," he said. "We'd just moved down from Crawford, and I didn't know anybody in South Philly, Casey."

"It's OK, you can cuss. Only to me, though," she told

113

him. "Our little secret. But with everyone else, you have to be respectful. We good?"

"For sure." Junior smiled. "So, yeah, I was fucked up when we got to South Philly."

"Mmmhmm." Casey nodded as she turned through his journal.

People treat love like a winter coat.
Put you on one season. Take you off for this or that reason.
Pack you inside a box. Shove you in the back
of a closet until they need you again.
I'm not a coat or a jacket that you zip and unzip.
My love is year-round.

LEONARD G. ROBINSON JR.

"So, I was watching this show on TV," he explained. "It's just crazy how people play with love like it's a toy, you know? Like a ball to be tossed around, but it's not!"

"Right." She nodded again, looking over his book.

As Junior waited on Casey to finish, he became nervous and chatty, wondering if his new friend really enjoyed his poetry or was just being nice. With each passing poem, Junior had an explanation – much like he did at home whenever Senior got on him. Senior was always on his case about something. He cut the grass too short. He ate too much. He used up all the detergent. Some days at home, it felt like Junior couldn't win. But with Casey, the mood was new. With just barely a day under his belt, Junior felt as if he'd known Casey all his life. He was at her heels, waiting on her validation as she read through his book. As the bell sounded for the first period, Casey handed Junior back his two journals.

"Whew, *child!*" she said. "So, you're on the fourth-floor. You got Mrs. Hawkins in 454. C'mon, I'll walk you up."

"What's Mrs. Hawkins like?" he asked. "She pretty?"

Casey rolled her eyes.

"Sorry, J.," she laughed. "Ain't no Halle Berry or Toni Braxton waitin' on you in 454."

"Shiiit," said Junior. "Man, how come I always get Jurassic Park?"

On the way to Mrs. Hawkins's class, Junior surveyed the students at Medgar, looking away as they made eye contact with him as if he was the newest inmate. Meanwhile, as curious girls popped on Now and Later candy, some of the boys sized up Junior, unsure of what to make of him.

"Why is everybody looking at me?" he asked.

"You're a new face," she told him. "This isn't like a regular school. Everybody here knows everybody. It's like a small town. Look J., Mrs. Hawkins is a little weird, OK? So, just try not to get on her bad side. You should be fine."

Junior looked down the hall to see an old, fish-eyed woman looking back at him with contempt, ready to devour him the moment he got close enough.

"I feel like I'm *already* on Mrs. Hawkins's bad side, and I haven't even walked in."

Unlike Franklin High, the students at Medgar spent the day in one classroom. There were no varsity or junior-varsity sports at Medgar. The only exception was gym class. Although Medgar's population was scarce, its student body, by all accounts, was considered the worst of the worst: Philly's rejects – the "hard-to-learn" and "most-likely-to-end-up-in-jail-or-dead" students.

As the bell sounded, signaling the start of first period, Junior waved goodbye to Casey and attempted to enter Mrs. Hawkins's classroom. With a palm to his chest, he was stopped at the door by his new teacher.

"Do I know you?" she asked him. "You one of mine?"

"Yes ma'am," he answered. "I was told room 454? Are you Mrs. Hawkins?"

Mrs. Hawkins, an older black lady with crooked makeup, grunted at Junior with a wicked scowl on her face.

"Well, go'on in!" she snapped. "Next time, I'm gonna mark you down as late!"

As Junior entered the room, Mrs. Hawkins followed behind him, cutting her eyes at him the entire way. When she asked him for his full name, Junior gave the woman his government name before asking to be called Junior. She then sneered at him and went on to introduce Junior to the class as Leonard.

"Now, go sit down!" She pointed to a chair at the front. "Call you what I *want* to call you."

Mrs. Hawkins didn't waste any time setting the record straight with Junior. Stunned by her candor, Junior took to his seat in the front row and didn't cough.

Mrs. Hawkins's class had a total of twelve kids: seven

116

Blacks, three Puerto-Ricans, and two white students (a boy and a girl). She treated the whites like gold and the other ten children like escaped animals from the city zoo. Often, she'd play the reverse-racism card, showing favoritism to her white students while condemning her minority students for minor infractions. She started and ended her day with book-work and snapped when the students had questions. During math, she told one kid to go to hell and called another class-mate a "jezebel". The only time Mrs. Hawkins even appeared approachable was when she discussed her bible, sitting on top of her desk. Even then, she likened the characters from her "good book" to the students in room 454 and did not quarrel with calling the kids "dogs" or "devils". According to Junior's classmates, Mr. Levy *loved* him some Mrs. Hawkins. Not only because she pacified the few white students at Medgar, but because she went to hell on the black students there.

During History hour that morning, Mrs. Hawkins became so irritated with Junior's class that she walked out of her room and left her coffee unattended. As she disap-peared down the stairwell, Junior saw the deceptive look on his classmates' faces as they eyeballed the unattended cup of steaming coffee on their teacher's desk. Junior then watched as one kid acted as a lookout, while another rushed to retrieve Mrs. Hawkins's coffee.

"Do it!" a kid yelled.

"Yeah, fuck that bitch!" a second yelled.

The kid holding Mrs. Hawkins's cup snorted and dumped a wad of gooey phlegm into her coffee. Junior gagged as he watched his classmates pass around the cup, each student taking a turn. Everyone took a turn – including the white kids on easy street – except Junior. One kid blew his nose with a napkin and stuffed it into Mrs. Hawkins's cup. Another student threw her grade book out of the classroom window and onto the roof of Medgar. The white girl passed gas in Mrs. Hawkins's chair, nearly burning a hole in the fabric, and then stole all her chalk. Junior couldn't believe it. One of the boys then placed Mrs. Hawkins's coffee onto Junior's desk.

"Your turn, Junior," the kid said to him. "Now hurry up before she gets back!"

Junior looked down at the swirling phlegm inside of Mrs. Hawkins's cup and gagged once again. He had every reason to spit inside her cup but couldn't bring himself to do it. Junior took a second look down at the cup and passed on the opportunity to get even with his teacher.

"Man, I ain't spittin' in no old lady's cup!" he said. "That's gross!"

"You're a fuckin' pussy, man," chimed another kid. "Mrs. Hawkins is a piece of shit!"

"So?" Junior raised his voice. "That doesn't mean we should spit in her coffee!"

As Junior went back and forth with his classmates over soiling Mrs. Hawkins's drink, the lookout waiting near the door alerted the class that Mrs. Hawkins was on her way back down the hall. With the world watching him, Junior took Mrs. Hawkins's cup and returned it to her desk. His peers all chastised him.

"Good Samaritan-ass nigga!" one kid said. "Teacher's pet-ass ho!"

"Fuck you," Junior shot back.

The second Mrs. Hawkins returned to room 454, she stood overtop of Junior's desk and accused him of using foul language in her class. It got him extra homework for the night, but at least he'd be able to sleep easier knowing he did the right thing.

New Kid on the Block

Later that afternoon, Junior loitered at his locker, wondering what he'd got himself into. Halfway through his second day there, he hated it at Medgar. At the door to the boys' bathroom on the fourth-floor, students exchanged roles, playing lookout as their peers ran a sex train on some impressionable freshman. The third-floor was much of the same but more blatant, with students exchanging money for drugs and other services. As Junior entered to use the bathroom, he startled one of the dealers there and got a knife pointed at him. Annoyed, the dealer put away his switchblade and confronted Junior near the door.

"You must be new. So, I'll let you slide this time," the dealer told Junior. "Piss and get out. And don't come in this motherfucka no more. This is *my* bathroom."

Junior quickly zipped up his pants and left without washing his hands.

On his way to lunch, Junior saw a kid get robbed of his beeper and K-Swiss sneakers. The robbers also took the boy's reversible NFL starter jacket. The assailants then stuffed the boy inside a locker. Outside of the lunchroom, Junior saw a girl's teeth get knocked out before she was dragged around by her hair until her roots were stripped out. Mrs. Patterson, the black music teacher who raised hell at Mr. Levy for attempting to dump Junior onto her, was knocked unconscious as she attempted to break up the savagery.

The food at Medgar looked awful – worse than prison food. On the menu for that day were roasted potatoes, corn, and a half-burnt chicken patty. The potatoes were frozen in the middle, and the corn tasted as if it'd come from outside and hadn't been washed. The chicken patty was rubbery, and Junior found a bone in his sandwich. At a table near the back door, Junior watched as his peers wolfed through their meals like Neanderthals. A girl passed by the table, asking Junior if he wanted his patty. As Junior went to hand it over, the girl took it off his fork and walked away without saying thank you. Discouraged, he left and went down to the main floor to look for Casey and found her eating at her desk.

"That look on your face, J.," she said to him. "It says it all."

To get his mind off Medgar, Casey asked Junior to take a walk with her down to the school library on the second-floor. He happily obliged. Junior followed her throughout, rambling about his day there so far and how different Medgar was from Franklin High as Casey inventoried a row of books. At one point, she lowered her clipboard down to her side when Junior told her what the kids in Mrs. Hawkins's class did to the old woman's coffee.

"They did *what?*" she asked. "Well, I don't like Mrs. Hawkins either, but I would *never* go as far as spitting into her drink. Hide her car keys? Maybe. Banana in her tail-pipe? Possibly. But spittin' in an old lady's coffee? Man, that's a *whole* different level of disrespect. Ewww." Casey shuddered. "So, how in the world did you end up here at Medgar, anyway?"

"Got into a fight," Junior told her. "This kid took my journal, and I just lost it. I didn't mean to...I'd been through a lot over the last year with Lawrence being gone and everything. I guess I just wasn't thinkin'."

"Tell me about it. Why? Who's Lawrence? Is he your brother?" she asked him.

Junior told Casey the story of his brother, handing her an old photo of Lawrence from his wallet. She stared into Lawrence's picture for an extended time as a tear leaked from her eye and down onto Lawrence's chubby face.

"This just did something to me because I think you're a good kid, and I hate that you had to go through some bullshit like that." She sniffed. "How old was he when he died, J.?"

"He'd just turned ten."

Casey stared down at Lawrence's picture again before looking onto the back. Behind Lawrence was a poem Junior had written.

Now that you're gone.

they stop by to visit.

They line up one-by-one, weeping while you're asleep.

Not a phone call or a Christmas card.

Not a call last year or the year before that.

But on the day of service,

they show up carrying their lakes & their rivers.

I will drown every day for the rest of my days, brother.

Love you,

Junior.

LEONARD G. ROBINSON JR.

"No, uh-uh." Casey caught herself between tears as she handed him back his picture. "Yo, you just wrecked me with that, Junior." Her voice cracked. "So…how are your parents holding up? How are you guys gettin' by?"

"I don't know," he said. "I guess just one day at a time, you know? Like everyone else."

As Junior put away his brother's photo, Casey took a seat next to him.

"I'm mad at myself," she said. "I wish I was here when you and Mrs. Robinson had taken a tour of Medgar. I would've told you to find another school. I've been lookin' for a job since May. It's so fucked up here, Junior, and Mr. Levy could give a shit."

Before they could finish talking, the bell sounded, signaling an end to lunch. As the two departed from the library together, Casey placed a hand on Junior's shoulder.

"J., look at me," Casey told him. "Man, if you need *any-thing* at all, you know where I am. Don't hesitate. We're family, and I don't use the word 'family' loosely. You're my little brother, now, and I'm gonna look out for you."

"No doubt." Junior smiled, his eyes reddening. "Man, Casey, you're the most real friend I've had since I moved here. It's so hard to meet genuine people sometimes, I just..."

"Not a friend," she interrupted. "I'm your sister, now. And right now, big sister says it's time for you to get upstairs to Mrs. Hawkins's class!"

Together, brother and sister ascended to the fourth-floor. At the door, Casey fist-bumped Junior and returned to the main office, leaving Junior in the hands of Mrs. Hawkins. As he attempted to enter her class, the teacher blocked him at the door.

"Go get me a TV from the library, boy!" she ordered. "And hurry up back!"

Careful not to further anger his teacher, Junior rushed down to the library and grabbed the closest TV he could find. Struggling, he pushed Mrs. Hawkins's TV cart up the handicapped ramp and onto the elevator by himself and up to the fourth-floor hallway, dripping sweat. As Junior returned to class, he was met with a chorus of teeth-suckers from his classmates. "Fuckin' boy scout!" one kid whispered. He then rolled Mrs. Hawkins's TV up to her desk and crashed into his seat at the front row. Before he could catch his breath, she ordered Junior back out into the hallway to question him about an incident from earlier.

"I know somebody did something to my coffee this morning. So, who did it?" she asked Junior, backing him into a corner. "Was it you? You little devil-heathen!"

"No ma'am; why would I do something to your coffee?"

"Well, who did it?" she raised her voice. "Tell me! If I have to, I'll call Levy up here and have him suspend everybody inside that damn classroom."

"If somebody *did* do something to it, I didn't see it. All I know is that I didn't do anything to it, Mrs. Hawkins. I would never do that."

Junior's teacher looked him up and down. With no proof that Junior was the culprit, she switched to a new topic. As Junior tried to enter back into her room, she started with him again.

"If I was you, I'd stay away from that white girl downstairs. She's trouble!"

Junior coiled his head at Mrs. Hawkins like a cobra.

"She ain't white, she was born an albino – you'd know that if you took the time to get to know Casey instead of judging her!"

"Dammit, *I* said she's white!" she yelled at him. "And it ain't a damn thing you can do to make me change my mind! Th'hell with her! And don't get sassy with me! You little no-good heathen! Go'on! Get back inside!"

As Mrs. Hawkins turned her back to walk in, Junior raised his middle finger at her.

For the rest of the afternoon, Mrs. Hawkins made Junior's class watch a documentary about the Victorian era in the

United Kingdom during the nineteenth century. Nobody paid attention, especially Junior. Kids were doodling on their desks, some falling asleep and snoring. Others used the movie time to roll up marijuana or pass notes about a fight scheduled to take place after school. Junior spent the rest of the afternoon inside his journal.

Halfway through the daunting film, Junior's eyes became heavy as he nodded and caught himself. Of course, Mrs. Hawkins went to the front of the room, stopped the film and turned on the light to her room. She then stood over top of Junior's desk with both hands on her hips.

"You think I'm stupid?" she hollered at him. "Hand it over!"

"Hand *what* over?" asked Junior.

"The journal! Give it to me! I saw you writing earlier, and if you don't give it to me, I'm gonna have you suspended and thrown out of here!"

Pissed off, Junior threw his journal down onto the floor.

"Thank you!" She snatched up his book. "You can have it back *after* the film!"

Sulking through the movie, Junior stared at the TV set, ready to explode on his teacher. He hated Mrs. Hawkins, who picked on him endlessly, making his life a living hell on just his second day at Medgar. At her desk, she opened Junior's journal during the movie, scowling through his body of work. Furious, Junior left his seat to confront her.

"You can't just read my stuff like that!" he told her. "It's personal, Mrs. Hawkins!"

Junior's teacher looked back at him with rottweiler eyes,

not blinking or speaking. After a short standoff, Junior returned to his chair, and Mrs. Hawkins continued reading through his journal. For the rest of the movie, Junior sat with his chin propped onto his palm, pouting.

When the final bell of the day sounded, Junior went straight to Mrs. Hawkins's desk and asked for his journal back. Before handing it back, she lectured him about being inattentive during class, calling Junior's poetry "the devil's work." She reached into her bag, pulled out her bible, and began rebuking him. Finally, she handed Junior his journal.

On his way down to see Casey before he left school, Junior opened his journal and noticed that Mrs. Hawkins had smeared his hard work with red ink, marking every grammatical and syntax error. Down on the main floor, he ran in to see Casey and showed her his journal.

"What the hell is wrong with that woman, Junior?!" she gasped.

"She's a bitch!" he fussed. "I *knew* I should've spat her in coffee when I had the chance. Look at this!" He held up his journal. "What am I supposed to do now?"

Casey looked into Junior's face and saw the hurt in his eyes. As Casey turned through his journal, Junior called his teacher every name in the book; he was practically jumping out of his skin.

"Stupid bitch. I hope she drops dead!" he said.

"She's got a broken spirit. Hurt people hurt other people, J.," said Casey. "But I can fix this. If you let me borrow your book for the night, I'll bring it back tomorrow. I promise the red will be all gone. Can you do me a favor, though?"

"Anything."

"Don't get into the habit of calling women 'bitches', OK? Scratch that from your vocabulary."

"Sorry."

"That's OK," she laughed. "Just wanted to make sure we checked that before moving forward. But I understand why you're angry. I'd be pissed too!"

Casey reached across her desk to fist bump Junior as he headed outside.

The moment Junior exited Medgar, he walked down to his mother's car parked at the curb. The sound of arguing emanated from the vehicle though the windows were up and the motor was running: Senior and Sandy were going at it.

Junior barely got in a "hello" during the firefight between his parents as they tore into each other like ravenous wolves, motherfucking this, and motherfucking that. At one point, Senior banged his huge fist onto the console so hard that the radio skipped. Of course, that incited another huge fight as Sandy accused Senior of ruining her stereo. Senior claimed that Sandy's '85 Buick Skylark was old as dirt, just like his wife.

From the main lot, Junior's parents quarreled all the way back to Kennedy Street. Junior sat in the backseat pretending to be a fly on the wall, listening to his parents argue over their savings account, living in Philly, the house, groceries, and other matters. Before Lawrence passed, Junior's parents had gotten along for the sake of their kids. After his death, they couldn't stand to look at each other. At the house, their dispute became so volatile that Senior ran Sandy's Buick onto the curb, threw it into park, and walked off down Kennedy street with Sandy hollering at him from the car window. During his walk, Senior punted the family's trash bin out into the street, sending recyclable plastics hurling into the air as bystanders scurried out of his way. Sandy shot from her Buick and went after him, chasing down her husband, reprimanding him for his theatrics as neighbors looked on.

"Where you goin' now, huh?" She marched beside him. "You ain't got no money, and don't nobody want your sorry black ass! So, you might as well come back home!"

As Junior watched his parents rage on like two pit bulls off their leashes, he reminisced about his last fight with Lawrence before his death. Their fight was similar, Junior chasing beside his brother, demeaning him as he attempted to pedal off. He remembered kneeling next to his brother as paramedics attempted to revive him. Ever since that moment, seeing his parents fight reminded Junior of how much he regretted his actions in the final moment of Lawrence's life. Lawrence was *not* a "stupid dummy" as Junior recalled saying to his brother. He was a shithead kid who had done something stupid, like every other ten-year-old around the world.

As Junior's parents came rumbling back up the street firing away at each other, he leaned against his mother's car, waiting for them to return. They walked up, still calling each other names as if Junior wasn't standing there. With his arms folded, he looked on, suddenly enlightened by the regret of having to see Lawrence take his last breath. Finally, when they acknowledged him, Junior took a stance against his parents' bickering. They were the only words Junior would have for them for the rest of that evening.

"Lawrence and I did that *just* before he died." He shook his head.

With his bag hooked onto his shoulder, Junior picked up the spilled bin which Senior had kicked over and walked inside, leaving his parents to settle their differences.

Love is like a Ferris wheel.
Go up high. Go down low.
Hang somewhere in the middle for a while.
Get off. Get on.
See the top of the world.
Then back on the ground again.
Stop. Hop off. Start at the end of the line.
Pay for a new ticket and do it all over again.

—LEONARD G. ROBINSON JR.

Money was the root of many tiffs inside the Robinson castle. Some nights, Junior would awaken to the sound of slamming doors and objects bouncing from the walls. Although both his parents would often threaten egregious bodily harm to one another during their scream fests, their threats were unsubstantiated. Arguing was Senior and Sandy's love language. They hollered at breakfast, cussed over the line during their respective lunch breaks, raised holy hell at the dinner table, and kissed each other goodnight. Someone always lit the dynamite first.

"What we eatin' tonight?" Senior once asked.

"Shit on a stick," Sandy replied. Ka-boom. The fight was on.

The days they didn't tear into each other about something were because they weren't speaking. The fights were almost always over the same thing: money. Some days, however, the subject matter was more personal: they fought over Philadelphia, Junior, Lawrence, and how their marriage was a sham from the second they met. It spiraled out of control, some days, with knife-like words hurled at each other. Usually, it was Senior who had the violent temper. Sandy once told Junior that the reason his daddy acted out so badly was due to his lack of education. "He doesn't know how to express himself at all," she told Junior once. "The man can't talk worth a damn! That's what happens when you don't finish school." Sandy's words didn't make sense to him at first. But as Junior got older, he referenced his mother's comment.

Five years before Lawrence passed, Junior had seen his daddy threaten to behead a neighbor back in Crawford over a late payment of twenty-eight dollars. Senior had changed the brakes in the neighbor's Nissan truck from the prior week. For seven days, the Robinsons' neighbor, Mr. Martin, ducked Senior, telling neighbors he had no intention of paying Junior's daddy the rest.

Hammer in hand, Senior drove down to the corner store where Mr. Martin liked to hang and caught him coming out of the liquor store with a case of beer. The second he saw Senior armed with a hammer, Mr. Martin walked back inside the store, returned the beer, and gave Senior the money he owed him. The scroungers who hung by the corner store cleared as they saw Senior, full of rage, exit his truck. Although on most days Senior said only a few words, he commanded respect and had no problem extracting it when necessary. "Never let nobody owe you too long," he told Junior. "I don't give a damn if it's twenty-eight cents. *Always* collect what's yours."

When Junior later told Sandy at home that his daddy almost beheaded a man over twenty-eight dollars, Sandy shook her head. According to her, Senior shaking down delinquent customers for late payments was nothing new.

"Is that all?" Sandy asked, laughing as she folded a batch of clothes. "I saw your daddy do worse things to people for less."

Sandy told Junior that when she was seven months pregnant with him, she stopped Senior from pistol-whipping a man on 14th Street over ten dollars. But it wasn't the money that got Senior hot. It was what happened afterward that sent Senior back to his car, looking for his pistol beneath the passenger seat. "Nigga, suck my dick!" the man told Senior in front of his pregnant wife.

"I was as big as a house. I wobbled out of the car with you kickin' inside me. Took me forever to get to him, but I did," Sandy laughed. "I've seen him whoop men for looking at me too long. Once, I saw him fight two cops and take away one of their guns. It's a wonder they didn't kill him. He had one *hell* of a temper when we were younger, and he still does," she continued, "but one thing I can't ever deny about him, Junior. We fight. We cuss. We argue like cats and dogs, but

I'll be damned if your daddy doesn't love me in his own little street corner way."

Sandy had told Junior she'd met his daddy on a cold, rainy night in March of 1971 when she was seventeen and Senior was twenty-two. Back then, Senior was part of a local street gang in North Philly – the 14th Street Gang. Known for shaking down heroin dealers and intimidating rookie cops, he was a formidable hood on the north side of town. In the trunk of his Burgundy '66 Cadillac El Dorado, under the wheel well, was a baseball bat and pistol-grip shotgun. Beneath the passenger seat was a loaded .38 revolver. At six-foot-five, Senior rarely needed a weapon to make his point clear. Like Junior, he began his life as a quiet kid who enjoyed drawing but hated school. His father, Russell, had been dragged from his car while on the way home from work and beaten to death by racist white cops and Klu Klux Klan members when Senior was just seven years old. Senior's mother, Gloria, died of cancer when he was ten. Before her death, she sent both Senior and his half-brother, Ossie, off to live with her sister in Whitfield, North Carolina. Aunt Odessa (or Dessie, as the boys called her) did her best to raise the boys on her own in rural North Carolina. Dessie got over easy with Ossie but failed to control Senior, the oldest and most impacted by the death of his parents. By the time Senior was twelve, he had dropped out of school. By thirteen, he stood over six-foot-one and weighed closed to two hundred pounds. At a farmers' market in the summer of 1962, he nearly killed another man he suspected was trying to cheat Dessie on a basket of cotton.

"Turn him loose, goddammit!" Dessie pried him off. "What in the world is wrong with you, boy?! What'd you go'on and do that for, Leonard?"

"He was tryin' to cheat you, Aunt Dessie!" Senior complained. "Look in his hands. Ain't nothin' in there but some skin. I bet it ain't nothin' in his pockets neither!"

As it turned out, Senior was right. The man had no intention of paying Dessie for the basket of cotton but had somehow overlooked her six-foot-tall nephew standing behind her.

In another instance, Senior had his way with a Whitfield police sergeant in a small river. While walking home from the store with his brother along a dirt road, the sergeant stopped the boys and accused them of robbing the store. Finding no evidence, he continued harassing the boys and reverting to racist Jim Crow rhetoric. Irritated, Senior dragged the flailing sergeant off the road, through the woods, and down to the river stream for a quick swim.

A year later, Senior placed the manager down at the gas station upside down in the trash for calling Ossie a "nigger" and broke a neighbor's jaw for putting the moves on his precious Dessie. When two cops showed up to arrest Senior, now fifteen, he feared no man. He bounced the cops around Aunt Dessie's house, destroying them both until they scurried from her devastated home. Scared for her nephew's life in the South, Dessie sent Senior off to live with an old friend in Philadelphia along with his brother. Ossie joined Senior soon after.

Trouble didn't come looking for Senior when he arrived in Philadelphia at fifteen. Instead, he went looking for it.

With his stellar street instincts and propensity to do whatever and whenever he wanted, Senior quickly attracted the attention of neighborhood gangs.

"Yo, where you from, big man?" a kid asked him.

"Norf Ca-liner," he answered in his thick country accent. By Senior's nineteenth birthday, he'd gained a reputation as the most prolific bone breaker in all North Philly.

And then along came Sandy...

Lonnie Sandra Woods was on her way to night school one rainy night in March of 1971 when Senior drove by in his Cadillac. Brother Ossie was passed out drunk, snoring in the passenger seat next to him. With his window down, Senior crept beside his future wife and offered her a ride.

"What you doin' out here, gal?" he asked. "Need a ride?"

Sandy didn't say a word.

"Gal, I *said* whatcha doin' out here," Senior repeated, cruising beside her. "It's rainin' like hell, *and* it's cold. Ain't you cold?"

Ignoring him, Sandy continued to walk.

Determined to win her over, Senior drove off up the street and whipped his big Cadillac around the block. He dragged his brother Ossie from the passenger seat, placed him inside the trunk, and returned to where he last saw Sandy walking.

"Hey there." He blew on the horn, "I just dropped my brother off. You sure you don't need a ride there, Ms. Lady? I ain't gonna hurt you. I just hate to see such a pretty thang walkin' in the rain. The least you can do is let me give you a ride. I'll even let you drive if you want to."

"No, thank you. I can walk," Sandy responded.

Senior then pulled his Cadillac over, shut off the engine, threw on his leather jacket from the backseat, and began to walk with her.

"What are you doing?" asked Sandy.

"Well, if you won't let me drive you, I guess we just gonna be wet together," said Senior.

Senior talked the whole way, boring Sandy as she attempted to walk ahead of him. At one point, he removed his leather jacket and placed it onto her back. By the time they made it down to Sandy's school, eight blocks from where they had first met, the two were soaking wet as they exchanged names and smiles.

"What time you get out of class?" he asked. "You got a man?"

"About eight," she said. "Yeah, I do," she giggled. "He's overseas fightin' in that white man's war called *Vietnam*."

"Mmmhmm." Senior put out his cigarette and exhaled a cloud of white dust.

"Well, I'm gonna be your new man, now," he said. "What kind of nigga lets his woman walk halfway across North Philly in the rain? That ain't right. I'll be back to pick you up."

Shocked by his candor, Sandy laughed as she disappeared into the building. Senior then ran back to his Cadillac in the pouring rain to find Ossie pounding on the roof of his trunk.

"Man, what the *fuck* is wrong with you?!" he hollered as Senior let him out. "What the fuck you put me in the truck for, Leonard?"

"Cool out, Oz. I got a girlfriend, now. Her name is Sandy. Sweet gal."

"Sandy? Sweet *gal*?" Ossie laughed. "What girl is dumb enough to date you?"

"Any girl dumb enough to be walkin' by herself in a place like North Philly at night without a man like me beside her. That's who."

After their riff, Senior dropped Ossie off at a friend's house not far away. He removed his .38 revolver from the floor of his Cadillac along with his pump shotgun and baseball bat in the well of his trunk.

"Hold these 'til I get back," asked Senior. "I don't want to creep her out. Not yet."

Ossie looked down at his brother's toys and shook his head.

"Damn, Leonard. Pussy got you already, huh?" he asked.

At exactly eight o'clock, Senior returned to pick up Sandy. When he arrived, she was still there, waiting for him in the lobby. Senior opened her car door and placed her books onto his backseat as Sandy smiled at him.

"So, where you live at?" he asked.

"You can drop me off right there in front of that house with the green mailbox."

Senior pulled his car up to the green mailbox and opened Sandy's car door. By then, the rain had eased up. At the door, Sandy's mother, Miss Elizabeth was waiting for her. Not recognizing the brooding black man standing next to Sandy, she answered the door in a haste, asking questions.

"Who is this strange man, Sandy?" she asked.

"Yes ma'am," he answered. "Leonard Robinson. From now on, I'm gonna be pickin' up and droppin' off your daughter to all her classes. What time should I come back tomorrow?"

Sandy's mother looked Senior up and down.

"So, uh, is that your Cadillac parked in front of my mailbox, Leonard Robinson?"

Senior looked back at his burgundy Caddy and smiled.

"Yes ma'am." He nodded, not taking his eye off Sandy's mother. "Paid for with honest money. Ain't a drug-sellin', dope-pushin' dollar used to buy that Cadillac, you see."

Sandy turned pink, chuckling at Senior before catching herself.

"Girl, get your happy ass in this house!" Miss Elizabeth pulled her inside. "Alright, Leonard Robinson. You can pick up my daughter tomorrow evening at six – and you better not be late."

"No ma'am," said Senior. "I'll be here at quarter-to-six. That's a promise."

The next evening, Senior returned to Sandy's house at exactly 5:45 p.m. with the wheels to his Cadillac shining underneath the sun. He was dressed in a sleek turtleneck, bell-bottom slacks with spit-shined shoes, and a matching flat cap. A heavy smoker, he forewent his usual afternoon snack of Newport cigarettes in exchange for mint gum. Miss Elizabeth answered the door, surprised to see Senior standing there. Before she could greet him, Senior removed his hat.

"Evenin' Miss 'Lizabeth," said Senior.

Soon after, Sandy pushed past her mother, grabbed Senior by the arm and whisked him down to his big Cadillac parked on the street.

"Whoa! Bye Miss 'Lizabeth!"

That night, Sandy skipped school for a night on the town with Senior. They spent their evening cruising throughout the city, listening to Isaac Hayes and eating funnel cake topped with strawberries. Later, on a park bench, they sat gazing up at the moon as they held hands. Sandy couldn't believe the size of Senior's hands. Her tiny hand fit inside his palm like a ball in a catcher's mitt. The two lovebirds talked for hours before kissing goodnight when Senior dropped her off.

Sandy skipped class the next night and the night after. Before long, she gave up her ambitions of becoming a nurse altogether to be with Senior. Senior, in the meantime, was attempting to kick his old street habits to begin a new relationship with Sandy. She first became aware of his lifestyle months into their union when a man made a pass at Sandy down at a drive-in theatre, unaware she was with somebody. When Senior returned from getting popcorn and saw the man leaning onto the door of his '66 Cadillac, he introduced the man's head to the door jamb...several times. A month later, a guy tried his shot at Sandy and ended up with a concussion and two orbital fractures. A third ended up with a broken leg. Word spread quickly across North Philadelphia that Sandy Woods was now Leonard's woman.

Sandy found her boyfriend's give-a-fuck attitude cute. Six

months later, after Sandy's eighteenth birthday, Senior proposed and she said yes. They wed inside a Philadelphia courthouse on September 20, 1972. Their cheap honeymoon was
spent at a rundown motel in New Jersey, watching the second
Ali-Patterson fight on a small black and white television.

For nine years, the Robinsons struggled with fertility.
Meanwhile, as Sandy grieved the passing of her mother, Miss
Elizabeth, Senior returned to the streets. With Ossie cheer-
ing him on, Senior busted out a man's teeth with the backside of his pump shotgun. In another heinous streak of street
justice, Senior beat a man with a stick down at the pool hall
for calling Ossie a clown – which he was. Ossie would start
trouble just to hide behind Senior.

In late November of 1980, Senior was on his way to help
his brother shakedown a group of hoods when Sandy phoned
him at Ossie's apartment. By then, she had been a city mail
carrier for five years with her dream of becoming a nurse far
behind her.

"I'm pregnant, Leonard," she told him. "Don't you think
it's 'bout time you cut out all that street shit you been doin'?
Sooner than later, it's gonna catch up to you." Sandy was right.

Senior walked outside of Ossie's apartment to the trunk
of his car. He handed his brother his pump shotgun, baseball
bat, and the keys to his beloved Cadillac, but kept his .38.

"You're gonna have to go on without me," he said. "Sandy's
having my seed, and I wanna be there. It's 'bout time I stop
all this shit, anyway."

"One more," pleaded Ossie. "For me, brother. I won't ask for nothin' else."

"Nope," said Senior. "Can't do it. Just drop me off back at the 'partment and leave me with the .38. You can have the rest." Senior was thirty-one.

So, Ossie did just as his brother asked. He kept Senior's tools and Cadillac and dropped him off at his apartment with Sandy and his soon-to-be son and went to rage war against the vandals who disrespected their 14th Street posse. (Ossie would go on to carry on the family business until he was murdered the day after Christmas in 1982.) Later, when Senior arrived home, he placed his .38 revolver inside his nightstand and kissed his pregnant wife.

"Where's the Cadillac?" Sandy asked him.

"I gave it to Oz," he said. "I'll get another ride. As much dirt as I've done in that thing, be my luck some damn fool roll up on me tryin' to get even. Besides, I'm a father now."

Nine months later, Junior was born. Lawrence came three years later in April of '84.

The latitude of my gratitude is ocean wide.
Atlantic. Indian. Arctic.
But to be Pacific.
I wish for my words
to reach every corner of the world.
Touch every heart of every walking soul.
That is my goal.

LEONARD G. ROBINSON JR.

Taming the Devil

When Junior returned to Medgar the day after Mrs. Hawkins smeared the inside of his journal in red, Casey handed him back his book; there was not a trace of red in sight. Casey had inscribed a short message for Junior toward the end of his book. "Keep going!" the message read, encircled by a huge blue heart. Junior turned through every page, looking for any sign of Mrs. Hawkins's red pen. He looked up at Casey, wondering where she got her magic. Casey told Junior she used a white-out pen to carefully remove Mrs. Hawkins's satanic markings from his journal. Junior placed his journal back into his bag, unsure of what to make of her unconditional support of him.

For the second day in a row, Casey elected to walk Junior up to Mrs. Hawkins's class on the fourth-floor. Along the way, Junior noticed the cutting eyes of staff members and his peers as they watched him and Casey move throughout the hall. Gossip chatter followed by snickering laughter pinched his ears as Junior turned. Suddenly, they were the center of attention and the talk of Medgar's violent hallways. A staff member approached Junior and Casey as they approached Mrs. Hawkins's classroom to forewarn them of the rumor mill surrounding the two. Casey, by all accounts, seemed just as confused by the environment as Junior.

"You guys haven't heard?" the teacher whispered. "Levy is so pissed!"

"Pissed about what?" Casey asked, looking down at Junior. "Why? What's wrong?"

Just as Casey began asking questions, Mr. Levy came marching up the hallway, charging toward both Junior and Casey. His porky neck was red with anger as he barked orders into Casey's face, shaking his fat, scaley finger at her as if she was a child.

"I warned you, Miss Haughton!" he barked, looking down at Junior and back at her. "This nonsense going on between you two is over!"

"What nonsense, Levy? What in the world are you talking about?"

"This inappropriate relationship you've been having with a student. You think I didn't know you took him to Domino's the other day? I watched you guys leave out on camera. It has to stop, Miss Haughton. From now on, you *cannot* walk Junior to class."

"But Casey didn't do anything," Junior chimed in.

"You shut up! I'll deal with *you* later. Hasn't your mother taught you any better?"

"Hey!" Casey raised her voice. "Don't speak to him like that – he's a kid! Junior, go to class."

Not willing to leave Casey on her own, Junior watched as students and staff members oohed and aahed as Mr. Levy dressed down Casey in the middle of the hallway. He called her incompetent and brought up things about Casey's past in front of Junior. Mr. Levy called her an addict and accused of her doing so much coke that she had sniffed her brains out. He ripped Casey so badly in front of students and colleagues, she began to tear up. Down the hall, Junior looked to see a smile painted onto the wicked Mrs. Hawkins's face. Humiliated, Casey covered her face and began to cry. Junior couldn't believe the way Mr. Levy spoke to his secretary. As childish laughter filled the entire fourth-floor, Junior's insides filled with fury. He looked into Casey's hurt face and decided to defend her.

"Man, fuck you!" Junior said to Mr. Levy, surprising himself as he shook with anger. "Casey is a good person and a good friend. And you ought to be ashamed of yourself for talking to her like that in front of all of these people!"

His peers all roared as Mr. Levy turned redder than ever. Steam boiled from his ears.

Removing her hands from her face, Casey tried to save Junior from himself.

"*Excuse* me? What did you say?" asked Mr. Levy.

"J., just let it go." Casey shooed him off. "It's OK. Go to class!"

Junior looked throughout the hallway at his peers who were all stunned by his candor. He seldom defended himself when confronted with trouble.

"You heard me!" said Junior as he shook. "Your mother should've swallowed you. Pork-sausage eatin' son-of-a-bitch!"

The hallway roared again as Mr. Levy showed his coffee-stained teeth at Junior. "Nobody talks to me like that at my school! *Go* to my office now! Both of you!"

Downstairs in Levy's office, Junior watched Mr. Levy scribe a whole book report of notes detailing his concerns about Junior and Casey's unsubstantiated "inappropriate" relationship. He added that Junior had called him a "son-of-a-bitch" in a note home that had to be signed by Sandy before Junior could return to Medgar. In the paragraph below, he wrote that Casey had taken Junior to Domino's during school hours, calling her "a major distraction to the faculty and learning environment of Medgar Evers Secondary School." He went on to accuse her of manipulating Junior and wrote that his teacher, Mrs. Hawkins, had caught Junior writing inside of his journal during class time. Adding insult to injury, he phoned Sandy at her desk to notify her that a letter was being sent home regarding Junior's behavior.

For the rest of the school day, Junior sat sulking and defeated. Although he had won the battle earlier, he had lost the war. Later that afternoon, Junior bumped into Casey and the two slipped into a vacant classroom to talk about what had happened earlier.

"Junior, you should've *never* shot back at Levy like that!" she whispered "Are you crazy?"

"But you're my big sissy," he said. "I hated to see you like that. It did something to me."

That afternoon during lunch, Casey gave Junior the scoop from a trusted source on rumors swirling throughout Medgar about the two of them. The word on the street was that the two were having sex in the school during lunch *and* after school back at Casey's apartment. Staff complained of nepotism between Junior and his new best friend, hoping to quell their uncanny friendship. Throughout the day at Medgar, Junior's classmates teased him, accusing him of falling for a white girl. They called him names like "House Negro", "Jungle Fever", "Uncle Tom" and other bi-racial or sell-out epithets. The allegations were upsetting to both Junior and Casey as the two cried together inside a vacant classroom.

"No matter how any of this bullshit plays out," she told him. "I'm *still* your big sissy!"

"Why'd Mr. Levy say those things about you earlier? What was all of that?" he asked.

"Man, ain't enough time in the *world*. Another day, OK?" she told Junior.

Junior and Casey waited until the coast was clear before disappearing in opposite directions in the hallway. Back in Mrs. Hawkins's class after lunch, Junior didn't help his case. Resentful of Mrs. Hawkins and his peers, he spent all afternoon writing in his journal, unphased by the enveloped letter addressed to Sandy inside his bookbag.

When Sandy arrived to pick up Junior later that afternoon, she gave him hell all the way from Medgar back to the house. She cussed from the second he opened her car door, through every traffic light, and into the living room where Senior was there waiting. She said the "F" word to Junior, certifying his eternal punishment.

"Pork-sausage?! Boy, what the *fuck* is wrong with you?" Sandy wolfed at him. "You have lost *all* of your mind the way you been actin' up at this new school, Junior. It ain't even been a *week*!"

Junior stood docile with his eyes looking down at the floor as veins bulged from his mother's neck. Sandy was furious, shouting at Junior about the struggle of supporting him through his expulsion and finding him a new school. Her anger towards him was backed by Senior as he shoved Junior around the room, threatening to castrate him for upsetting his mother.

As Sandy went on to read Junior's note home from school, she inquired about Casey.

"And who the *fuck* is this Miss Haughton person? Is she the lady that bought you the pizza a few days ago? Huh? Well, is she?!"

"Yes, ma'am," Junior muttered.

As Sandy continued to read through Junior's note, he trembled under his daddy's hot breath as he waited for sentencing. Soon after, she rendered her verdict.

"I want that Nintendo, and I want the TV out of your room, *and* I want that library card because you ain't goin' nowhere no time soon until you learn how to behave. And when you go back to school tomorrow, you tell Miss Haughton that *I* said she is too goddamn grown to be your friend. You're only fourteen years old. You're a child. She's an adult."

"C'mon, Ma," Junior pleaded. "None of this me. Think about it. Mr. Levy is just an evil man trying to make things up, and y'all are falling for it. This is stupid."

WHAM! Down went Junior. Sandy then stood over top of him.

"You are *not* so grown that I won't knock you down on your ass!" she shouted. "Now, get off my floor and get out of my goddamn face before I slap you again. Go'on. Go!"

With his face still burning, Junior rose to his feet and retreated upstairs to his bedroom for the night. In his room, he wrapped up his Nintendo console, small television, and library card and handed them to Senior as he waited outside his room door.

Later in the bathroom mirror, Junior dabbed at the tender pink on his face from where Sandy had slapped him. Staring at his reflection, he exhaled, upset and angered. Most of the time when Junior got into trouble at home, Sandy would stop by before the night ended to educate him about his punishment. That night, however, neither Senior nor Sandy came to talk to him.

Unable to sleep, Junior thought of Casey the entire night. Earlier, he had tried to write but was too upset to formulate a meaningful poem. The thought of ending his friendship with Casey was overwhelming to him. He laid there, imagining his own heart breaking as he anticipated telling her the news that they could no longer be friends.

The next morning, Sandy dropped Junior off at Medgar without a word the entire way. As Junior closed her car door, Sandy called him back over. With his hangdog expression, he stood there with his hands stuffed inside his pocket.

"Aren't you forgettin' something, Junior?" she asked.

With his arms flaccid and weak, he leaned in to embrace Sandy and pecked her on the cheek.

"Thank you, sir," she said. "Now, go'on inside and be the young man that your daddy and I raised you to be – and don't forget what I said last night."

"Yes, ma'am," Junior murmured as he climbed the stairs into Medgar.

On his way to class, Junior passed by the school's main office and glanced through the window. From the corner of his eye, he noticed Casey's cubicle was missing and thought the worst. Ignoring his mother's conditions, he marched into Mr. Levy's office and demanded to know what he had done with Casey. Mr. Levy looked up at Junior and smiled. He placed his two pig legs up onto his desk and leaned backward in his chair. The chair cried for mercy under Mr. Levy's wide body.

"You know something, Junior?" He folded his hands behind his head as he laughed. "You're a goddamn genius! I figured out a way to take care of a little issue we've been having here at Medgar Evers. It came to me yesterday afternoon."

Believing Mr. Levy had fired Casey, Junior clenched his fists and tightened his jaw.

"Relax, kid. Besides, you don't have the balls to hit me. I'll throw your ass out of Medgar so fast that your mommy's head will spin. Then what would she say? So, anyway, between the little shithead, dope-pushing kids, and future jailhouse birds running around here at Medgar, I've finally found a solution.

See, I've been looking for a new Director of Security here. So, who better to promote than Miss Haughton?"

From a walkie-talkie next to his feet, Mr. Levy radioed for Casey to report to his office.

She showed up wearing a gray security uniform and badge with her orange hair slicked into a neat bun. Her slacks were stuffed inside black military-style boots. Her gold nameplate shone, blinding Junior as she stood there with a subdued look.

"Say hello to Officer Haughton, Junior," Mr. Levy formally introduced the two.

Life is difficult to explain.
How can something so remarkably beautiful
be so cruel and unfair to us all?

—LEONARD G. ROBINSON JR.

Seven

With the two of them together in his office, Mr. Levy put out the official word: if he caught them interacting, Casey would be fired on the spot, and Junior would be suspended for ten days. It tore them in half, forcing Junior to save his skin at home and Casey to save her job. Before dismissing them, Mr. Levy ordered the two to shake hands in front of him. Casey extended first as Junior followed behind. As their palms met, Junior felt the folded note she had prepared beforehand. Shortly thereafter, Casey left and Junior shoved the note inside his coat pocket as Mr. Levy looked on, unaware of their transaction. "Remember, Junior – " he opened his flaky hands " – ten days. What would Mrs. Robinson think to see her boy sitting at home that long?"

Out in the hallway, Junior removed Casey's note from his pocket. *Yo, meet me in 328 after this.* There were tiny hearts written next to her signed name.

Rushing, pushing through his peers, Junior raced down the hall toward the staircase. Juking, spinning, he whisked onto the third-floor before waiting for the perfect time to slip into 328. Less than a minute later, Casey showed up looking somber as Junior had expected.

"J., I'm really sorry for all of this." She began to cry. "I didn't mean for any of this to happen. You seem like such a nice kid who'd gone through something so fucked up, and I just wanted to take you under my wing a bit. I didn't mean to get you into trouble at home. Can you forgive me?"

"*Forgive* you?" asked Junior. "You didn't do anything, Casey! That was all Mr. Levy and that fuckin' Mrs. Hawkins, man! She's in on this shit, I bet!"

"Yeah," Casey sniffed. "So, look, maybe we just ought to cool off for a while, you know? I don't want you to get suspended, and I can't afford to get fired. Just for a little while?"

"No, Casey! I don't care if I get kicked out of Medgar – you're my big sissy, remember? Th'hell with 'em. We're still family, right? We straight?"

"Junior…"

"Casey, c'mon," he interrupted. "That's just Levy flexing his power. He ain't about nothin'."

"You don't know Levy like I do. He's a real asshole."

Together, they sat in silence as they tried to come up with a resolution to continue their friendship among Mr. Levy and his adjoining cronies. Junior paced throughout the tiny classroom, unable to settle down.

"So, we good?" he asked. "We're still family, right? Right, Casey?"

"You're right! Fuck 'em!" she said. "Look, we have to be careful how we meet up. I'm not gonna get fired and you can't get suspended. We just have to be smart, that's all. I said it before, J. We're beyond poetry at this point. What we have is divine and special. No one can take that away from us. We'll get through this."

Junior exhaled a sigh of relief, laughing himself away from crying as he eyed Casey's security uniform and touched her badge.

"I got a new job!" She extended her arms, jokingly, as the two laughed.

As the bell rang, signaling a start to the day, they booked to meet in room 328 every morning before the first bell and after school. For Junior, it was better than not having Casey in his world at all. As planned, Junior exited first, dipping into the nearest stairwell towards Mrs. Hawkins's classroom. Casey left minutes thereafter. Junior barely made it in time before Mrs. Hawkins closed her classroom door. Once inside, he took a seat near the front row, relieved. Casey was still his big sissy.

In the weeks following Casey's involuntary promotion to Director of Security at Medgar, Junior had no choice but to watch from the side as Casey succumbed to Mr. Levy's mind games and mental fuckery. With Thanksgiving fast approaching, the two relegated their friendship to meeting in vacant classrooms and exchanging notes. As always, Junior ended each note with a poem for Casey. In her response, she vented about Mr. Levy.

Casey's fancy title as director didn't endear her with her security colleagues. To show their disdain, they allowed Casey to earn her stripes. In a note to Junior, she wrote how they'd purposely show up late to roll calls and take forever to answer her back on the radio. When a fight broke out inside the school, Casey said she was always the first officer on the scene and that her colleagues would be slow to help her. *One kid popped a razor from underneath his tongue*, Casey wrote. *I was like 'fuck!'* she scribed to Junior with a smiley face. Junior couldn't believe her bravery. If it was him who had been forced into accepting such a promotion, he told Casey he would've quit. Mr. Levy spared no expense at finding new ways to fuck with her. For instance, he had Casey's cubicle moved down to the basement level and revoked her staff card to use the elevator. One morning, he put out an emergency page onto the fourth-floor. When Casey got there, sweat glazing across her forehead, she was the only officer to show up. Mr. Levy then told her he was only checking to see if her radio worked correctly. It was the first in a series of mind games to force her out.

"I don't get it," Junior said to her one morning. "If he hates you that badly, why doesn't he just fire you? Why all this?"

"J., you're so intelligent, but still so young," Casey explained to him. "That's some people for you. That's the evil of the world trying to disseminate the good in people like us. Levy could fire me any day, but seeing me suffer gives him greater satisfaction. You'll understand when you get older."

Enforcement, as it turned out, was Casey's kryptonite. Gullible and kind, the students ran over her as Mr. Levy gave her every shit detail he could find. One morning, after Junior got dropped off, he saw Casey standing outside attempting to make peace with the dice shooters at the front of the school. He watched as the boys humiliated her, laughing in Casey's face and belittling her authority. They called her "fat yellow-girl" and other mean names she had heard all her life because of her albinism.

"C'mon y'all, gimme a break," Casey pleaded, smiling warmly at the boys as they surrounded and mocked her. "Look, I'm just tryin' to do my job; help a sista out."

"Bitch, you ain't no sista of mine," one of the boys yelled.

Junior then watched as one of the boys threw a soft drink into Casey's face. Another boy then rushed Casey and ripped the aluminum badge right off her shirt and chucked it onto the roof of the school. Mortified, with Coca-Cola dripping from her hair, Casey slogged back into the school. The story spread around the school by lunchtime.

During lunch, Junior saw a group of girls playing with a strand of orange hair that looked like Casey's. Out in the hallway, he saw a row of red bloody droplets and followed it down to the nurse's station to find Casey there. With her head tilted toward the ceiling, the school nurse was attempting to stop her nose from bleeding. Her shirt was badly torn, eye puffy and a shoe impression was left on her shoulder as she winced in pain.

"They jumped me in the girls' bathroom on the third-floor." Casey spat blood down into the sink "I'm OK. I got beaten up worse in Jersey."

Enraged, Junior barged into Mr. Levy's office.

"You win!" said Junior. "OK? You win, Mr. Levy. Suspend me. Expel me. Whatever you have to do. Just stop messin' with Casey. She doesn't deserve any of this!"

"Ohhh, you mean that?" he laughed. "Well, it's part of the job, son. Too bad."

"They're kickin' her ass in here. She ain't no security guard. She's your secretary!"

"Th'hell if she is!" he yelled. "She's Director of School Security! It's her job to get her ass kicked as long as I *say* it's her job. Now, get the hell out of my office!"

By the afternoon when Junior had met with Casey, her eye was purple and there was a hematoma near her temple. She showed Junior where a student had cut a lock of her hair with a pair of scissors and said that Mr. Levy had provided her with a list of truant names and ordered her to call their parents. He then demanded she cite staff for the smallest of infractions like forgetting to close the windows in their classrooms or parking on the lines in the school's lot. In less than a week, Casey became the most hated faculty member amongst students and staff members. By the end of her second week as Director, a group of students had stolen the hubcaps from her car and spray-painted "FAT BITCH" across the windshield of her Toyota. Beaten, bloodied, and purple, she had had enough. One morning in room 328, she met with Junior with her right eye swollen shut and told him she was leaving.

"I have to leave," she told him with her good eye welling in tears. "I can't stay here another minute, J., it's just… not… safe for me, anymore. I'm sorry."

Sitting next to her on the floor, Junior then placed his arm around Casey as she leaned onto his shoulder and wept. Junior held his own.

"I get it," he said. "Don't worry, you'll always be my big sissy. No matter what."

As they parted ways, Junior watched as Casey vanished down the stairway towards Mr. Levy's office with her bag in one hand and her security badge in the other. He returned to Mrs. Hawkins's class on the fourth-floor, believing he had seen the last of Casey Haughton.

Family Forever

Later that same morning, a brawl broke out inside Mrs. Hawkins's classroom when one of the boys slashed a kid across the jaw with a butterfly knife. The boy's wound turned white before a river of blood began streaming down his face and onto his desk. Soon after, the fight was on between four boys who were opposing gang members. Desks were strewn throughout the class as the boys tussled, bouncing from wall-to-wall and rolling across the floor. At one point during the brawl, Mrs. Hawkins tried to separate the boys and was knocked to the floor. Her frail body hit the floor like a wet pancake as Junior's peers cheered on the barbarity. Acting instinctively, Junior rushed out into the hallway.

"Yo, we need help in here!" he yelled.

Within seconds, nearly half the school was gathered outside of Junior's classroom. Pushing, shoving, security swamed through a sea of curious onlookers hoping to disperse the melee. Smartly, Junior waited outside of the room – Senior and Sandy had once taught him to get out of the way if ever a fight broke out. "Don't stand and watch," Senior told him. "It'll be your luck somebody pulls out somethin' and then you get hit."

Out in the hallway, Junior watched from the background as a voice called to him from the stairwell. Turning to look, he noticed Casey waving him over. *Three-Two-Eight* she motioned to Junior using her fingers. Nodding, Junior crept down the back stairwell.

At their secret hideout on the third-floor, Casey checked on him.

"You OK?" She looked him over. "What the hell happened up there?"

"I don't know!" he said. "It happened so fast, man! I thought you were leaving?"

With her eye still engulfed, Casey grabbed him by the hand. "I just couldn't leave you here by yourself, J.," she told him. "Not with that kind of shit happenin' upstairs. One way or another, we'll get through this together, OK?"

With their friendship under the radar, the two remained close from afar. They spoke in passing, swapped notes, and met in room 328 whenever they could. In a note dated Monday, November 13, 1995, Junior wrote to Casey, thanking her for staying at Medgar, calling her his godsister. He followed with a magnificent poem to convey his heart for their genuine friendship. Her heart melted as she read through Junior's poem with one and a half eyes.

> *It feels good to have a friend in you.*
> *To go through it all, in you.*
> *To experience the world, in you.*
> *To talk, laugh, cry and share things in you,*
> *Thank you*
> *for the friend in you.*
>
> LEONARD G. ROBINSON JR.

That same Monday, Junior saw a kid at Medgar get pummeled by another student in the hallway for stepping on a kid's sneakers and failing to say 'excuse me'. The victim was an Indian kid named Aadrik. He was new to Medgar. His parents had just moved from Philly's west side after his father lost his job as a salesman and could no longer afford Aadrik's private tuition. His adversary was a kid named Donovan. It happened during the break. Aadrik had attempted to pass by Donovan and smudged his new shoe by accident. When Donovan asked him to wipe it off and Aadrik smiled back at him, the annihilation ensued. Donovan grabbed Aadrik by the throat and proceeded to bash the boy's head into the locker repeatedly. Aadrik, no taller than 5'1 and 125 pounds, crumbled to the floor instantly, bleeding from both ears, seizing violently. It wasn't until later that students and faculty learned Aadrik didn't speak great English. His smile wasn't meant to be harmful. Unfortunately for him, he couldn't comprehend the value his peers in the United States put on tennis shoes. Donovan was expelled initially. But later when it was learned that Aadrik was now blind in one eye, the police arrested Donovan at his home and charged him with aggravated assault. It took Junior months to rid the sight of seeing Aadrik seizing on the tile floor with blood draining from both his ears.

In the aftermath following the brawl in Mrs. Hawkins's classroom, Junior became the most loathed student at Medgar. His peers detested him for summoning for help and not allowing the fight to continue. They called horrible names and within days, Junior had developed what was known as a "snitch jacket" for interfering in what was considered official business. Concerned for his safety, Casey offered Junior a small Swiss army knife for personal protection.

"Man, shit is crazy. Take this." She handed the knife to him. "Just don't do nothin' stupid."

Junior looked over the small, concealable weapon and tucked it into his pocket.

"Thanks, Casey."

As the mindlessness at Medgar continued, the chaos happening around Brooke's Rowe was equally as devastating.

On the street over from where Junior lived, twelve-year-old Baylor Mack was shot dead by police when officers mistook his black pager for a weapon. In the days following the fatal shooting, an attorney assigned to the case determined there was not enough evidence to indict the officers responsible for shooting the boy. Junior was sitting between his parents when the announcement was read from a podium down at City Hall. Senior leaped to his feet, disgusted with the decision. It triggered a war inside the Robinson castle as both Senior and Sandy had it out for each other. Fed up with city living, Sandy had given all of her forty-one years to Philly and wanted out. Senior countered that what happened in Brooke's Rowe happened everywhere else in the world. But in the back of Sandy's mind was Medgar. In just two months, Junior's school had seen more than its fair share of violence. Kids were being assaulted and staff members were being beaten for interfering. Most recently, a teacher was taken out on a stretcher after being sucker-punched with brass knuckles. Letters were sent home to parents by Mr. Levy, ensuring that he'd get a handle on things. With no available school willing to take Junior so late into the year, Sandy had no choice but to leave Junior enrolled.

"You can still be the first man in our family to graduate high school," she told him before bed that night. Yet, later that same evening, Junior overheard his mother crying in the kitchen as she worried about her son. As if losing Lawrence the year before wasn't enough, she now had to contend with sacrificing Junior for the sake of breaking a generational curse. Sandy had spent her entire life living in the ghetto and wanted better for her surviving son.

The more violence that happened inside Medgar and throughout Brooke's Rowe, the more Sandy worried, and the more Junior felt the weight of his mother's worry. Soon, she was back at the kitchen table looking at houses in places far away from Brooke's Rowe. Cities like Autumn Hills, Maryland were a two-hour drive south from where the Robinsons lived, and with a populace of 6,400 residents, it seemed like the perfect escape. Yet, still, the war over money raged on.

"So, where you runnin' off to now?" Senior asked Sandy one night after finding news clippings of cities scattered atop the kitchen table. "Woman, you know good-and-goddamn-well we can't afford to move out of here. It's just a shitty pipe dream. Might as well give it up! Junior ain't goin' nowhere and neither are we! Philly is our home!"

At the door of Medgar one morning, Sandy held Junior's face with her hands.

"Junior, I *need* you to take this school thing seriously," she told him. "I need you to work hard so that you can have choices in life and don't end up stuck in Brooke's Rowe or some damned place like Crawford like your momma did. Do you understand?" Then, before Junior could answer, Sandy kissed him and left. That kiss added more pressure on Junior than any other kiss Sandy had given him any other morning.

Everyone is not your friend.
Your enemies will dress in disguise
right before your very eyes
if you don't soon realize.
Everyone is not your friend.

LEONARD G. ROBINSON JR.

Normal Sin

On the Tuesday before Thanksgiving, Junior could barely stay awake in Mrs. Hawkins's class. That morning, Mrs. Hawkins, with her wrist in a cast from the melee the previous week, introduced a guest speaker to Junior's class. The man's name was Oswald Darrius. He claimed to be from North Philly before migrating to the NFL during the 1970s. Hobbling on a cane, he boasted about his career as a starting lineman for the New York Giants and the Buffalo Bills. As he moved throughout the classroom, he spoke with both hands in flight like Donald Trump. At one point, Mr. Darrius stopped at the front of the room, allowing Junior to get a closer look at the guest speaker. His crooked fingers were covered in championship rings and one of his legs appeared longer than the other. He wore an orthopedic shoe on his right foot and walked with a deep limp which the kids all later mocked him for. He claimed that football had saved him from living on the streets.

"You see," he began, "I was worse than y'all could *ever* be." The man hobbled by Junior's desk, touching him on the

163

shoulder as he passed. "I used to be a little bad somebody. Always in the middle of things. Robbin' folks. Stealin'. All kinds of shit." He touched another boy on the shoulder. "But I had a goal and that was to get out of Philly."

In Mr. Darrius's back pocket was a photograph taken during his youth; he passed it around the classroom. In the picture was a group of boys that had since passed or were serving life terms in prison.

"See him," the man said. "That's my buddy right there. We played football together in college. Football is a beautiful sport. I made some good money in those days."

Unimpressed by the man's narrative that sports entertainment was their only hope for the future, Junior opened his journal to write. Fortunately for Junior, Senior had long since killed his dream of playing professional sports.

"Look here, you don't need no goddamn football to be somebody to white people. That's bullshit," Junior recalled Senior telling him when he didn't get picked to play intramural football back in North Philly.

Hoping to win over the rambunctious class, Mr. Darrius showed Junior's class his battle scars on both legs from having two of his knees replaced. Finding little spark, he pulled out two hundred in cash and counted it as Junior's class suddenly came to life. He offered to pay a kid a hundred bucks if they could name which NFL team won the championship in 1960.

"Do *you* know?" the man asked Junior.

"Know what?" Junior answered, irritated.

"Which team won it in 1960?"

"I don't watch football, sir."

Junior's class all blew out air, groaning at him as Junior carried on in his journal, unmoved by the presentation. The one time Junior did glance over was to look at Mrs. Hawkins's evil face. Her eyes slanted at him behind her bifocal glasses. By then, Junior was numb and could care less about what Mrs. Hawkins, Mr. Levy, or anyone else thought. He used the hour-long presentation to write a new poem to Casey. Ever the perfectionist, he erased until the rubber on his pencil wore into the metal, scratching a hole inside his sacred journal.

As soon as Mr. Darrius left, Mrs. Hawkins reamed Junior in the hallway.

"You gotta be the most *disrespectful* little boy I've ever seen in my entire life!" she hollered at Junior, her voice echoing throughout the fourth-floor. "How dare you sit there and *write* during Mr. Darrius's presentation? You ought to be thankful someone took the time to talk to your little narrow ass. Damn devil!"

Already on punishment, Junior had nothing to lose. Fed up with Mrs. Hawkins and the underworld at his school, he lashed back.

"Fuck you!" Junior screamed back. "*You're* the devil!"

Mrs. Hawkins gasped as she held her chest with one hand and stumbled backward into the wall like Fred Sanford, unable to believe Junior. He had had enough.

"Lady, you got some nerve! You're the biggest bible-preachin' hypocrite I've ever seen! Yeah, I said it!" Junior continued. "Call my mother. Call my daddy. Just leave me the fuck alone!"

Downstairs in Mr. Levy's office, Sandy shouted at Junior through the phone line. "What did we *just* discuss a few days ago?!" she went off. "Boy, are you crazy? Are you on PCP or something? Because you gotta be on drugs to talk to an old lady that way!"

Sickened by his behavior, Sandy hung up on him. Junior was later issued afterschool detention for disrespecting Mrs. Hawkins. With a subdued look, he returned to Mrs. Hawkins's class to the celebration of his peers. They patted Junior on the back as if he'd finally crossed over to the dark side and had done some good by cussing out Mrs. Hawkins. For Junior, however, it was the lowest point of the school year for him. He had gone from being a quiet, shy kid to someone who would curse out a woman old enough to be his grandmother.

At lunch, Junior barely ate as he stared down at his cold corndog and mashed potatoes covered in diarrhea-colored gravy. Sulking, angry, a kid walked by and asked if Junior planned on eating his lunch. "Man, just take it," he flapped at the kid. Minutes later, a teacher bypassed Junior at the table, shaking his head at him in disgust, followed by another teacher. Bothered by the events from earlier, Junior looked up toward the door of the lunchroom and noticed Casey staring right at him with her arms folded. Soon after, she disappeared into the hallway – his cue to leave. Junior headed down to room 328. When he got there, Casey was waiting for him. Her arms were still folded.

"I know…" he greeted her. "She started it first, though."

"Junior! C'mon, man!" she fussed at him "You know you're not supposed to be writing poetry when a guest speaker is talking. It's rude! And *then* you cuss out Mrs. Hawkins? Who in the hell do you think you are? Samuel L. Jackson or somebody?"

Junior leaned against the wall and sighed.

"C'mon, J. You can't be cussin' out your teacher and gettin' into trouble. You're just giving Levy more ammunition. We gotta be smart, remember? How many days did Levy give you?"

"What does it matter?" he asked. "I'm already in trouble. Besides, who cares?"

"*I* care Junior." She looked into his eyes. "Why do you think I'm still here?"

As Casey walked over to the window, using her reflection to straighten her hair and uniform, Junior followed behind her.

"So, let me get this straight," he asked. "You stayed… because of… me?"

Ignoring him, Casey tied her hair into a ponytail as if to avoid the sentimental moment between them. Unable to do so, she turned to face him. "Yeah…I uh…I love you, man." She giggled as her voice began to hoarsen. "You're like the little stubborn brother I never got to have. Like the family I'd dream about having as a little girl. Like the little… homie from around the way that you knew was gonna grow up and be somebody special someday."

Junior was speechless.

"I don't know what to say. *You love me*? Shit, my own daddy won't even tell me that," he said.

"You ain't gotta say it back to me or nothin'." She wiped her eyes. "But that's just…how I feel, OK? I don't want to see you hurt or get into any trouble, J. You got it, man? I'm fuckin' serious, Junior," She grabbed him by the arm. "I ain't playin'!"

Staring into her green eyes, Junior nodded.

"I won't, Casey. I promise I'll fly straight."

"Good." She smiled. "OK. Go away. You made me cry — I'm mad at you!"

Don't want your money or what isn't mine.
But if you don't mind,
I would like a little more of your time.
Don't care what's on the outside
because that'll eventually fade away.
And I pray, our souls become as inseparable
as your sun is to my day.

LEONARD G. ROBINSON JR.

Fuck Detention

When the day was over, Junior stayed behind in Mrs. Hawkins's class to serve detention. She put him to work immediately, dropping a huge filing box loaded with old test papers onto Junior's desk. The second it landed, a

168

sheet of dust overwhelmed him. She sneered at Junior as it landed. Between sorting papers, rearranging desks, washing boards, and beating erasers probably not used since the 80s, Junior spent the next hour mumbling expletives to himself.

Mrs. Hawkins made the experience hell for him. She double and triple-checked Junior's work, making him redo each task just to prolong his agony. Then, as if she was enjoying his misery, she sat near the back of her room with her bony legs crossed, sucking on candy, teeing off insults at Junior. She called him a "rotten bastard" and shouted at him every time he missed a spot. At one point, Mrs. Hawkins threw an empty juice bottle at him. It had been left behind by a student. The bottle bounced from the wall, nearly missing Junior's head before it landed at his feet.

"You heathen! Here!" She flung the bottle. "Catch this!"

"Yo, don't throw nothin' at me," Junior barked at her. "That's rude, Mrs. Hawkins!"

"Shut up. I throw whatever the hell I want! Hurry up!"

Child-like, Mrs. Hawkins threw whatever she could scrounge on the floor at Junior. Fortunately for him, her delicate arm could only get so much wind behind her throw. Throughout detention, she berated Junior, snickering like a dying cat as he grew angry at her antics. She dared to quote scripture from the bible before asking Junior if he was "saved" as she claimed the world would end on December 31, 1999.

"I feel sorry for your mother," Mrs. Hawkins told him. "She's got an ass for a son."

"Is that right?" Junior indulged her to pass the time. "What makes you so sure of that?"

"*How* you ask? You ask *how* do I know? 'Cause you ain't nothin' but a lowdown heathen!" she scoffed. "I'm gonna work the devil out of you! Go'on. Work!"

Junior was no saint by any stretch of religion, but he was also no heathen. He was misunderstood, just like Casey was often mistaken for being a white girl, he once thought. As Mrs. Hawkins carried on in her foolish torture, damning Junior's future and blaming his parents for raising such a "shithead son", he ignored his teacher. Near the end of his punishment, Mrs. Hawkins approached him at the front of the room to check his work. She eyeballed the clean board and grunted before finding a dime-sized smudge in the far corner.

"It's clean, Mrs. Hawkins," said Junior. "Can I go now?"

"Clean?" she yelled at him. "Look at that smudge! What's all this stuff here? You're about as useless as a limp dick."

After Mrs. Hawkins pointed out the smudge on her board, she walked over to the filing cabinet where Junior had sorted through a stack of papers and emptied it onto the table.

"These are all wrong!" she fussed. "Forget it. Just leave. You're worthless like everybody else in this damn school. Go away before I change my mind."

Before she tried keeping him overnight, Junior grabbed his belongings and headed toward the door. Having a change of heart, he decided to confront Mrs. Hawkins about her attitude. Biting his tongue, he was mindful of his behavior.

"How come you hate me so much?" Junior asked her. "What've I ever done to you?"

Marching over to him, Mrs. Hawkins slammed her hand down onto the desk. She stood directly in Junior's face as he towered over her. Her mean bug eyes fixed on him and her breath smelled like coffee and menthol cigarettes. To get away from her hideous breath, Junior leaned backward.

"I hate all of you kids equally. You're all heathens. Especially you. You're just like my son. You think you know *every* damn thing."

As Mrs. Hawkins trolled back to her desk, Junior put two and two together.

"So, I get it now. This ain't about me. It's about your son." He softened. "I didn't know you had a son, Mrs. Hawkins. Did something happen to him? Is he OK?"

"Why don't you mind your damn business?" She suggested.

Junior approached Mrs. Hawkins at her desk.

"I'm sorry for cussin' at you earlier, OK?" he apologized. "But if you're gonna throw scriptures from the bible at people then you've got a lot to learn about treating people better than the way you do, ma'am. I don't know a lot about God, but I know he doesn't like ugly. And I don't know what happened to your son, but I hope you can find it in your heart to forgive him...and me. Have a good Thanksgiving, Mrs. Hawkins."

With the last word, Junior threw on his Walkman and headed out the door.

I breed forgiveness,
though I remain savvy with my heart,
unaware of the direction
to which sinister winds might blow.

LEONARD G. ROBINSON JR.

Down the Barrel of a Gun

Darkness had befallen Brooke's Rowe as Junior stepped out of Medgar and into the cool night air. That evening, with the holidays keeping Sandy busy on mandatory overtime and Senior tied up with his handyman business, Junior would have to catch the city bus back to Kennedy Street. Unfortunately for him, the nearest stop was a six-block walk from Medgar's doorstep. With his headset blaring Nas's *Illmatic*, Junior carried on into the Philly darkness, drowning out the city sounds surrounding him. Earlier, Casey had offered him a ride home before remembering Mr. Levy's strict order for them to not socialize.

Up the block, Junior passed by a green Jeep Cherokee with tinted windows parked along Sunnyside Avenue. Humming to himself, Junior bypassed the small SUV, unsuspecting of the four masked individuals approaching him from behind. With his guard lowered, he stopped to flip his cassette tape when suddenly he felt a sharp blow to the back of his head. The pain dropped him to his knees. Unaware of what happened, he palmed his scalp to find his hand covered in blood.

Junior turned to look and saw four masked men standing there, one of whom brandished a silver handgun. Before Junior could surrender, the gunman shoved Junior into a steel shutter and raised his gun into Junior's face. His hands went up immediately.

"You the nigga that called for help in Mrs. Hawkins's class the other day?" the gunman asked him. "That didn't have shit to do with you. You should've minded your business."

Crying, Junior begged for his life. "C'mon man! Look, I ain't with none of that, I'm just trying to get home!"

"Shut the fuck up!" The gunman cocked his pistol. "Empty your pockets!"

Trembling, Junior dumped the contents of his pockets onto the sidewalk and raised his hands again. As the gunman's goons scrounged through his wallet, they dumped his school ID onto the pavement and removed ten dollars from inside his wallet. Another boy went through Junior's pockets, patting his legs and ankles and checking inside his school bag.

"That's all I got is that ten dollars." He pointed with his toe. "I ain't got shit else."

Junior looked on in fear as the robbers looked around at each other, deliberating on whether or not to spare his life.

"Ten dollars ain't enough to pay for what you did!"

The robber then struck Junior across the jaw, hard, knocking him down onto the pavement as the others proceeded to beat him. They kicked and punched Junior mercilessly as he crawled out into the street, desperately trying to get away. As he tried to run, one of the boys tripped him, causing Junior to fall. Helpless, he covered his face, begging for his attackers to leave him alone.

One of the robbers took Juniors' headset from around his neck, a beloved Christmas gift Lawrence had bought him two years before. Another ripped off his tennis shoes and bulky jacket. The robbers pummeled Junior some more as the gunman placed the barrel against Junior's forehead, threatening to kill him if he told anyone what happened.

Battered and bloodied, Junior laid there with a gun pressed against his head, wondering if he'd ever see his family again. Staring at death, he overheard a car come gunning up Sunnyside Avenue to his rescue, succeeded by the flickering of high beams and a car horn. It was none other than his big sissy, Casey Haughton. Startled, the gunman let Junior go.

Casey, still wearing her security uniform, exited her car hurling sections of broken brick from Medgar's mural toward Junior's attackers. The first brick hit the gunman square in the face.

"Get off him!" she screamed. "Step the fuck back! Back up!"

As pieces of brick reigned on the robbers, the gunman dropped his pistol. Thinking quickly, Junior, bleeding from the mouth, knocked the gun into a nearby storm drain, disarming the assailants. Casey then grabbed her pepper spray off her duty belt and sprayed the robbers as they coughed and retreated back to their getaway car and fled.

Limping, falling over, Junior struggled onto his feet as

Casey and a bystander helped Junior up. Sobbing, he could barely talk.

"They fuckin' robbed me," he moaned. "I can't believe they fuckin' robbed me."

Wasting no time, Casey hoisted Junior onto his feet, shoved him into the back of her car and raced to the nearest hospital.

Don't get misinformed by the uninformed.
Miseducated fools swim together
Like a school of dumb fish
waiting to get eaten
by the sharks of their oppressors.

—LEONARD G. ROBINSON JR.

Eight

Junior appeared in the lobby of Children's Hospital, lagging onto Casey's shoulder, swollen, crying, and bleeding from his mouth. He was aided by a desk nurse who quickly summoned for a gurney. Knots lined atop Junior's forehead and scalp like anthills, and his eyes looked like golf balls with slits for his red eyes. There was a gash on the bridge of his nose, and his lips were bloody and puffy like undercooked sausage links. Missing a sock, the toenail on his right pinky toe was snapped back to the cuticle. He struggled to make his way onto the gurney. Wincing, whining, writhing in pain, he held onto Casey's hand before a team of hospital staff whisked him away into Intensive Care, breaking the hold.

Aching all over, doctors administered Junior extra-strength Tylenol. When that failed, they gave him morphine to slow down his restlessness and anxiety. Within minutes, his pain subsided, and he was out. When Junior awoke an hour later, he was surrounded by his parents, Casey, and a police detective. Still out of it, Junior could barely keep his eyes open as Sandy tried to talk to him. His jaw and head throbbed, and the room was spinning from the combination of drugs and the four-on-one ass-kicking.

"Junior? Baby?" Sandy leaned over him. "Honey, can you hear me?"

Nodding his head in response, Junior winced as his headache suddenly grew worse. He cried again which also made Casey cry.

"Honey? This is Detective Engram. He needs to ask you about what happened, OK? I need you to talk to the detective for us. Can you do that for me?"

Slow and more precarious than the first time, Junior nodded again.

"Hello Leonard, I'm Detective…"

"He prefers Junior!" Casey interfered. "Please, call him Junior, sir."

Irritated, the detective exhaled as both Senior and Sandy looked at one another, surprised by Junior's big sissy.

"Very well." He fake-smiled. "Junior. I'm Detective Engram with the Philadelphia Police. I need to ask you some questions about what happened earlier. Can I get you to talk?"

Junior sluggishly extended his arms so Casey and Senior could hoist him up in bed. He grunted in pain. Through the slit in his gown was a large scrape across his back from where he had fallen to the asphalt. With his right hand, Junior reached for the controller to his bed to raise himself to speak with Detective Engram. Meanwhile, the detective jotted notes on Junior's injuries onto a clipboard. Sandy offered him a sip of ice-cold water to help him wake up.

"I can come back tomorrow if you guys think that'll be better?" Detective Engram said.

As Sandy went to speak, Casey beat her to it.

"Give him a damn second, OK?" she hissed as she straightened Junior's pillow. "The kid just had his brains beaten out of him. He's in a lot of pain, Detective."

Sulking and impatient, the detective backed into the corner of the room as Junior's family tended to him. To nurse his delicate jaw, Senior fed him a bowl of chicken noodle soup with crushed crackers and a box of fruit juice. Junior barely stayed awake during the feeding as the antsy detective constantly changed positions, crossing his legs and folding his arms. At one point, the man excused himself to take a phone call from his cell phone, leaving Junior's room.

"I mean, what's the hurry?" said Sandy. "Our son was just attacked! Can't we get any help?"

"You see?" said Senior. "There's that niceness in you, I be talkin' 'bout! You *always* want to see the good in people, Sandy. Ain't nothin' good 'bout *none* of 'em. Same thing with Lawrence. All of a sudden, you wanna *call the police*. Motherfuck the police! I'll say it to the bastard's face!"

"Look, don't you start that shit in here!" Sandy fired back. "Not now, Leonard, OK?!"

As Junior's parents began to argue, he sat there watching half-awake. A nurse walked in and asked for the Robinsons to take their fight outside, which they did. Smartly, Casey stayed behind to wait for the detective. Minutes later, Detective Engram returned to Junior's room with an emergency and had to leave. The Robinsons returned to Junior's room, noticed the detective had left, and began to shout again in front of Casey. They blamed one another for Junior getting hurt and for the detective having to leave. As Sandy went to thank Casey for her help and to relieve her for the night, Junior came to life.

"Can she stay a little while longer?" he mumbled.

Before either of Junior's parents could answer, Casey was right by his bedside. She then leaned over and grabbed Junior by his splinted hand.

"I'll do whatever you want me to do, J., as long as your parents say it's OK," she told him. "If you want me here, I'm here. Whatever you need. I got you."

With his face still scuffed, eyes like golf balls, and the top of his head looking like the Appalachians, Junior turned to look over at Senior and Sandy for approval. They scowled at one another before finally giving Junior the nod.

"Sure, Junior," said Sandy. "If you want her to stay, well, then we want her to, also."

As Junior slowly rolled over onto his side, Casey thanked Junior's family for their hospitality and excused herself to use the restroom, leaving the Robinsons alone.

"So, is she the white girl from Junior's school?" asked Senior.

"She's not white, Leonard – she's black – she's an albino," said Sandy.

"A what? A who? You said she's a rhino?!"

"Lord Jesus! Will you just go away? Go have a cigarette or something!"

Sometime after 1 a.m. in the early morning hours of Thanksgiving Eve, Junior awoke to the sound of J. J. Evans's voice on a re-run of the 1970s television show, *Good Times*. Still in pain, he turned to survey the room and noticed Senior asleep next to him in a chair with his ball cap cocked over his face. His daddy's long legs were outstretched as if he was on a long flight. Across the room in the corner, Casey was curled into a ball beneath Senior's jacket. Meanwhile, out in the hallway, Junior overheard his mother's voice as she conferred with staff about his condition and treatment upon his discharge. According to what Junior overheard, he had sustained no broken bones during the attack but would need to miss seven to ten days of school. Junior tried to stay awake to hear more but drifted back into sleep.

Three hours later, Junior awoke to Casey and Sandy talking; Senior was gone. He could tell from the tones of their voices that they were enjoying talking with each other. To keep them bonding, he pretended to be asleep, eavesdropping on their conversation.

"I can't believe what you just told me!" Sandy fussed. "Mrs. Hawkins did what?! Why didn't Junior tell me all of this? How could he not tell me all of these things?"

"He didn't want to upset you," said Casey. "Look, I was wrong to carry on having a friendship with your son after you told him not to. I take responsibility for that, Mrs. Robinson. But I do understand Junior's dilemma. Growing up as the only albino girl in my neighborhood in Jersey, I know what it feels like to be different than other kids. So, we bonded on those similarities."

With his sausage lips somewhat smiling, Junior drifted back to sleep. He awoke again two hours later to the aroma of a bacon, egg, and cheese biscuit from McDonald's. With a plastic knife, Senior sawed Junior's sandwich into four bite-sized sections to accommodate his achy jaw. Across the room, Casey and Sandy stood together near the window to Junior's room, sipping hot coffee, looking at the sun as it crept over Philadelphia.

"Girrrrl, I gotta give it to you," Sandy said to Casey. "I thought *I* grew up bad. You've had it hard your whole life."

"Had *what* hard?" Junior snaked into their discussion.

"Ha! He's awake!" laughed Casey.

"I forgot to tell you that he does that." Sandy shook her head. "Feelin' better, honey?"

"Here and there," said Junior.

Some prefer the lake while others prefer the ocean.
I prefer the motions of a body of water to cleanse my soul.
Let the rain pour down soon
with streams that run into my wildest dreams.
Lakes & Oceans.
What waters must I swim?

LEONARD G. ROBINSON JR.

Uninspired

When Junior was discharged the following morning, doctors handed him a packet of mandible exercises to nurse his injured jaw along with a prescription for Percocet. By then, the small slit between his engulfed eyes had opened enough for him to cry as he recollected what had happened to him. As suggested, Junior would miss between a week or more of school to allow his injuries to heal. Down at the Save-a-Lot, Sandy bought Junior a cart full of chicken noodle soup, oatmeal, and apple sauce. As the Robinsons parted ways with Casey that morning, she hugged Junior and left him with her cell number in case he wanted to talk.

At home, Junior limped in front of the bathroom mirror, surveying his battered face. Most of the swelling in his scalp had subsided, but his eyes were still enlarged and dried blood caked the inside of his nostrils and corner lip. Using his finger, he dabbed the patch of swollen skin surrounding his orbital bone. Pain shot through his body and he yelped in agony. Feeling sorry for himself, he shut off the bathroom light and wept in the dark.

Later that afternoon, a police detective arrived at the Robinsons' house to interview Junior about his attack. Downstairs at the kitchen table, the detective spent more time jotting notes than questioning Junior about the incident. Fed up with the injustices her family had received since the previous summer, Sandy became irritated with the detective, questioning the officer about his interview skills.

"Do you mind telling me what you're writing?" she asked. "Because you've been sitting at my kitchen table for over an hour, and you haven't asked my son anything noteworthy, sir."

"What would you like for me to ask him?" the detective asked.

"I don't know, perhaps, 'Can you tell me what they looked like? What were they wearing? What kind of vehicle were they driving?' You know? *Something.*"

Sassy and smart-alecky, the detective rolled his eyes at Sandy.

"OK, Junior." He shook his head. "Can you tell me what they looked like? What were they wearing? What kind of vehicle were they driving? Is that good enough, Mrs. Robinson?"

Infuriated, Sandy threw the detective out of her home.

"Get out of my house!" she barked at the man as she followed him to the door. Shortly thereafter, Junior retreated upstairs to his bedroom.

Uninspired to write, he relegated himself to read some of his past works during his time off from school. Angry, Junior's poems read to him like litter floating downstream. Before long, he began ripping and tearing out the pages to each of his journals, one by one. On his first night home from the hospital, Junior destroyed eleven of his journals from the summer before.

Thanksgiving came and went that year, much like it had the previous year after Lawrence had died. Senior stayed out of the house most of the day, on his ladder or out on his truck, while Sandy prepared Junior a short plate of collard greens, thinly cut ham, and candy yams. As he tried to open his tender jaw to eat, pain ripped through his body, forcing him to drop his fork down onto the floor. Touching his lumpy face, he started to whimper.

"I need you to be strong for me." Sandy held him. "Don't let yourself get too low."

For Junior, there was no other place for him to go except down low. He spent all day sleeping or tearing up his old journals. At night, he stared out the window into the world, contemplating revenge for all of the injustices of the past year.

The day after Thanksgiving, three days after Junior's attack, the swelling around his face had gone down, and the cut on the bridge of his nose finally scabbed. To get him out of the house, Sandy took Junior along with her for a quick drive into Philly's west side. Sandy waited until they arrived back in front of the house to apologize to him for being hard on Casey several weeks back and not giving her a chance.

"I should've believed in you," she told him. "I was wrong about everything. I had no idea what was happening at Medgar all this time, and all that you had been going through. But I got something to tell you," she went on. "I'm thinkin' about pullin' you from Medgar. At least next fall you can start again at Franklin High."

"Franklin High?" asked Junior. "Then that means I won't see Casey again! I'll stay back a year. I won't graduate on time – I'll be behind. Ma, please," he begged. "I can go back to Medgar. I'll be fine. It'll all work out."

"Junior – "

"Ma, please!" he interrupted. "I'll do anything!"

"It's just not safe. I know that you'll miss a year and that you're worried about not being able to see your friend, but we'll find a way to make it all work out. OK? But I may have to do this, Junior. Those boys could've killed you that night. Then what?"

Afterward, Sandy hopped out of her car and went inside, leaving Junior in the passenger seat to mull over his predicament. He did so without tears, but with heaviness. As the rigors of life's injustices weighed on his heart, his poetic mind became dark with vengeance. Instead of phoning Casey to talk, Junior phoned the malevolent spirit reigning within him.

The world is not my oyster.
Things do not happen for a reason.
Practice does not make perfect.
Nice guys will not finish last.
Lies given to me by my ancestors shall be abolished,
like rusted chains given to slaves.
You must take what's yours while you still can.
I've decided to take what's mine
and whomever else is weak enough to let me take theirs.

LEONARD G. ROBINSON JR.

.38 Revolver

Days later, while standing in the doorway of his parents' bedroom, Junior noticed Senior's nightstand partially open and saw a glimpse of his daddy's loaded .38 revolver. As he returned to his bedroom for the night, he paced back and forth, hoping to ward away his thoughts of revenge. To take his mind off of his daddy's gun, he tried to write but found his world filled with nothing but pain and hatred. He hated the police for dumping on his case and for treating Lawrence's death as just another black person shot dead. He hated running away from Crawford afterward, and the grief his peers had given him since moving to Brooke's Rowe. He hated Franklin. He hated Medgar, and all that had been associated with his stumbling blocks since day one. Suddenly, the only light illuminating his sinister world, Casey Haughton, was being taken away from him along with the school year. Tired of losing, Junior slipped into a world of darkness. He returned to Senior's nightstand the next night, and the night thereafter.

In the bathroom mirror, Junior role-played with his daddy's gun, aiming at his reflection. Admiring its chrome finish, he fingered its solid grip before feathering the trigger. Then, before his daddy noticed it missing, Junior returned the revolver to his nightstand. Back in his room for the night, he fantasized about the .38 revolver, and the power it gave him. He was no longer a boy, but a man. He would never be a loser again.

One afternoon, Senior placed a bowl of chicken noodle soup and pain medication onto Junior's nightstand and closed his son's door. The second he left, Junior hurled the bowl into the wall, shattering the fine porcelain and soiling his wall with soup. As Senior opened the door and saw the mess, he looked at Junior's lumpy face and thought twice about beheading him. If it had been any other day, Junior's daddy would've buried him beneath the house. Not that day. Instead, he left and returned to clean up the mess while his son sat sulking on his bed. "If you ain't gonna eat nothin', at least take your medicine," Senior told him. Heeding his daddy's advice, Junior reached for the melted tablets swimming in his spilled soup.

Sandy didn't sleep for two whole nights after learning what had happened. Under duress, she succumbed to her old, filthy habit of smoking – a habit she had given up when she'd become pregnant with Junior. Unable to sleep, she slipped out into the backyard long after her family was asleep to indulge in her new favorite pastime.

Meanwhile, the Robinsons were still at war over Brooke's Rowe. At odds with their decision was Sandy's tenure down at the post office. With only ten years left until her retirement, she spent her twenty-year celebration sobbing into the arms of co-workers who were unaware of her troubles at home. The Robinsons' two-bedroom townhouse was crumbling on top of them. The roof was old and needed repair. Beneath the basement drain outback, underground roots had torn through a drainage pipe, causing it to clog often. The cost to have the old piping replaced was $8800 – more than the family had managed to save in nearly five years. Not to mention, both cars needed major repairs.

With the holidays fast approaching, Senior's handyman business had begun to stagger, tightening their overall income. Whereas he usually averaged five to six jobs per day, he was now lucky to make two in one week. With tempers short, arguments were often and volatile. The worst problem was Junior's dilemma. Not a single public school (or alternative) in all of Philadelphia would take him until the fall of '96. Adding more misery to their problems, this would be the Robinsons' second Christmas without Lawrence.

The weekend before Junior was due to return to Medgar, his face and sore jaw had healed significantly, and he began to come around. Returning to writing, however, proved to be an arduous task. Beside him on his bed was a pile of crumpled paper that reminded him how his artistic talents continued evading him. On his mind was the barrel of his daddy's .38 revolver tucked away in his nightstand. Although writing had given Junior his path to understanding the world, nothing could compare to the power he felt when holding his father's gun. Desperate for a new identity, he entered his parents' room, removed his daddy's .38, and placed it into his pocket. Shortly thereafter, he was distracted by a knock at the door.

"Honey, can you get that?" Sandy called to him from the kitchen. "My hands are full!"

As Junior attempted to return the gun, Senior got on him.

"Boy, didn't you hear your momma callin' you?" he

seconded. "Get the door, dammit! Th'hell are you doing up there? Hurry up!"

Rushing, stumbling, Junior shoved the revolver back into his pocket and rushed downstairs. As he neared the door, his parents exited the kitchen and stood in the living room, watching him. Alarmed, Junior stopped in his tracks.

"Don't look at me!" growled Senior. "Open the door, knucklehead!"

As Junior went to open the front door, waiting for him on the other side was Casey. She was holding his favorite meal: Domino's pizza with extra cheese, pepperoni, and sausage. Before Casey could get a word in, Junior grabbed his big sissy and hugged her. He then turned to look back and see his parents grinning with guilt. He had been set up – in a good way.

Keeping Casey

After a late lunch, Junior and Casey stood out on the porch, overlooking Brooke's Rowe as they enjoyed an unusually warm November night. On the sidewalk in front of them, walkers strolled up and down Kennedy Street, some without a destination and some waiting near a shattered bus stop. Across the way, hands begged for loose change as snaggle-toothed, cold-beer sippers skipped checkers along a dingy checkerboard.

For Junior, seeing Casey was rejuvenating to his fractured world. As she happily chattered on about nothing, he looked over into her pudgy face and could see her sibling-like love for him. She was his best friend in all of Brooke's Rowe, Crawford, all of Philly, and the entire world. Each time she attempted to leave, Junior would ask her to stay and Casey would oblige him. "OK, ten more minutes. For real this time, man!" she'd say before an hour would pass by. "But I gotta get going after this!"

The more Casey talked, the better for Junior. Her energy was warm and magnetic, and having her over for dinner was a much-needed break from his dreaded head. She had a cute, dimpled smile that shone, and her infectious laugh let everyone in the room know that Casey was there. It was beyond Junior why the staff at Medgar treated his big sissy with such disregard. As she got up to leave him, Junior begged her for another ten minutes.

"Junior… C'mon, man!" She giggled. "I got shit to do. It's almost six o'clock!"

"I know, but the last ten minutes went too fast!" he said. "Yo, please? Last time, for real. Then you can go. Please… Casey? Besides, I wanted to ask you something. If you don't mind?"

Falling for his puppy-dog eyes, Casey took a seat next to him.

"Boy, you better be lucky you're like my little brother – what is it?"

Searching for something meaningful to keep her around, Junior cycled through his brain.

"The other night in the hospital, I heard you talking to

my mother, and uh…it made me think about something Levy said to you in the hallway on the day I got in trouble. He called you an addict and some other things. I was just wondering…did something happen to you some time ago?"

Lost for words, Casey exhaled and stared into the street lamp above them.

"…Really can't believe you asked me that right now, J."

Unsure of where to begin her story, she started from her childhood growing up as an albino kid in Newark to living in foster homes throughout the tri-state area. It took Casey an additional two hours beyond her ten-minute window to share her story. She choked at times, using a ball of napkins she found inside her coat to dry her eyes as she re-lived the horrors from her past.

"Maaaan, I lived everywhere," she explained to Junior. "New York. Boston. Philly. Jersey. Bridgeport. Providence, Rhode Island. The social services system just couldn't get it right for a girl like me. I went through a lot, Junior. Tried suicide a bunch of times. Drugs. Man, I did it all."

Bundled beneath her wintry coat, a slight chill blew down Kennedy Street as Casey recalled her life before meeting Junior. Born an only child, Casey told Junior that her biological parents had abandoned her when she was just seven years old. Her earliest memories of her parents were being referred to as "the ugly white baby" by her father, and that her mother overdosed on heroin in the summer of 1974. Nearly twenty years to the day Junior's brother was gunned down on a busy North Philadelphia street corner. Casey told him that she knew something was wrong when her father didn't pick her up from school the next day.

"I cried for like six days," she laughed to shield her emotions. "Nope. He never came back."

In the middle of the precinct, she wailed upon learning that her mother wasn't coming to get her, either. From there, Casey moved in with her aunt in Newark, New Jersey where she lived for the next three years. At school, she was picked on and beaten up by her classmates and called names like "fat", "ugly", and "little orange-haired white girl" because of her albinism. Her aunt Tyler had a boyfriend who was an alcoholic and he had groped her one day when they were alone together. When Casey tried to tell her aunt about the incident, her aunt slapped her across the face and gave her away to social services. Casey told Junior that night that from the time she was ten years old until her fifteenth birthday, she lived in thirteen different houses before finally moving to Providence, Rhode Island, where she met the Haughton family.

"I've had every fuckin' last name you can think of, Junior. I've been a Robinson." She nudged his elbow. "Johnson. Smith. Williams. Thomas. Capies," she went on. "But the best last name I ever had was Haughton. So, I changed it to that."

Casey said that along with her new name came her sister, Courtney.

"She pretty?" asked Junior. "C'mon man, hook me up!"

"Yeah, she's thorough," Casey laughed. "Rangy. Tall with long hair. Cute. You probably saw the picture on my desk?

That's her. I met the Haughtons when I lived on the west side before they moved to New York. I should've gone with them, but I ended up here in Philly. It was the worst mistake of my life…until I met you. Before that, I was a train wreck. My demons had caught up to me. I was afraid I'd screw it up. The Haughtons treated me like royalty. I took piano lessons. Culinary classes. I learned how to drive. The whole nine."

To Junior's surprise, Casey removed her arm from her coat to show Junior a slew of old cut markings on her left wrist, buried beneath a "Laugh now, cry later" tattoo.

"Even though I had Courtney and her family, I was still a wreck because of what I had gone through," she explained. "I got married *and* divorced all in one year. Had a miscarriage. Got arrested a few times. I tried to kill myself by jumping in front of a train until my fat ass slipped on a sheet of ice and I broke my foot," she laughed away her tears. "I tried slicing my wrist up with a razor. When that didn't work, I tried drugs – all of this before I was twenty-two. Plus, I couldn't keep a job. I was just in so much pain, Junior. I didn't want to be here."

Junior hung on her every word. Their connection seemed divine as he attempted to process Casey's past in comparison to his. Losing Lawrence was hard enough, but not nearly as bad as the hand Casey had been dealt since she was a little girl. Junior then hooked his arm through Casey's and leaned his head on her shoulder.

"Thank you," she sighed before continuing. "So, eventually, I got myself together. I got help where I knew I could get it. My family. The Haughtons. They believed in me – even when I didn't believe in myself. And Courtney? My sister?" Her voice cracked. "I don't know where I'd be if she wasn't around."

Looking down at her watch, they saw it was 7:51 p.m. Two hours had passed since Casey had promised to stay for her last ten minutes. As the two went to embrace, Casey inadvertently patted Junior on his coat pocket and noticed his bulge.

"Yo, that better not be what I think it is, homeboy!"

Concerned, she went to touch Junior's coat pocket again, but he bladed himself away from her. Casey became angry.

"Junior, get over here!" she ordered. "I ain't playin'. Now, what is that?"

Busted, Junior reached inside his coat and removed Senior's .38 revolver, which he had been hiding since Casey first got there. Lost for words, she gasped and a look of guilt painted itself onto Junior's face.

"Yo, what the *fuck* are you doing?!" Casey ripped him. "Junior, are you crazy?"

"Man, aren't you tired of getting pushed around all the time?" he asked. "I am! I'm sick of this shit. Sick of always having to run. I ain't runnin' no more, Casey – been runnin' my whole life. The next person that fucks with me," he fingered his daddy's gun, "I'm gonna blast 'em. Not gonna be anybody's bitch anymore."

"Stop talkin' like that! You're not!" She lunged for his coat pocket. "Now, gimmie the gun, Junior. I'm not gonna sit here and let you ruin your life!"

"No!" Junior pulled away from her. "No more baby shit, man! I'm gonna start puttin' niggas in body bags. Nobody is ever gonna jump me again!"

"Shut up-shut up-*shut* up!" Casey slapped him. "Oh my God! Look at what you made me do, Junior! I just hit you!"

Frozen in time, Junior stared back at Casey in disbelief of himself and that she had just slapped the taste from his pitiful mug. Stunned, he took a seat on the porch and sagged his head. Neither Junior nor Casey said a word for five minutes. Within that time, an ambulance came flying down Kennedy Street, adding the perfect reference to Junior's dilemma. The noisy siren seemed to revitalize him; he veered away from the raging, vengeful teenager he had become and returned to his former innocence. Somewhere in the center of the Robinsons' yard was Casey, incredulous that she had slapped Junior.

"I'm sorry," he apologized. "Can you forgive me, Casey?"

Pouting, Casey turned to look at Junior and looked away like an angry school girl who'd lost out on playing at recess. As Junior tried to sweet-talk his way back into being her brother again, Casey stuffed her hands inside her jacket and threw her hood over her head. As Junior tried to approach her, she turned away from him to hide the fact that she was crying. Before long, her worry for him came gushing out.

"You're scaring me!" Her lips started to quiver. "I don't *like* all of this, J.!"

As Casey began to cry, Junior slowly removed his daddy's .38 revolver from his coat pocket and looked it over. When

Casey saw the gun once again, she plopped down onto the steps in front of him and wept inside both her hands.

"I'm sorry," Junior apologized again. "I promise, I'll get rid of it. I'll put it back where I got it, OK? Will that fix all of this, Casey?"

Unable to catch her breath, Casey sniffled as she looked up at Junior with runny makeup streaming down her broken face.

"Do…you…pro-promise?"

"I promise!" Junior sat beside her as she leaned onto him. "I promise!"

Still distraught, Casey sniveled onto him as they braved the night air together, thinking over what could've been their unfortunate end.

Just after 9 p.m., Sandy blinked the lights to the front porch, indicating that Junior and Casey's visit had come to an end. Casey took one last breath before they hugged one final time. Junior apologized about a dozen times for hurting her as she took responsibility for slapping him. Together, they decided that the story of Senior's .38 revolver would be their secret.

"You know what to do?" she asked him.

"I do now," Junior replied.

Casey took a deep breath, fired up the engine to her car, and drove off into the night.

As soon as Junior entered the house, he bypassed Senior and Sandy watching TV in the living room. The moment Junior entered the foyer, Senior scowled at him, forcing Junior to rub the bulge inside his coat. Without warning, his daddy got up from his chair and glared at Junior. Believing he'd been caught, Junior melted instantly.

"Come here," Senior called him over.

Unsure of what to expect, Junior slow-walked to his daddy as Sandy turned to observe whatever her husband had up his sleeve. As Junior stood in front of him, Senior leaned inward.

"The next time... you leave your room light on with nobody in there, I'm gonna remove the light from your wall, and your head from your shoulders. You got me? Electricity is expensive!"

"My bad, Daddy." He smiled.

The second Senior turned his back, Junior raced up the staircase to his parents' bedroom where he returned his daddy's .38 to the nightstand.

I'm a story with no ending.
I am a poem with debatable clarity.
I am asleep but conscious
behind my own wheel.
I am dead to everyone, including myself.
I am a loss for words. I am speechless.
I am beyond repair.
I am a life taken for granted.

—LEONARD G. ROBINSON JR.

Nine

While Junior played video games inside his room late on a Sunday, attempting to forget about Senior's .38, Sandy interrupted his game. Her stance on Medgar had changed; she reiterated her goal to see Junior walk as the first man in the family to graduate high school. Without word or notice, she cracked open his bedroom door and began to speak. Her tone was commanding, yet delicate and organic.

"If I keep you out, that's another year here in Brooke's Rowe," she told him. "School leads to opportunities, and opportunities lead to better choices in life. It's selfish," she explained. "Your daddy is gonna drive you to school tomorrow."

As Sandy went to close his room door, Junior placed his game stick down on the floor and met his mother by the door.

"Thank you." He placed a hand on his mother's shoulder before she left.

Anticipating his return to Medgar, Junior rummaged through his closet for something to wear. In the bathroom sink, he used an old toothbrush to clean his sneakers and asked Senior to touch up his hair with Wahl trimmers. Laughing, joking, Junior's daddy seemed nothing like his typical self that night or any other night. He winked and smiled, showing all his teeth, and even allowed Junior a taste of his precious fireball scotch from his minibar to celebrate his return. Junior took a shot Senior poured for him in an old mason jar. The second the hot whiskey touched his juvenile tongue, he darted into the bathroom and spit it into the sink. Roaring, Senior clapped Junior across the back and invited him back into the barber's chair.

Later that evening before bed, Junior returned to his room to write, penning about his inevitable return. Unable to sleep, his artistry which had avoided him over the past week, finally returned.

Early the next morning, Senior's rusty truck rolled in front of Medgar for Junior's triumphant return. As Junior went to get out, Senior reached his wide hand out for Junior to shake. "I think you're gonna be good." He extended his hand. As

Junior went to shake Senior's hand, thanking him, his daddy jerked him back inside the truck and closed the door. With all his might, he clamped down onto Junior's hand like the jaws of a vice. Helpless and imprisoned, Senior began slapping him across the back of his head and checked Junior with a shot to the ribs.

"You little crab motherfucka!" Senior pressed harder. "You think I'm stupid?! You think I don't know you been inside my nightstand fuckin' with that .38? *Huh*?"

Senior squeezed onto Junior's hand so hard that his son's nailbeds turned purple.

"Arghhh-arghhh! No, sir!" Junior screeched in agony as his daddy cranked up his torment. Unable to defend himself, Senior pulled out every trick to pay Junior back for touching his gun. He plucked him across the ears, back of the head, and used his knuckle to poke Junior in the ribs. Occasionally, Senior popped him across the back of his head for good measure as Junior yelped in agony, begging him to stop.

"C'mon Daddy, let me go!" he pleaded. "Man, you hurtin' my hand!"

The more Junior complained, the harder Senior clutched. He then rolled Junior's knuckles together like marbles as his son winced and patted his foot against the floorboard in pain. Then, just before Junior began to cry, Senior released him – but not before slapping Junior across the back of his head one last time.

Ripping his hand away, Junior stuffed his hand inside his chest pocket and doubled over. Senior then took an ice cube from his soda resting in the center console and dropped it down Junior's back. Just to fuck with him, Senior sped off in his truck, whipping around the block with Junior unbelted in the passenger seat. Just before he arrived back in front of Medgar, he stomped on the brake, sending Junior rocking forward in his seat.

"Boy, if I *ever* catch you with my .38 again," he threatened, "they're gonna have to do a full autopsy on your ass so that they can remove my foot from it! You hear me talkin' to you?" he whacked Junior in the chest. "Stay the *fuck* out of my nightstand!"

"Yes, sir," Junior grimaced.

"Good." Senior straightened Junior's coat for him. "Have a good day."

Slowly, Junior crawled out of Senior's truck and limped toward the staircase of his school. Halfway up the stairs, Junior headed back to Senior's truck. He stood at the passenger door, holding his neck, stomach, and head. His hand still throbbed from Senior's anaconda-like grip. As Junior stood there waiting for his father to acknowledge him, Senior cracked the window.

"How'd you know?" Junior asked.

Senior looked at Junior glaringly as he exhaled a cloud of cigarette smoke.

"Do you think your daddy is stupid, Junior?"

"No sir."

"Yes, you do. You think I'm a goddamn fool."

"No, I don't," said Junior. "I don't think that at all."

Junior's daddy looked him up and down. Soon after, he reached over to open the door to his truck, allowing Junior to sit inside. Afraid that Senior would hit him again, Junior sat as close to the door as he could in case he needed to escape. Senior put out his cigarette in the ashtray and fanned away the smoke.

"So, why'd you take it?" he asked. "And if you lie to me, I'll break every bone inside your tiny little body, nigga. Now, why'd you touch that gun, Junior?"

Knowing his father was capable, Junior thought long and hard before he answered. He decided he needed his bones to get up the staircase to Medgar to see Casey once again. Junior also didn't know just how much his daddy knew about him taking his .38. He elected to play it safe, sparing his life.

"I guess I got tired of feelin'… like a bitch," Junior cussed, raising Senior's eyebrow. "Man, so much is expected of me all the time but so little of everyone else. Those kids jumped me over nothin'. I wanted to get even. I wanted to feel like for once, I could give back all that I'd been given. But I can't 'cause that's not who I am. So, I put it back…where it belongs."

Pleased with his honesty, Senior nodded his head.

"I killed a man when I was nineteen years old," Senior blurted. "Never told your mother about it. Police said it was self-defense, but it wasn't. I could've walked away. I could've not gone there in the first place. I haven't slept in twenty-seven years, Junior…Maybe one day I will."

Junior sat staring into his daddy's face as Senior glared at his reflection through the windshield. As father and son sat in awkward silence, the bell to Medgar rang, signaling a start to first period. Fearing Mrs. Hawkins would get on him, Junior reached for his backpack on the floor.

"You got a better path than the one I had," Senior said. "Don't go that road, Junior."

"You're not gonna tell Mom about this, right?" asked Junior.

"Yeah, I am," said Senior. "One day, though… just not today. Go'on, get out."

Junior scooted out of his daddy's truck and hurried up the stairs into Medgar.

You and I,
we're beyond poetry.
Beyond words. Beyond blood.
Beyond Brooke's Rowe or any part of Philly.
We're two souls brought together in tragic harmony.

LEONARD G. ROBINSON JR.

Brother Gay

Running, rushing, Junior zipped up the hallway staircase and down to Mrs. Hawkins's classroom expecting her door to be locked. When he got there, however, he saw no sign of the evil, bat-faced woman and noticed a different teacher was sitting at her desk. Junior looked around the room and noticed every single artifact of Mrs. Hawkins's classroom along with her desk plate was missing. As he poured into his seat in the front row, a bearded black man sporting an African Kufi hat stood up and introduced himself. With a sharp voice, the man wrote his name on the blackboard in fancy, bold letters: BROTHER GAY. Junior's classmates all snickered except for him. His peers carried on as if he hadn't got jumped a week earlier.

"I know y'all are used to Mrs. Hawkins closing her door at a certain time," he explained to Junior's class of twelve. "But I believe that no door should be closed on a child's education. If you're late, you will still be permitted to enter my class – but it'll be your responsibility to find out what's going on – not mine. As many of you know, Mrs. Hawkins has moved on. So, I'll be your teacher for the remainder of the school year. If you need anything, Brother Gay or Mr. Gay is fine."

Junior's class all laughed again. Brother Gay then passed around a sign-in sheet for each student to fill out and promised to memorize their names before the end of the day. Unlike Mrs. Hawkins, he didn't react to the gossipers in the back, the way their former teacher would have.

During first period break, Junior approached Brother Gay with the sign-in sheet and politely asked to be addressed as "Junior" rather than Leonard. The man looked down at Junior's school ID and back up at him.

"Something wrong with the name 'Leonard'?" he asked.

"I ain't too fond of that name," explained Junior. "So, everyone calls me, 'Junior'."

Brother Gay opened his wallet and pulled out his Pennsylvania State Driver's License to show Junior. To his surprise, Brother Gay was also named Leonard.

"Well, I happen to like that name quite a bit." The man winked. "But sure, Junior it is."

> *Proudly free to be me.*
> *Free to think. Free to dream.*
> *Free in my heart. Free to cry.*
> *Free not to care what others think.*
> *Free to be me – the only way to be.*
>
> LEONARD G. ROBINSON JR.

Beyond Poetry

For Junior, returning to Medgar was more than just seeing Casey. It was returning to the scene of a gruesome crime – and not batting an eye. It was about confronting his fears without retreat. He was not a product of his environment but a victim of it, both at home and in school. Back in Crawford, the boys would chump Junior over his video games or figurines, and they'd bait Junior by starting fights with Lawrence. Picking on his brother was the only thing that would provoke Junior to fight. During the contest, however, he'd cry so pathetically that the boys would all mock him. One day, Lawrence had come home with a swollen eye, and Senior made Junior go fight the boy responsible. Junior later found the kid but didn't fight him. Instead, he paid Lawrence his entire allowance for a month to tell Senior that he had won the fight. Junior knew he wasn't a fighter; he was a writer. It was poetry that refined Junior's purpose, and through poetry, he would rebuild himself. The thrashing he'd received the Tuesday before Thanksgiving would be his genesis. Bloodied and stripped of his pride on a city street, his healed face failed to show the stitch marks on his young heart. Taking Senior's .38 was Junior's breaking point. Putting his daddy's gun back was his baptism. Casey was an anomaly. A delicate black woman, born white as snow, who he'd call his big sissy and who would lead him to overcome the traps inside his mind. The first true friend he'd had since moving to Brooke's Rowe. Sandy, his mother, was Junior's rock to lean on. Senior was Junior's balance between the parallel worlds of poetry and life in South Philly.

On his first break that morning, Junior went looking around for Casey but was unable to find her. Afterward, he returned to class and tried again on the second break, lunch, and afternoon break. Desperate, he phoned Casey's cell phone from a payphone outside the cafeteria before leaving school that day but couldn't get an answer. Looking for answers, Junior went tracking for Mr. Levy inside his office, but he wasn't there. Confused, he climbed into his mother's car parked in front of the school.

"Look, I'm sure she'll be in tomorrow," Sandy assured him. "You guys can talk then."

The next day at Medgar was the same result, Junior dividing his break time between looking for Casey and spying on

Mr. Levy. Out of options, Junior went to Brother Gay during break to ask if he had seen or heard from Casey.

"Not too familiar with her. You'd have to check with Mr. Levy on that," he advised.

When the day ended, Junior went down to Mr. Levy's office to ask if he had seen Casey. His mouth stuffed with tuna fish and mayonnaise, Mr. Levy glared at him.

"I thought I banned you two from being together," he said. "Haven't you heard by now?"

"Heard what?" snapped Junior.

"She quit earlier this morning," he said nonchalantly. Mr. Levy then pointed down at Casey's security badge sitting atop his desk. Junior picked up the badge and looked at his best friend's imprinted name. On the back of her old badge near the needle was a piece of cotton left behind as if the badge had been abruptly taken off. Immediately, Junior envisioned Casey ripping the badge from her shirt in protest. Incensed, he tossed the badge down onto Mr. Levy's desk. It bounced, landing next to his sandwich.

"If she quit then it's because of you!" said Junior. "You *made* her quit!"

"Th'hell if I did!" he yelled. "She quit this morning, I said. It happened earlier. She said she couldn't handle it, and that's the truth!"

Junior looked down at Casey's badge on top of Mr. Levy's desk.

"If Casey was leaving, she would've told me! She wouldn't just leave suddenly."

"Bullshit," he shot back. "It's one of the more reasons she chose *not* to tell you. Look at you, Junior. You're like a damn little puppy who lost its owner. She didn't want to hurt you."

As Junior digested Mr. Levy's story that Casey had abruptly quit, it began to make sense to him. On the night he had taken Senior's gun, he recalled her life story and wondered if her past had caught up to her again. Disappointed, he trudged out of Mr. Levy's office and into his mother's car. With a lump wedged between his throat and his broken heart, Junior could barely tell his mother what had happened to Casey. Sandy, always the optimist, uplifted him during the drive home.

"Maybe she just needs time to process it all, Junior," Sandy explained. "Leaving a job can be devastating for some people. She'll reach out to you. Just give her time."

"*Give her time*?" Junior asked. "How could she just leave like that and not say nothin'?!"

When Junior and his mother returned home, Senior was outside attempting to replace the light fixture on the front porch when Sandy told him about Casey. Unphased by Junior's predicament, he skipped right to the point.

"Well, wouldn't you've quit if you had to work for a sumbitch like that?" Senior asked.

"That ain't the point, daddy!" Junior complained. "She left and didn't even tell me!"

"Adults have reasons why they don't tell kids certain things," Sandy chimed in. "Just give her a chance; I'm sure Casey will explain everything when the time is right."

That night, Junior paced across the floor of his bedroom wondering where Casey had gone off to. At the dinner table, he picked through his food while both his parents carried on as if nothing happened. On his nightstand was Casey's cell phone number which he usually carried inside his wallet. From the kitchen phone, Junior called three times and left three messages on her voicemail service. Just after 7 p.m., Senior came upstairs to ask Junior to ride with him down to the hardware store.

As Senior's truck cruised up Kennedy Street, Junior stared off into the holiday air, wondering where Casey had gone. Images of their first day together at Medgar to the last time they had seen one another flashed through his mind. Suddenly, it dawned on him. The prior week, Casey had told Junior about her past struggles with suicide. Was she dead? he wondered. Was she in a hospital somewhere in his big city after finally losing it? As the night wore on, so did Junior's mind which began playing tricks on him.

At the hardware store, he asked his father if he could remain inside the truck which Senior obliged. Out in the parking lot, he saw a blue Toyota resembling Casey's car and exited Senior's truck to investigate. The inside of the car looked exactly like Casey's. Junior moved from the driver's window to the passenger side looking for any artifact that would resemble his big sissy. Suddenly, a dog, a rat terrier, sleeping beneath its owner's coat whisked into the front seat and began barking at Junior from the window. Startled, he fell backward onto the asphalt. Shortly thereafter, Senior exited the shop and saw Junior lying on the ground next to the blue Toyota.

"Pretty sure the owner wouldn't 'preciate you lookin' in his ride," Senior joked. "You mind tellin' me what in the hell you're doin'? Are you crazy?"

"I thought it might be Casey's car," Junior replied.

"Well it ain't!" his daddy woofed. "Now, get your ass back in that truck."

On the way back home, it seemed that every passing car was a blue Toyota, and every driver behind the wheel looked like Casey. Senior could care less about a blue Toyota and its operator. Riding down Kennedy Street, he chatted on about a neighbor who had promised to help swap the transmission inside his Ford pickup. It was one of the only times he seemed to say more than just a few words when it came to fixing things. As Junior's daddy carried on about the transmission to his truck and the fluid needed to get it up running like new, Junior stared out into Brooke's Rowe, wondering about Casey. When he returned home, Sandy was waiting for him at the door with a message.

"Casey called, said she was on her way," Sandy told him. "She asked if she could see you for a few minutes. I told her that's fine. Make sure it's quick; it's still a school night."

With his coat still buttoned, Junior waited by the window for Casey to arrive. At one point, a blue sedan parked near the front of the Robinsons' house. Believing it was Casey, Junior charged from the house before realizing the driver was a delivery person in a blue Geo Prism, similar in make and model to Casey's vehicle. Frustrated, he returned to the front steps before Sandy asked him to come in from the cold. An hour went by with no sign of Casey until just after 8:35 p.m., her car arrived in front of the Robinsons' house. By then, Junior was fed up with Casey toying with his emotions. With a scowl worse than his daddy's, he marched down the walkway, opened Casey's car door, and slammed it behind him. Her pleasant smile turned to a look of bereavement.

"Man, what the fuck is your problem?!"

Junior hollered as if she was his out-of-control, teenage daughter. "I been lookin' all over for you! How could you just leave like that?"

"First of all," she barked back. "I might be your friend, but I'm *still* your elder...*and* your big sissy! You will *not* talk to me like that, young man! Now, what the fuck is *your* problem?"

Realizing he had barked up the wrong road, Junior eased off the gas.

"I-I'm sorry, Casey," he fumbled for an apology. "I didn't mean to...I was just...I miss you at school. How come you didn't tell me you were gonna quit?"

"I didn't quit, J. I got fired."

"You *what*?"

"Levy called me Sunday night. We got into it, and he fired me. I didn't *quit* anything."

"What about your cell phone? I called a bunch of times, left messages too. How come you never called me back? Didn't you get 'em?"

"No, I didn't," she told him. "I lost my phone. I had to get a new one *and* a new number. Can you believe that? A new number? I've had that number since last year! I was so pissed. Of course, I was pissed about Levy, but I can't say that I didn't see it comin'."

Junior looked off into the distance, relieved to know that Casey was all right and that he and Casey would still be together post-Medgar. Soon after, Sandy stood near the living room window before flickering the light on the front porch, indicating their time had come to an end. Concerned, Junior tried to coax Casey into staying longer.

"Yo, ten more minutes – ten more minutes!" he begged.

"Not this time, J., I gotta go," she laughed. "Look, we'll talk again soon, OK?"

"No, Casey!" he threw on his seatbelt. "You can't just..." his eyes teared. "What am I supposed to do with you not around at Medgar? I'll be alone again..."

As Junior lowered his head, Casey grabbed him by his pointy chin.

"You think this is goodbye?" she asked. "You ain't gettin' rid of me that easy."

Casey then reached into her bag, lifted out an ink pen and an old receipt, jotted down her new cell phone number, and passed it to him. She placed a row of change into Junior's hands. Before sending him inside, Casey removed a poem she kept inside of her bag, placed it into Junior's hands, and closed them as he stared back at her.

"This way, no matter where you are," she pinched him

on his bubbly nose, "you can reach me. I'm sorry for making you worry. I won't run off like that again. I promise."

As Casey placed her hand on Junior's shoulder, he leaned onto Casey's wrist as if her touch and presence rejuvenated him. Junior took a deep breath, relieved. Despite what had happened, he still had his big sissy. As the two embraced, Senior opened the door to the house standing next to Sandy in the window. Junior looked at the clock on Casey's dashboard and noticed it was 9:03 p.m. Twenty-eight minutes had passed since Casey arrived, but it seemed like twenty-eight seconds as the time magically quickened whenever the two were together. With his change and poem, Junior exited her car and returned to the house. As he entered the foyer, Casey dabbed at her car horn and drove off.

"Everything all right?" asked Senior.

With his hands filled with change and a poem from his big sissy, Junior nodded.

"It is now," he said.

Upstairs inside his room, Junior unfolded Casey's poem and read it. Moved, Junior re-folded Casey's poem and placed it in his wallet behind Lawrence's photo.

Dear Junior,
You're the moon that balances my waters.
The sun that lights up my sky.
The blood that runs through me.
You're the sail in my winds.
The strength to keep me going.

You're the brightest star I've ever seen skip across the galaxy.
You and me?
We're beyond poetry.

CASEY HAUGHTON

The "L" word

To showcase his students' flair, Junior's teacher, Brother Gay, invited every child to the front of the room for a mock talent show to celebrate the upcoming Christmas holiday. "Since you all won't be exchanging gifts," he explained, "your gift to one another is to share your talent."

Brother Gay's commitment to camaraderie was succeeded by teeth-sucking groans as Junior's peers threw up their arms in disgust and leaned in their seats. The first kid up was a girl named Shannon Jackson. She trudged to the front of the room with hair covering over her beautiful face and sung lyrics to Groove Theory's hit "Tell Me". Junior couldn't believe the perfection of the girl's voice as his peers all clapped to celebrate her. It was the first time Junior had seen his classmates at Medgar encourage another student. His only experience of encouragement was on his second day in Mrs. Hawkins's class when his classmates tried to goad him to spit into her coffee.

The next eye-opening act came from a boy named Mario who conned the class, telling them all that he was a master illusionist. More like the king of bullshit, Junior thought, as he watched Mario walk to the front of the room donning a folded dollar bill in his hand. Holding it high for the class to see, he passed the crumbled bill to Brother Gay to inspect. Finding nothing off about the dollar bill, he handed the bill back to Mario who re-folded it. "Y'all wanna see it disappear?" he asked, egging on the class. Shortly thereafter, he stuffed the bill inside his mouth and swallowed it.

"Ta-da!" he said before marching back to his chair. "This is so stupid!"

When it was Junior's turn to perform, he was met with a litany of teeth-sucking and eye-rolling from the peanut gallery. Anxious, he surveyed the room, acknowledging his peers' displeasure with him. Just as Junior was about to quit and take his seat, Brother Gay approached Junior at the front of the room and whispered into his ear.

"I believe in you, Junior," he told him. "Don't be afraid of your fellow students."

Swallowing his fears, Junior opened his journal and began to read.

Plant a seed, water it, and birth a tree.
But some young seeds don't get the water they need.
Instead, they get forgotten by other forgotten seeds.

LEONARD G. ROBINSON JR.

"Yes!" Brother Gay began to clap. "That was terrific, sir! Impressive!"

Junior took a look around the room to see his peers slouching from their chairs with faceless expressions. Invalidated, he quickly closed his journal and took his seat, wishing a black hole would open in the center of Brother Gay's classroom for him to fall into. As the bell sounded for lunch, Junior's classmates passed by his desk, mocking his poetry with typical belligerence. "Faggot-nigga," one boy mumbled on the way out. "Fuckin' loser," another boy muttered. Embarrassed, Junior opted to be the last one out the door. As he attempted to leave, Brother Gay asked him to stay behind for a few.

"That was an incredible poem, Junior," he complimented. "You have a gift for words."

Shrugging, Junior tucked his hands into his pocket.

"Nobody else thought so," he said.

Brother Gay then motioned for Junior to take a seat as he sat on the edge of his own desk.

"So, you and Miss Casey Haughton got along pretty good, I hear?" he asked, surprising Junior. "Received a call this morning. Still don't know how she got the number." He laughed. "She told me you were special. I never met her, personally, but I heard about what happened to her. How are you holding up?"

Exhaling in defeat, Junior sagged his head.

"Man…sometimes I feel like I can't breathe," he said. "But I wouldn't have made it this far here at Medgar without Casey. *She's* the one that's special. Not me. I'm just a broke kid from Philly."

Pausing, Brother Gay nodded in sanction of him.

"Your humility is out of this world, Junior," he said. "Do you love her?"

"W-What?!" Junior stuttered.

"Now, don't get cute with me, son." His tone straightened. "Do you or not?"

Turning pink with teenage awkwardness, Junior's stomach began to boil as his soul rose from the depths of him, dancing inside of his body at the thought of Casey's impact on him. Looking for words, Junior found none.

"You do, don't you?" he pressed. "That's OK, son. Love is good a thing. I'm not accusing you of being *in* love. Loving someone and being *in love* are two different things."

Relieved, Junior exhaled again as Brother Gay laughed and touched him on the shoulder.

"Don't ever wait to tell someone you love them." He handed Junior a row of quarters from his pocket. "The opportunity that exists today may not be here tomorrow. Enjoy your lunch."

On his way to make a phone call, Junior stopped at the door.

"Oh, one last thing," Junior asked. "Yo, whatever happened to Mrs. Hawkins?"

Brother Gay approached Junior at the door.

"Like I told you, she moved on," he said. "To the House of the Lord. Passed away while you were out. See what I mean? Life moves fast." He clasped Junior on the arm. "Why don't you make that call to Casey?"

Heeding Brother Gay's advice, Junior pulled out the receipt with Casey's phone number and approached the payphone outside of the school's cafeteria. Unfortunately for Junior, there was a line of six students ahead of him. The closer Junior got to the phone, the more the "L" word became a reality, and the more nervous he became. As soon as he reached second in the queue, the bell sounded, ending lunch. Discouraged, he returned to his class on the fourth-floor. As Junior approached the door with a look of defeat, Brother Gay stopped to ask him about his recent phone call.

"Line was too long," said Junior. "I'll call her later."

Brother Gay reached into his pants pocket and handed Junior his cell phone for him to use. He scrolled to his recent calls to highlight Casey's number, raised the antenna on his brick phone, and passed it to Junior.

"My nighttime minutes don't start until six." He eyeballed Junior. "Can you make it quick?"

Armed with Brother Gay's cell, Junior raced down to room 328 where he and Casey used to meet and placed a call. When she didn't pick up, junior started to leave, dejected. But just then the phone rang and when he answered, it was Casey.

There, in his secret hiding space, Junior revealed to Casey what had been on his heart.

"I love you, Casey," he told her. "I should've told you the other night when you stopped by, but I was too nervous. I didn't want to make you uncomfortable or for things to get awkward. But you've done so much for my life. I just can't imagine life without seeing you every day. You're my best friend…hello? Yo…are you there?"

"You know you just killed me with that, right?" She chuckled into the line. "Got me cryin' and stuff — you know I don't like to cry, J. Only for you. And I love you, too. Of course. How'd you convince Brother Gay to let you borrow his cell?"

"I told 'em what was on my mind," Junior charmed. "He said 'love shouldn't wait.'"

"Nope," she sighed. "So, what are you doing Friday? We should go see the tree at Rockefeller Plaza. Wanna go?"

"Man, my folks ain't gonna let me go to no New York! We barely leave Brooke's Rowe, let alone Philly. Plus, it's expensive."

"Will you just *ask*, please? Let me know by tomorrow. If so, I gotta get bus tickets."

After the two hung up, Junior's heart felt lighter as a smile appeared on his face. He loved Casey, and she loved him back.

Later, when Junior's parents arrived to pick him up from school, he asked if he could see the Christmas lights at Rockefeller Plaza with Casey on that Friday, just a few days before Christmas. Surprisingly for him, Sandy didn't say "no". She told him "hell no". New York was too far away for him to stray from home during the Christmas holidays at age fourteen without being accompanied by either of them. Senior doubled down in agreement. He said that New York City was twice the size of Philly and "full of crazy-ass motherfuckas worse than the ones we got here in Brooke's Rowe." As a consolation, Sandy offered to extend an invitation to Casey to come by the house for a chaperoned pre-Christmas dinner.

"Why do I need an extra chaperone with Casey?" asked Junior. "She's over twenty-one."

"Because girls are *much* faster than boys!" said Sandy. "We don't know that woman *that* well, Junior. Suppose she tries to kidnap you? Take you somewhere in an alley up there and nobody knows where the hell you are?"

"Man, Casey ain't gonna kidnap nobody. That's crazy!"

"Hey!" Senior howled, pounding onto the wheel. "What did your mother just say?!"

Sulking the rest of the way home, Junior avoided his parents for much of the night. With his lips buttoned, he floated around the house in anger over the ruling. Disappointed, he decided to make a sacrifice by not eating dinner that night. Instead, he loaded his belly with a bag of stale popcorn from beside his bed and a flat can of Coca-Cola on his nightstand. Later, as Sandy entered to kiss him goodnight, Junior returned a lipless kiss to his mother. As he went to brush his teeth for the night, he passed by his daddy in the hallway outside his bedroom. Senior glared at him throughout the awkward confrontation, refusing to back down from the Mexican standoff. As Junior attempted to squeeze by, Senior eventually moved to the side.

"New York my ass," Senior muttered as Junior went by.

In the bathroom mirror, Junior contemplated breaking

the unfortunate news to Casey that their plans for New York had been canceled. Unable to find the words, he returned to his room window, threw on his Walkman, and frowned into the chilly, Philly night.

True love hurts sometimes
like new shoes out of a box.
Some shoes fit just right.
Some shoes don't fit at all.
Some shoes last a lifetime,
and some shoes only a nighttime.
Yearn a love that feels good
to stand and walk in
with warm cushy soles
that escort you to your dreams.

—LEONARD G. ROBINSON JR.

Ten

It was just after 3 a.m. Thursday morning when Junior awoke to Sandy busting through his bedroom and turning on his room light. With her favorite plaid suitcase in one hand and her winter coat in the other, she ordered Junior out of bed. "Get dressed! We're leaving!"

Junior, still bleary from the abrupt disturbance, rose out of bed to fetch the closest pair of wrinkled jeans and hooded jacket he could find. He barely got one leg inside his pants before Senior came gliding up the staircase in a wrath. Knocking pictures from the wall, his wide nostrils flaring like a rabid bull, he charged after Sandy who was attempting to take the one thing he had left in this world, his surviving son and namesake, Junior. "Fuck you!" he hollered.

"Fuck me?! Nigga, *fuck* you!" Sandy screamed back at him. "I should've never married your sorry black ass!"

Half-awake, Junior thought he was seeing things that morning, as he watched his daddy go to his nightstand and retrieve his .38 revolver. With his finger on the trigger, Senior pointed it at their bedroom television set.

"I'll shoot every TV *in* this motherfucka!" he threatened. "You ain't takin' my son!"

"You ain't gonna shoot shit!" dared Sandy. "You ain't got the heart!"

For the life of him, Junior couldn't understand why his mother would say such a thing knowing his daddy was a lunatic. Sweat glazing from his greasy forehead, Senior fired one round into their thirty-two-inch, color television inside their bedroom. Sparks danced and sizzled inside the mangled box for nearly a minute before a teepee of smoke withered the air. The shot startled Junior awake as Sandy ducked behind Junior's dresser. Her eyes were as big as a goldfish.

"You're a crazy son of a bitch!" Sandy gasped.

From the master bedroom, Senior continued his rampage throughout the house as Sandy carefully followed behind her unstable husband. Senior didn't shoot any more TVs that night, but he lifted the living room couch over his head and punched a hole through the drywall. Their tiny rowhouse began to cry as dust fell onto the rug. Soon after, he grabbed the keys to his pickup truck and marched outside as Sandy went running after him.

"Where you goin'?! Don't nobody want your dumb ass but me!" She marched behind her salty husband, talking shit. From his room window and with one leg hanging from his jeans, Junior watched his parents argue in the middle of Kennedy Street. At one point, Sandy picked up a piece of brick from their garden and threaten to bust Senior over the head. Ignoring her, Senior started up his truck and left. Soon after, the cops arrived with flashing lights and sirens loud enough to wake all of Brooke's Rowe. Later, Junior found out that a concerned neighbor had phoned the police. The argument between Junior's parents had begun over Christmas lights.

On his way to school that morning, Junior rode next to his mother without a word, careful not to set her off. It took nothing to set Junior's parents ablaze. Over money, they'd tear into each other like ravenous wolves. Over him, he worried next time they might kill each other. For Junior, it was all the more reason he realized he hated Philadelphia – and why a break to see the tree at Rockefeller Plaza in New York sounded to him like a voyage around the world.

When Sandy's Buick arrived at his school, Junior leaned over to kiss his mother on the cheek and told her he loved her. The night before, he had thought about smooth-talking his way into visiting New York with Casey. After the blow-up between his parents, however, Junior decided to settle for pre-Christmas dinner at the house with Casey. All that was left on his mind about Friday's dinner was to hope that a roach wouldn't show up to celebrate.

As Junior went to get out of the car, Sandy called him back to the door.

"I'm really sorry about last night, Junior," she apologized. "We shouldn't have been actin' like two animals. That's unacceptable, and I'm sorry – for both of us. Have a good day, OK?"

Junior kissed his mother again and then walked into Medgar. After all that, *have a good day*? He laughed to himself.

Remove every cloud from the sky.
Give me the sun.
Let it shine bright over me,
shadowing my every move,
illuminating my awakened soul
from the horrendous cold night.

LEONARD G. ROBINSON

Empire Lie

In the afternoon before Junior's class was dismissed, Brother Gay passed around a blank sheet of paper to each of his students and asked them to write down the name of a relative or friend close to them. Junior wrote: Senior, Sandy, Lawrence, then added Casey. Brother Gay asked every student to hold the paper high so he could walk around and see these names. When he got to Junior, he glanced at Casey's name and smirked at him. He then asked each student to crumble up their paper. The kids enjoyed this part of the lesson. Some made makeshift joints or paper airplanes while others did as was instructed. Brother Gay then challenged the class to straighten their papers. Junior's OCD kicked in immediately. He worked overtime as he attempted to unbend the sharp creases – all to the amusement of his peers. Brother Gay walked over to him and placed a hand on Junior's shoulder to stop him.

"As you all can see," said Brother Gay, "Brother Junior here is serious about restoring the things most dear to him, as evidenced by his resiliency."

Junior got the joke and stopped.

"But you can't restore what's taken away from you!" Brother Gay raised his voice as he circled around the room. "That's how a victim feels! Crumbled. Lost. Dead to the world! They'll never be the same, no matter how much you try; the hurt will always be there. Think about that when you're out there in the street. Look down at the papers in front of you with the names of the people dearest to you, young brothers and sisters," he continued. "What paper is *your* name on? Will it be a diploma or a death certificate before your twenty-first birthday? Which one?! Take control while you can."

Most of Junior's class didn't get Brother Gay's dry sense of humor, but Junior did. To some, Brother Gay was just an uppity cat with a fancy vocabulary who referred to God as "Allah" and overused analogies. Like Casey, he was crazy about Junior and the direction of most young black boys there at Medgar Evers Secondary School. Despite his candor, he commanded the attention of Junior's class with his realness and diction. Unlike Mrs. Hawkins, he talked *to* his students and not *at* them. One morning, Brother Gay was summoned into Mr. Levy's office, leaving his steaming cup of gas station coffee unattended. Junior's classmates eyed one another, seeing who would be the first to welcome Brother Gay to Medgar. Surveying the room, not a single student left their seat. Shortly thereafter, Junior's teacher returned and finished his unsoiled beverage.

Brother Gay was the perfect balance of adult and mature youth, which made him relatable to the students at Medgar. For Junior, his new teacher was a blend of both his parents and Casey: he had an educated, take-no-prisoners attitude with an amicable spirit. His good-natured character would eventually thrust him into the crosshairs of Mr. Levy, who seemed more interested in recruiting robotic staff members to his infantry.

When the day ended, Junior climbed into Sandy's car and asked his mother if she had heard back from Senior. The look on Sandy's face told him that his daddy hadn't called. Junior spent the remainder of the ride home wondering if his parents' overdue breakup was a reality. For years, the Robinsons had flirted with the possibility of separating. After twenty-two years of marriage and the death of a child – all while living barely above the poverty line – a divorce seemed imminent.

Occasionally during the ride home, Junior attempted to make conversation with Sandy but failed miserably. Again, he thought of bringing up seeing New York with Casey but decided against it. Watching his daddy shoot out the TV the night before along with the silent car ride was convincing to Junior to let it go. Having Casey over for dinner, he decided, would be better than not having Casey at all.

As Junior and his mother turned onto Kennedy Street, Junior spotted his daddy's truck parked in front of the house. A smile grew on his young face as he stared down Senior's truck.

As soon as Junior and his mother exited the car, the door to the Robinsons' house opened and Senior stood on the porch, glaring at Sandy as she gave it back. Unsure whether his parents would fight or make up, Junior positioned himself in the middle of his parents in case a brawl ensued. As they sized up each other, Senior walked down the stairs and over to Sandy as she slowly backed away, unsure what was on her husband's mind. Towering over her, Senior pinned Sandy against her Buick; she cracked into an inviting smile as Senior smiled back and the two embraced and kissed. It was their first kiss since burying Lawrence the summer before. Just as their lips came together, the Robinsons' phone began to ring. "Junior, get that, will ya?" Senior asked him, preoccupied with his wife's reunion. In the kitchen, Junior looked down at his caller ID. The caller was none other than his big sissy, Casey. She was calling to confirm their New York appointment scheduled for the next morning.

"So, what'd they say?" she asked him. "What time am I pickin' you up?"

Disappointed, Junior breathed into the phone. "Maaaaan," he began.

"Uh oh," said Casey. "What happened? They shoot us down?"

"Shoot us down?" he laughed nervously. "Nah, I was saying 'maaaaan' as in, '*Maaaaan,* I can't find anything to wear!'" he explained. "I-I'm good. I can go...yup. Can't wait... Can you meet me at Medgar before the bell?"

"Of course. I'll give Mrs. Robinson our itinerary in the morning. Yo, we're gonna have so much fun, J., I've got a whole day planned for us. You're gonna love it!"

After dinner that evening, Junior paced throughout his bedroom, knowing he had twenty-four hours left to live if his parents found out about New York. Right before bed, both Senior and Sandy entered his room to apologize for the other night. Holding hands, they assured Junior they would stay together and that the new year would be better. Sandy then kissed Junior on the forehead as Senior looked on proudly.

"Been a little rough, but things'll get better for us, Junior – and you too," he said.

Just as his daddy said that a moth landed in Junior's belly as he attempted to work up the nerve to tell his parents of what he'd done. New York was a big city. Bigger than Brooke's Rowe or any other part of Philly he'd seen. As his parents left the room for the night, Junior decided to spend the final hours before his execution indulging in his favorite pastime.

From the shoreline, I sea waves that gladly wave back at me. I am ready to sail the world.

LEONARD G. ROBINSON JR.

New York

On Friday, December 22, 1995, Junior arrived at Medgar Evers Secondary School for his last day of class before winter break. As he mulled over the decision whether to go through with his big lie along the way, he kissed Sandy on the cheek and headed straight to room 454 to ask Brother Gay for advice. With Casey on the way to get him, there was still time for him to do the right thing.

"As an adult, as a teacher, and as a parent, *hell* no!" Brother Gay began. "However, as a friend, as a mentor, and a dreamer," he continued, "it's a great opportunity to see something new."

"So, what should I do?!" Junior asked. "If I go, I'm just as good as dead when I get back."

"I can't answer that, Junior. That's a tough one. But what-ever you decide to do, this conversation never happened between us – let's shake on that."

Brother Gay extended his hand out for Junior to shake. As they slapped skin, Junior's teacher winked at him, leaving him on his own to make the decision. Thinking, deciding, Junior lifted his bookbag onto his shoulder and headed out of Medgar before he could be seen. As he neared the door of room 454, Brother Gay spoke once again.

"Brother Junior," he called to him. "New York is a beauti-ful city. Make the best of it."

Smiling, Junior disappeared down the back staircase undetected and slipped into Casey's car in front of the school. As he approached her car tip-toeing like a cat burglar, Casey cocked her eyebrow at him before looking around for Sandy.

"Yo J., where's your mom?" she asked.

"She said not to worry about it. She'll see us when we get back."

"See us when we get back, huh?" Casey repeated. "Hmmm. Interesting…"

"Yeah, she was uh, late for work. She told us to go ahead."

"…OK. Well. As long as she's good with it that's alright, I guess. We better get going."

At the Broad Street bus terminal, Junior and Casey boarded Greyhound Bus 808. Once inside, Junior stuffed his book-bag beneath his seat and piled next to Casey as she handed him an arrival and departure receipt. When Junior realized he wouldn't get back to Brooke's Rowe until after 8 p.m. that night, his eyes nearly blew from both sockets. Medgar generally let out around 3:20 which meant Sandy (or worse Senior) would be there to pick him up shortly afterward.

"Shit, Casey!" he freaked. "It says we won't get back to Brooke's Rowe until after eight!"

Pushing past Casey, Junior went to confront the bus driver.

"Man, you sure this bus can't get back to Brooke's Rowe any quicker?!" he asked.

The bus driver, who looked every part of Samuel L. Jackson from *Die Hard: With a Vengeance*, glared at Junior. The man then looked down at Junior's big feet as Junior's eyes soon followed down to the yellow line; one of Junior's sneakers had breached the toe line. As Junior moved his foot back, the driver cranked the engine to his bus, keeping his eye on Junior until he returned to his seat next to Casey in the ninth row.

"What is with you, Junior?" she laughed. "Who do you think you are? Barry Sanders or somebody? You almost knocked me over. Why are you so edgy this morning?"

"Sorry, just a little nervous," he said. "I promise, once we get moving, I'll be fine."

"Good. You're gonna have so much to tell your folks about when we get back!"

Exhaling, Junior agreed. "Yeah, tell me about it…"

Junior had seen images of New York on TV before, but he soon learned that New York on TV was nothing compared to New York in person. Just after noon, their bus passed the bright blue signage welcoming them to the Empire State. From the interstate, Junior saw some of the tallest buildings he had ever seen in his life. Next to his window in the opposite lane, was a green Dodge Minivan with New York plates. The driver was wearing a New York Yankees ball cap as he dangled his arm from the car window in the wintery air, unusual for a December day. The second he spotted the tall buildings lurking in the background, Junior forgot about his scheduled execution for later that evening. With the day ahead of them, he decided to spend his remaining hours immersed in his new favorite city.

As Casey rode beside him, Junior leaned in to steal a kiss on her puffy cheek. Flabbergasted, she quickly jerked away. "Junior?! C'mon, don't do that!" she gasped, blushing.

"Sorry," he apologized. "Just wanted to say thanks." Reaching into his backpack, Junior cycled through some of his favorite rap cassettes, searching for the perfect listen as Casey looked down into his bag.

"So, who is it today, J.?" she asked. "Eric B. & Rakim? Nas? Biggie Smalls? The Roots?"

Junior popped open the deck on his Walkman to show Casey a single from Bone Thugs-N-Harmony.

"Man, you can't understand shit they say! They rap too fast for me!"

"I know, but it sounds so good!"

With his Walkman blasted high, Junior cracked open his window and took a whiff of the cool New York air. Emerging from the Lincoln Tunnel, Junior saw a glut of city cabs and buses at every street corner, just like at home. But Philly traffic was nothing compared to New York traffic – not even close. There were enough traffic lights at each street corner to fill every Christmas tree back on Kennedy Street. In a one-mile radius, Junior thought he saw nearly every ethnicity. Back in Brooke's Rowe, Black and Puerto-Rican families dominated the ghetto genre with a sprinkle of poor white folk.

Somewhere near Times Square, a pre-Christmas parade was taking place for a group of elementary school children. Junior leaned out of his seat to catch a glimpse of Cookie Monster and Big Bird waving to a crowd of kindergarteners as they waved back. A few lights down, a man dressed as Superman braved the cold in a pair of blue tights. Meanwhile, Batman took on Joker in a corny Kung-Fu exhibition to the cheer of a festive holiday crowd. Above it all, light snow trickled from a white sky. Junior wondered if heaven was anything like New York City. Back home, the only exhibitions Junior saw were cops slamming a man's head into the ground or junkies tripped out on dope.

When their bus arrived at Rockefeller Plaza in Midtown Manhattan, Junior rushed off to get a look at the Christmas tree. The fifty-foot-tall tree towered so high, it hurt his neck to look up. Adults, some with their children, were dressed in ugly Christmas sweaters as they glided across the ice in skates, some twirling magnificently. The bus driver told his riders to be back no later than 5 p.m. to depart for Philly at the scheduled time.

Junior stood near a wall, admiring a gang of ice skaters as they floated by him, waving as a crowd of visitors gathered to cheer them on. Back when Lawrence was around, he and Junior would go to a school not far from the house to sled down a hill with the other North Philly kids when it snowed. They didn't own a sled, but Senior allowed them to take the trash lids from out back, provided the boys returned them to the house. At the school, the neighborhood kids would make a makeshift ramp that would send them hurling into the air and into a batch of snow. The sledding came to a stop when Junior and Lawrence lost their lids.

As Junior watched the group of skaters, in awe of New York's Christmassy bliss, Casey offered to rent him a pair of skates for twenty dollars.

"Casey, black people don't ice skate!" he laughed. "Don't they have any lids?"

"Lids?!" she asked. "I'm black too, fool! And we're not in North Philly anymore – we're in Manhattan – and don't you believe that! Black people can do *whatever* black people wanna do as long as they don't worry about what *other* black people think about them. Here, take this."

As Casey handed Junior a crisp twenty, he challenged her to join him.

"OK, but you gotta do it with me, Casey," he negotiated. "I ain't going by myself."

"Look negro, *my* fat ass is *not* gettin' on that ice!" she laughed. "Not for all these people to see me! Besides, I'm rusty. If I fall, I might break the ice. I'll fall right down to hell. It'll be a shit show. I won't be allowed back in New York. Hell, I might get kicked out of the country!"

Junior used Casey's wit against her. "*Black people can do whatever black people wanna do as long as black people...*"

"Oh, shut up!" she interrupted. "Gimmie the damn money! And don't be laughin' at me!"

Junior had never seen ice except for when it snowed back in Brooke's Rowe. The second his feet touched the glassy surface, he went down. As he tried to get up, he went down again...and again. Casey fell once on her big butt but managed to recover as she glided down the ice, twirling like a beached whale on skates. She then went over to Junior to encourage him as he went down a fourth time. Frustrated, he crawled back to the bench, ducking incoming traffic before ripping off his skates and placing them next to his soggy socks. After a few minutes, Casey skated over to him, spraying him in the face with chipped ice from her blades.

"Fuck it, man." Junior shook his head.

"Yo, just take your time," she stumbled. "Don't give up, OK? Look, we came up here to have fun, right? So, let's have a good time. C'mon, we'll hold hands."

Cussing, pouting, Junior put back on his skates and braved the ice as he held onto Casey. As he reached out for her gloved hand, she grabbed onto his, teaching him the basics of footwork and balance. It took a while, but Junior got it. On wobbly legs, he began to smile as Casey wrapped her arm around his waist, gliding beside him.

"See!" she laughed. "I told you! Look, you're doing it!"

As his stumbles minimized, Junior melted into a sweet laugh next to his best friend. "So, how'd you get so good?" he asked.

"My sister taught me."

Holding hands, the two bladed slow and steady across the ice, soaring gingerly. Over-confident, Casey tried to dance and fell. As Junior began to laugh, his karma followed and he landed on top of her. Embarrassed, Casey laughed loud enough for all of New York to hear. After floating around a bit more, the two returned their skates to the rental booth, slipped on their tennis shoes, and returned to the viewing area. As they enjoyed their festive afternoon in Manhattan, admiring the glow of Christmas decorations and seasonal holiday colors, Casey sat Junior on a nearby bench to share her heart.

"I got a confession to make, J.," Casey told him. "There's something I've been meaning to talk to you about. I don't know how this is gonna go, so bear with me."

Turning to face her, Junior tuned in.

"So, look, I got offered a new job. I won't be in Philly much longer. Couple more weeks or so into January, but I'm gonna be moving in with my sister, Courtney. She's got a townhouse over in Fort Foote – not far from here." Casey grabbed Junior by his hands and looked into his eyes. "Listen, this isn't an easy decision to make – you'll need to talk it over with your folks, and there's a lot more to it – but I'll just say it anyway," she continued. "So, there's this… school in my sister's neighborhood. It's privately run, but I think it'd be perfect for you. They take kids all year. All you need is a New York address, and you're good." She paused to catch her breath. "I was thinking…maybe…you know… you'd like to come and live with us? You know? For school?"

Taken aback, Junior swallowed. "…So, you mean like, you wanna adopt me or something?" he asked.

"Not *adopt* you-adopt you," Casey explained. "You'll still go home on the weekends. But during the week, you can crash with us for school. My sister, Courtney, she's on board with it. You'd have to get used to living with two women, but I already talked to her about it before I asked you. I'd just need to know if Mr. and Mrs. Robinson could agree to that. What do you think – are you interested? Would you like to come and live with me?"

Junior looked into Casey's green eyes and saw his deceitful reflection looking back at him: His parents had no idea that he had just finished ice skating in New York. Unbeknownst to Casey, she was harboring a fugitive on the run from justice. In theory, New York was an opportunity of a lifetime. For Junior, however, getting his parents to agree to terms on a joint residency would be a tall order as the Robinsons seldom agreed on which roach spray to buy or what gas to use in the cars. Not to mention, in the year since Lawrence had passed, Junior's family had become a tight ship. Not only had Sandy become overprotective of him, but Junior was also Senior's right-hand man for his handyman business. He was also the buffer between his parents to keep their marriage from collapsing after being held together with a safety pin for the last year. For Junior, leaving Brooke's Rowe meant his parents would lose another son. As he flirted with the idea inside his head, he soon came to the reality that living in New York beside Casey was a pipe dream.

"I'd love to live with you, Casey," said Junior. "But there ain't *no* way my parents would let me stay here in New York. Then, I think about Lawrence and it's like… I don't know – I feel like I don't deserve all of this sometimes. I guess I'm just bound to Brooke's Rowe, you know?"

Casey became angry with Junior, angrier than when he had taken his daddy's .38.

"Yo!" she barked. "You are *not* bound to anything, J., and you *damn* sure ain't bound to fuckin' Brooke's Rowe! Brooke's Rowe is where you live, but it's not who you are. Even if you don't *ever* come back to New York, I don't want to *ever* hear you say some dumb shit like that again. You hear me?" She raised her voice. "Do I make myself clear?"

"I didn't mean to make you upset, Casey," Junior explained. "But it's just a reality for kids like me in a Crawford or a Brooke's Rowe situation. It is what it is, you know?"

"No, it's not!" She leaped from her seat. "It's not, OK? You're not bound to Brooke's Rowe. That's stuff that's inside your head that we need to get rid of. Man, you can go *any* damn where in the world, Junior! All you need is a plane ticket and some hope," she carried on. "I've seen you write – I've seen you dream – I've seen you come up with poetry that no other fourteen-year-old kid has ever done in my life, J. I've lived in the ghetto longer than you've been alive. I've been around that mentality my whole life. I'm here to tell you that you can break these curses right now if you want to. OK?"

As Casey rejoined hands with Junior, he took a deep breath.

"Just think about it for me?" she asked him. "Can you at least just think it over?"

"Sure, Casey." He smiled. "I'll think it over."

But Junior did more than just think about Casey's invitation that day. He internalized what it would be like to live with Casey. In his mind, he felt unworthy of such a tender soul willing to take him under his wing and wondered if he was even good enough for the opportunity. Off in the distance, a tower clock nearby read 1:36 p.m. Two hours had passed since they arrived at Rockefeller Center. With their stomachs grumbling, they traded in their skates for a bite to eat.

To change gears, Casey offered him to lunch at the exquisite BuBoy's Café & Lounge on the corner of West 44th and 7th Avenue. Through a glass elevator that glowed green and red, Junior followed Casey to the top floor. At the door, a hostess eyeballed Junior with suspicion as Casey requested a table with a window seat. The woman looked Junior up and down as he played the role of a civilized adult.

"He's my little brother," Casey giggled. "He just turned eighteen...it's his birthday."

Sharing a small booth, Junior and Casey sat overlooking the city from the nineteenth story. Peering into the snowy air, Junior wondered what Lawrence would have thought of

New York. He thought about Brother Gay back in Medgar, wondering if his new teacher could keep a secret. He thought about the other kids from his neighborhood and imagined how different life would look if they could gaze down at the world from the nineteenth floor.

For lunch, Casey treated Junior to a delicious ham, egg, and cheese melt with hot chocolate and marshmallows. Out in the lobby, next to the hostess stand, a pianist softly tickled Claude Debussy's "Clair de Lune", to Casey's delight. Enjoying the serenity, she closed her eyes and swayed from side to side, sipping on her toasty latte. Junior couldn't believe the genius of the artist behind him. He watched as the man's fingers raced crazily across the piano in unison, each digit responsible for dishing out its melodic tune. He glanced down the other end of the street, staring out at the World Trade Center's huge structure off in the distance; he wished the day would never end.

Sometime after 2:30 p.m. on a crowded New York Street, Casey flagged down a cabbie for their next excursion.

"So, where to now?" Junior asked her. "Empire State Building?

"Even better," she told him. "While sitting in BuBoy's, I realized seeing the Empire State Building only gives you a view of New York. But this school I'm about to show you, J.," she touched his arm, "will allow you to see the world."

Casey handed the taxi driver a ten-dollar bill.

"Driver, Langston Hughes School of Art, please."

Don't drown in your miseries.
Paddle your fears.
Kick your legs. Tread the bayous
of your subconscious.
Survive the wave and float to ~~shore~~ sure.

—LEONARD G. ROBINSON JR.

Eleven

From the cab window, the Langston Hughes School of Art in New York was a stark contrast to any school Junior had ever seen. The tall and immaculate structure looked like a mini-mall from the outside with large stone-cut walls and elegant landscaping. Unlike Medgar, no gamblers were loitering near the entrance to give Junior and Casey a warm welcome. As their cab arrived at the front of the building, Junior stepped out onto the campus driveway, removed his hat, and held it against his heart as if someone had died.

The inside of Langston was nothing short of breathtaking. In the middle lobby was a small reflection pool with a running fountain, and a bust of the late, great writer and influencer. Next to Hughes was a collection of his embroidered poetry and passages. Junior's favorite, "The Negro Artist and the Racial Mountain" was encased at the bottom of the pool along with the hopes and dreams of the students there. Unbeknownst to Junior, Casey had arranged for a tour that afternoon with a school recruiter. While waiting in the lobby, Casey handed Junior a shiny nickel from her bag and asked him to make a wish. Taking forever and a day, Junior closed his eyes, made his wish, and launched his dream into the pool. Casey doubled his wishes with a dime.

"What *is* this place?" he asked her. "It's incredible."

Pleased with his enthusiasm, Casey placed her hand onto Junior's shoulder.

"Hopefully your new school," she told him. "I really hope you can come live with us, J."

Admiring the inside, Junior hoped so also. Looking down at his watch, his stomach began to boil as he realized school at Medgar had just let out; he pictured Sandy out front waiting on him. He knew he'd be a dead man when his parents found out about New York. In the meantime, however, with Casey by his side and a tour of Langston at his fingertips, he relished the moment. His tour guide was a bushy-gray-haired man named James. He greeted Junior with a firm shake and walked over to Casey and hugged her.

"Ah, yes," he said, gleaming. "Thank you so very much, Miss Haughton, for bringing your son to us. I'm sure he'll love the tour."

The second James turned his back, Junior looked over Casey.

"*Son?*" he whispered.

"Play along!" she muttered back.

The school was nothing short of a phenomenon to Junior. Glass doors encased in marble that opened at the push of a button. Computers in every classroom and at every student's chair. Vending machines that actually worked and were serviced daily. A built-in help desk for both student and faculty members' technological needs. Not to mention, the staff members were all pleasant, including the school's dean, Roberta Evans. She shook Junior's hand with her own two hands and hugged Casey as if they were friends who hadn't seen each other in fifteen years.

The inside lobby looked like the headquarters of Chase Manhattan Bank. Langston had two floors with a theatre, library, cafeteria, and basement. It serviced approximately 134 high school kids, and every classroom had two full-time teachers. The building was patrolled by one security guard, an older black gentleman with a steep accent like Morgan Freeman. His weapon of choice was his intellect and a long flashlight, and he didn't carry cuffs or pepper spray. On every floor was an elevator that was accessible to students and every floor had a large television that ran nonstop with world events, stock market lapses, and other daily news to keep students and faculty abreast.

"Big-ass TV," Casey said under her breath to Junior. "Can you believe that?! Fifty inches!"

As Junior and Casey followed James throughout the first-floor hallway, Junior saw illustrations of some of the most brilliant black minds of the twentieth century: James Baldwin,

Harriet Tubman, Frederick Douglass, Nelson Mandela, Dr. King, Malcolm X, George Washington Carver, W.E.B. DuBois, Marvin Gaye, Sam Cooke, and more. Under each illustration was an inscription of their accomplishments. Strapped for time, Junior breezed over a few before returning to Casey and Mr. James near the first-floor elevator.

"So, what's it like here?" Junior asked the man. "Are the kids nice?"

"Well, at the end of the day, they're kids," said James. "I've been here since '89, and I can count on one hand how many fights I've seen. The rules are strict here. If you fight, you're gone. Misbehave? You're out of here. The accountability tends to deter the kids from getting into too much trouble. For the most part, the kids are respectful, well-behaved, and get along well with other students and faculty."

As James led Junior and Casey out of the elevator onto the second-floor, Casey chimed in with a question of her own.

"Can you elaborate just a *little* more on the environment here, sir?" she asked him. "Sorry if I sound pushy. But what's a typical day here like for a student?"

"Classes start promptly at 7:55 a.m., not a minute later and ends at 4:10 p.m.," said James. "Each class has about six or seven kids with two teachers in each. It's an art school for talented kids but still a high school. The students get one hour for lunch with breaks in between." He then pointed to a menu on the wall. "The food here is not what'd you typically see on a high school menu. Bison, lamb chops, venison, organic vegetables. Stuff like that. The kids wear uniforms

Monday through Thursday. Fridays are dress-down days – with limitations, obviously." He winked at Junior. "For Saturdays, we have a tutor available from 8 a.m. to 2 p.m., and a shuttle service which runs every day from 6 a.m. to 6 p.m. The library is available at the same time."

Casey looked at Junior; Junior looked at Casey. Not a word was exchanged, but the look on Junior's face said it all: If he could, he'd move to New York tomorrow.

As the recruiter led Junior and Casey onto the second-floor known as "Artist Way", Junior peeped into room 219 where acting was being taught. Across the hall in 234, another teacher taught playwright for African-American film. Down the hall in 239 was Junior's favorite: African-American Literature and Contemporary Poetry. With drool sliding from his pitiful face, Junior stood at the door pane of 239 and watched as students dissected poetry and debated music. On the agenda for that day, written on the board was a poem by Tupac Shakur. Back and forth, the students deliberated as they tried to come up with the meaning of their hero's artistry. Loud and somewhat obnoxious, they argued in good fun as their teacher shushed the class, allowing every student a chance to speak. Unlike Medgar, they didn't bash, name call, or threaten to pull out razors from beneath their tongues. The only weaponry used for that day was their brilliant and spongy minds. Junior could've fainted.

"Casey, look! 2pac!" Junior pointed. "They're studying 2pac!"

"What?!" she said, shoving him. "Let me see!"

What was also shocking to both Junior and Casey that afternoon was the number of black students in attendance at Langston. On his way down the hall, Junior expected to see a surfeit of preppy white kids with moussed hair and cream-colored sweaters tied around their necks. He was happy to learn from his recruiter that Langston was a diverse populace with black students dominating at a 54% majority. As classes let out for the afternoon, Junior stood in the center of the hallway next to Casey and watched as kids who looked like him blew by him and out the door.

"*Now* do you see what I was tellin' you earlier, J.?" Casey asked him. "Man, look at these kids runnin' at us. They ain't no different than you – or me when I was your age."

Aside from Langston's charming glamour, James assured Junior and Casey the staff was *all* pleasant and proud to serve as members of an elite school. Not to mention, Langston was slated as having an 83.6% scholarship ratio to some of the nation's top art institutions in the country. Down in his office, James computed the average G.P.A. at Langston was 3.587. Every quarter, recruiters from colleges and the armed forces came to speak with students about possible career paths. James handed Junior a brochure with his card attached and pitched Casey a breakdown of Langston's tuition. Her eyes exploded inside her head as she stared down at the price: $7800 per semester. At roughly eight grand per year, Langston was a no-go. At home, Junior's parents went to war for far less. Junior looked down at the circled cost at the bottom of the form and walked out of James's office, leaving Casey there by herself. Another dream diminished. Outside, Casey found Junior leaning against the wall. The instant he saw her, he began firing away at his big sissy.

"Man, what'd you do that for?!" he asked, irritated. "You *know* my parents can't afford for me to go here. Eight g's?! Thanks for gettin' my hopes up for nothin'!"

"You think all this is for fun?" she asked him. "You think I'm just bullshittin' you – pulling your arm when I tell you how special you are and that things can happen for you? I *believe* in you, Junior. I've *always* believed in you." She patted on her chest. "You think I'd bring you up here just to throw this in your face? Well, I didn't! Good things can happen sometimes."

"How?!" Junior clapped back. "My parents can't afford no fancy Langston education. We're not exactly rich, Casey. Don't you get it? All these ideas and stuff you come up with some-times, I can't do them! You're just wasting your time on me."

"STOP TALKIN' LIKE THAT!" Casey howled at him. "Stop saying things like that to me! You're not a waste of time, J.!"

"Look, I'm just trying to be realistic about this," he wolfed back. "Eight g's per year is a lot of money when your parents ain't got shit. You should've *never* brought me here, Casey. I can't move to no New York. There's no way."

The cab ride back to Rockefeller Plaza was awkwardly silent. Junior sat in a slumber, playing with a string on his jacket. Beside him, Casey looked out into the dense air, hurt by

Junior's rhetoric on Langston. The two siblings sat for close to a half-hour without a word. Junior sulked and tossed on his headphones to drown out the silence around him. Closing his eyes, he laid his head back on the seat and exhaled. Before long, he felt one of his earplugs removed and Casey's voice inside his head.

"I'm sorry about earlier," she apologized. "I didn't mean for our trip to be such a disappointment, J. I didn't want *any* of this, especially since this could be one of the last few times we get to hang out, you know?"

"No, Casey." He shook his head. "*I'm* the one who's sorry. You're so good to me. I loved New York, and I loved Langston, too. There was no disappointment. I just wish there was a way for me to go, that's all. Sorry for being such a jerk to you earlier."

As the two waited by the bus terminal for 808, Casey came up with another idea.

"What if I were to help?" she offered. "Could that change things? I could pay part of it."

"No, Casey. I can't let you do that," said Junior. "That'll just hold you back. It's too much."

"But I want to, J. What if we split it down the middle? I take half, and your parents do the other? That could work, right?"

Junior looked down at his watch and noticed it was 5:02 p.m. – well past his pickup time from Medgar. His scheduled execution was not a matter of 'if', but 'when', the moment his parents found about New York. Accepting his fate, he turned down Casey's invitation to sponsor him. As they boarded bus

808 in Times Square, Junior kissed his big sissy on her cheek.

"Casey, you're the sweetest big sissy any kid could dream of," he told her. "But I can't ask you to pay part of my tuition at Langston. It's not fair to you. New York was a dream and experiencing it all next to you made it even better. But as much as I hate to admit it, Philly is my home. I'll never forget you."

Holding onto her hand, a tear rolled from Casey's eye down her cheek.

"You love me, don't you?" he asked her.

Gasping, Casey wiped her eyes. "With all my heart," she chuckled away her tears. "Fuck man, you got me cryin' again. You're like the little brother I never had. I'm really... fuck... hold on. God this is hard...I'm gonna miss you, Junior."

"Not like I'm gonna miss you," he told her.

You can fix broken. But you can't fix done.

LEONARD G. ROBINSON JR.

The Last Son

Halfway home, just after 7 p.m. that evening, Junior was sleeping on Casey's shoulder when he was awakened by the sound of her cell phone going off in her bag. Casey missed the call before it went to voicemail. Checking her phone, Casey looked down at the screen and noticed six missed calls from Junior's residence. Concerned, she showed Junior his home number on her screen.

"Shit! Six miss calls!" she griped. "Hope everything is OK!"

As Casey went to dial back Junior's house, he grabbed her cell phone and closed it.

"Casey, wait a second," he sighed. "I have to tell you something."

"Well, can you tell me *afterward?*" she asked him. "This could be important."

As Casey reached for her cell phone, Junior pulled it away from her reach.

"C'mon, J., stop!" she snapped. "Gimmie back my phone, man!"

Closing his eyes, Junior looked up to the heavens and sighed again, anticipating his impending doom. The jig was up. In less than an hour, he would be executed by guillotine by none other than his undertaker for a father, Senior. With six missed calls in the last two hours, his parents were more than just concerned; they were on the verge of losing their minds. As Casey continued to give Junior hell, he finally cracked and gave back the phone. Casey got halfway through one ring to Junior's house before he came forward with the truth.

"They don't know I'm up here." He sagged his head.

Casey closed her flip phone immediately. "They *what*?!"

"I asked; they told me 'no'. I should've told you earlier."

Soon after, Casey's cell phone began to ring again. The number was from Junior's house. Disappointed and with her hands on both hips and her mouth flying open, she dropped her cell phone into Junior's lap. Her arched eyebrows were slanted in evil anger. "There you go! You got yourself into this shit – you get yourself out!"

Junior looked down at Casey's cell in his lap, knowing what fate awaited him on the other end of the phone. He lifted the small box and then turned off the ringer, leaving his parents in the dark about his whereabouts.

"One day," he said to her. "I just wanted *one* day to hear 'yes', instead of being told 'no'. If it wasn't for you, I would've never got to see a city as beautiful as New York. I'm sorry I lied to you, Casey. I hope you can somehow forgive me for all of this."

Scowling at Junior, Casey's phone rang once again. As Junior looked down at her phone resting on his lap, Casey took back her phone and placed it back inside of her bag.

"You were right," she told him. "This *is* a waste of my time."

By the time Junior and Casey arrived at Brooke's Rowe terminal and arrived at her car, Casey was still not speaking to him. She said little to Junior on the way back to his house as he rode in silence, staring from the car window at what was his reality: Brooke's Rowe, the decrepit bowels of South Philly. There was no BuBoy's Café & Lounge, holiday parade, or piano man playing "Clair De Lune". There was no Langston Hughes School of Art. The only school Junior was accustomed to was the School of Hard Knocks. Kids carrying razor blades for protection and a janky police force that would continue making poor folks into an example.

As Casey's Toyota turned onto Kennedy Street, Junior's stomach bubbled with intensity. The game was over. After a day that meant a lifetime to him, he wondered if he'd ever see Casey again for lying to both her and his family. As her car came to a stop in front of the house, she turned to him.

"This hurts us, J.," she told him. "I thought taking your father's gun was bad, but this takes the cake – the fact that you lied to me. I'm crushed. I wish you all the luck with your writing and everything. But I can't...I just...I can't do this anymore..."

"I understand." He sagged his head. "I had a great friend in my life, and I fucked it up. Just like I did with Lawrence."

Junior slithered out of Casey's car and up the sidewalk to meet his doom. His lips began to quiver as he attempted to make up with Casey as she waited next to her car, teary-eyed.

"Casey, I'm sorry. Please..." he apologized.

"...Go, Junior." She waved him on.

The second Junior stepped foot on the front porch, the outside light came on, and Sandy opened the door. As the makeup on his mother's face began to melt at Junior in the doorway, Senior came marching down the steps, half-twisted on alcohol and remembering Lawrence. He then jacked Junior by his jacket and slammed him into the living room wall. Unable to control his rage, he slapped Junior hard across the face, knocking him down onto his backside.

"Where you been, huh?! You think you're grown?!"

WHAM, Senior slapped Junior across the pus again, lifting him onto his feet and tossing him over the sofa as if he was a pro wrestler. Meanwhile, standing at the door, Sandy howled and cried for Junior as if her son had been sold away to a new slave owner. WHAM, Senior slapped Junior again, tossing him back onto the floor as Junior's mother attempted to stop Senior from killing him. Soon after, Junior recalled Casey running over to the door in place of Sandy. The second she got there and saw the Robinsons entangled on the floor, she sobbed with the agony only a true friend could muster.

"Please, it's my fault! I should've known better!" Casey hollered. "Don't hurt him!"

The neighbors on Kennedy Street thought someone had died inside the Robinsons' house the way both Sandy and Casey cut up, worried Senior was on the verge of killing Junior. He picked up Junior by his jacket collar again before smacking him down onto the floor one last time for good measure. Standing over his son, he roared.

"This is my fuckin' house! I run this motherfucka – not you!" Senior screamed at Junior as he laid beneath, a trickle of blood coming from his mouth. "Hang up on me? I'm your father, nigga! New York? Huh?! You think you can go to New York without our consent?!"

Reeking of alcohol and rage, it took *all* of Sandy to cart away Senior long enough to allow Junior onto his feet. By then, Casey had intervened in the Robinsons' affairs, forgetting Junior's empire lie, taking on the role of his big sissy. With Senior pinned to the closet door by his linebacker wife, Junior wiped away the trickle of blood from his swollen mouth.

"I'm sorry, y'all..." He cracked in half. "Man... I'm sick of Brooke's Rowe! I'm sick of Medgar – and I'm sick of Philly, too! I HATE IT HEREEEE!" He shook with indignation before racing past his parents and up into his bedroom. With the door shut to his room, Junior crumbled onto his bed, biting into his pillow to drown out his wretched cries. He was done with life in Philly and wanted out. Downstairs, Casey was inconsolable. The gruesome sight of seeing Junior knocked around by his daddy destroyed her. Before leaving she handed Sandy a pamphlet to Langston Hughes School of Art in New York. It was soggy with creases.

"I thought he'd like the school." Her voice hoarsened. "Please don't be mad at him."

From his bedroom window, Junior watched as Casey trudged down the sidewalk and into her car. As she closed her car door, she folded onto her steering wheel and cried again before pulling off. Shortly thereafter, Junior pulled his curtain closed for the night.

I was once blind, now my eyes can see,
this wondrous world, and all that was waiting for me.
My heart was jaded. I'd fallen asleep.
For days I would weep.
Now, I know where I must be.

LEONARD G. ROBINSON JR.

A Dream Not Deferred

White covered every street corner in Brooke's Rowe on Christmas Day. Despite the joyous occasion, beat cops worked overtime chasing dealers pushing powdered cocaine. With holiday money in hand and the city's open-air drug market booming, cocaine stuck to asphalt more than snowfall that Christmas. For the Robinsons, the holiday was gray and dull, the same as every year since Lawrence had died. The day before, Junior's daddy draped a cheap set of old red and green lights around the doorway. Feeling satisfied with himself, he then took a chug of eggnog before wiping his mouth with his sleeve and tossing the bottle into the garbage. Before Lawrence's death, the Robinsons would get a tree from the mall lot. Both Junior and Lawrence each got a hundred dollars to blow on gifts in the days leading up to their holiday. That year, however, with bills cutting into the Robinsons' budget, Junior got fifty dollars along with a new jacket and a pair of snow boots from Payless Shoes. That Christmas morning, Junior slept up until 10 a.m., indifferent to his unwrapped jacket and cheap boots hanging on the rack in the living room closet. Downstairs, Sandy spent her festive morning watching the Christmas Day parade taking place in Manhattan on TV while Senior worked outside on his truck, mumbling to himself. Sipping on her cup of coffee, she looked through old family photographs, laughing to herself as she reminisced.

In the days since New York, Junior noticed his parents had been quiet to a fault – as if they were hiding something.

Meals were square and quiet as Senior kept his eyes buried down into his plate. To break the awkward silence amongst them, Sandy attempted to squeak something toward forgiveness for Junior's big lie.

"Well, I'm sure glad that you're here," she said to Junior, rubbing his hand. "Don't know *what* I would've done without you around. I'm sure your daddy feels the same way."

As Junior looked up from his plate into his daddy's face, Senior glared at him, chewing his meatloaf like a deranged prisoner waiting to shank him. Lowering his head, Junior sighed.

"I know, Mom," he replied. "I know."

Junior had barely written in his journal since New York happened. For three days, he struggled to put something noteworthy together before giving up writing altogether. Brooke's Rowe was his home. Casey was forever gone. Feeling hopeless, Junior placed his latest journal into the garbage bin next to Senior's eggnog. Sandy would find it later that evening, covered in gunk and cranberry sauce.

The day after Christmas, Sandy called Junior down into the living room to answer for his crimes of treason and deceit from his escapade in New York. For days, she had bummed in awkward silence, trying to concoct the most befitting punishment for him.

When Junior arrived in the living room that morning, he saw his soiled, abandoned journal on the coffee table. Sandy almost always got on him for wasting things. Considering his journal was half full, he hoped his mother would tab it as time served. Frustrated, Sandy offered Junior a seat on the couch next to Senior as she stood in front of the TV. Junior thought it was a wonder his daddy hadn't shot the TV out like the one in their bedroom. He thought he'd never again see the light of day or Casey's pretty smile as he took his seat on death row. Usually, when his parents spent days before sentencing him, Junior's punishment was long and harsh. If he was lucky, he'd get away with a two-week punishment and give up his Nintendo console again.

"What you did to our family last Friday was disheartening," Sandy scolded him. "You deliberately disobeyed us – and you could've got Casey in a lot of trouble. Suppose something had happened to you? Then what? It was selfish and irresponsible – and you're gonna pay for that."

Junior looked over at his daddy for clarity as Senior stared back at him with his trademark glare.

"On the other hand," Sandy continued, "even though I'm pissed with you, I just can't help but admire your courage. You *knew* you'd get killed for what you did, and you did it anyway. Why? Because there was something in your heart that said, 'I have to do this'. What you did wasn't meant to be mean-spirited. It was for the betterment of you. That was courageous, Junior, and I respect that a whole *hell* of a lot. Just because we're your parents doesn't mean we're always right about everything. In fact, after thinking it over, I was wrong *not* to let you visit New York with Casey."

Junior glanced down at his soiled journal and back up at his daddy whose face softened.

"So, I'm not on punishment?" he asked.

Sandy reached into her pocket and pulled out Junior's pamphlet from the Langston Hughes School of Art and placed it next to his book on the coffee table.

"Your daddy and I had a *long* talk with Casey on Christmas Eve," she told him. "And *we* think that going to Langston is…a great opportunity for you. Besides, just because we're not able to leave Brooke's Rowe doesn't mean you shouldn't. It's not fair to hold you back."

Senior placed his wide arm around Junior and pulled him in close.

"I was wrong for jumping on you the other night," he apologized. "But I did it out of love, son. You scared the *shit* out of me. I can't lose another son, Junior. You're my everything, and I love you…Yeah, I said it," he joked. "Maybe I ought to say that more from now on."

Junior's eyes watered the moment his daddy told him that he loved him. He seldom showed the boys affection. Senior then kissed him on the back of his head and patted his firstborn son on the back. Senior began to laugh with tears in his own eyes.

"Maaaan, you got to be a *brave* motherfucka because I was gonna kill you for hangin' up!"

As the family shared a quick laugh, Sandy ushered Junior off to his room to prepare for a surprise visit from Casey. That morning, he would sit at the head of the table as their chief investment. With his future on the line, Junior ran off to his room to change clothes.

Our Little Investment

On Tuesday, December 26, 1995, Casey, and her sister, Courtney, arrived on Kennedy Street dressed like CEOs headed to a business meeting. At the door, Junior suffocated Casey with a hug so tight Senior had to pry him off. The two women entered the Robinsons' residence, looking stunning in black excellence.

"Yo, this is for real, man," Casey told him. "So, I asked Courtney to dress up."

Senior couldn't keep his eyes off of Courtney, and neither could Junior. She was dark complected like Senior, tall with stallion legs and long, pretty black hair. The disparity between the two sisters perplexed Junior's daddy: Casey was white as snow and Courtney dark as he was. Unable to interpret the contrast between both sisters, Senior, in embarrassing fashion, posed the inevitable question: How? It cost Senior an elbow from Sandy, but he got his answer.

"I'm an albino," Casey laughed, unphased. "It's a defect when the skin has no color."

"So, you mean like a white person?" Senior asked.

"That's right. Both my parents are black."

As Senior tried to put Casey's explanation into context, Sandy interrupted: "She's a black woman like every other black woman that's in this living room right now. Now, perhaps we should get to what this meeting is about and *not* focus on what color Casey is or isn't."

To kick off their business meeting, Sandy brewed a fresh

batch of hot coffee for Casey and Courtney, while Senior blazed on a cigarette near the foyer. Junior sat between both sisters, unable to remove his eyes from Courtney's stock-inged legs. With her hair slicked into a neat bun, she looked every bit an actress from the big city. Occasionally, Junior stole a peep at her long, powerful legs before rolling his eyes elsewhere throughout the room. At one point, he went to look again and noticed Courtney noticing him. Ashamed, he re-focused on the prospect that was ahead of him.

As Sandy and Casey negotiated terms for Junior to move to New York, he took a bathroom break and stared at his reflection in the mirror. Back during the summer, he had got himself expelled from Franklin High and barely made it into Medgar. Now, he was on his way to a fancy art school in New York. Through it all, Casey had been by his side. His best friend and big sissy. After his short break, Junior returned to his office down in the living room and listened to the details the adults were discussing.

"We'll rotate; I'll pick him up every other Sunday," said Casey. "He'll stay with us at the townhouse in Fort Foote from Monday through Friday for school and then come home on the weekends – if that's OK?"

Casey then presented the Robinsons with a map of their sub-section of Fort Foote, New York, in conjunction with the school. From a library computer, she had printed the Robinsons the directions to their house along with two house keys: one for them and one for Junior. Junior placed his key inside his wallet as he listened in on his new life ahead of him.

"He'll have full access throughout the house," Courtney spoke up. "Access to a computer. Local parks. Eateries within walking distance. A public library. My boyfriend is at the house right now building Junior a desk where he can do his homework."

As a New York resident, Junior would pay significantly less in tuition at Langston than an out-of-state student. Not to mention, with Courtney's military background, Junior would receive a break in his tuition of $1,000, bringing the Robinsons' total to $6800 per semester. Across the room, with Senior hovering over her, Sandy worked out a monthly budget for Junior's tuition – it totaled around $600 per month for him to attend.

Carefully, Junior studied his mother's face for a reaction. At close to $600 per month for him to attend Langston, he knew his parents couldn't afford it. He thought about the many nights he had stayed up listening to his parents argue over money, and the time Senior destroyed the boys' fan over eighty dollars that had gone missing from his nightstand. As Sandy punched and crunched numbers on a calculator, attempting to find the space for Junior to leave, he suddenly got cold feet.

"Maybe this isn't such a good idea." He shrugged. "It seems like a lot."

Junior's backing out was met with silence. Across the room, at the bottom of the staircase, Senior puffed on his cigarette while sipping on a bottle of lukewarm Colt 45 malt liquor. Meanwhile, Casey and Courtney worked together on a weekly planner of household chores for Junior. Hearing no affirmative response, Junior tried again.

"Um, *hello*?" he said to no effect. "It's just a lot of money, and maybe we ought to…"

"Boy, shut up!" Senior interrupted. "*Damn!*"

Shortly after Senior put a muzzle on Junior, Casey introduced her original idea she'd offered to Junior while in New York.

"What if we split it, Mrs. Robinson?" she offered. "Would that help? I can chip in $200."

Courtney tagged in next. "I can do $150."

Junior then suddenly came to life.

"I'll be fifteen next summer," he declared. "I could find something part-time at the grocery store or McDonald's. Or I could help daddy with business on the weekends."

With $350 covered upfront along with Junior's room and board, there was still an additional $216 remaining for Sandy to pay each month on Junior's tuition. She looked down at her calculator one last time and powered it off.

"I'm sure I could do a day of overtime to make up the difference."

Last but not least was Senior.

"Business should pick back up in the new year. Count me in on that."

Three hours and two pots of coffee later, the vote was unanimous. After an official visit from Sandy and Senior to Junior's second home, Junior would stay in New York to attend the Langston Hughes School of Art.

Saying 'yes' was harder than Sandy had thought it would be. Her hands shook as she hugged and thanked Casey and her sister for offering to take on Junior and help out with his schooling. Then, with their jackets bundled up, the Robinsons followed the two sisters back to New York. With Senior behind the wheel, Junior watched his mother's face as they crossed the threshold into the Empire State. It was the same look he'd had on December 22. In all of her forty-plus years of hell-raising in North Philadelphia, Sandy had never been as far as an hour and a half's drive into New York. It was a frightening reality for Junior that most of his extended family had not been further than the City of Brotherly Love.

As Sandy's crusty Buick arrived along the cobblestoned roadway of Courtney's Fort Foote, New York townhouse, the Robinsons piled into Courtney's Nissan Maxima for a brief tour. From the top of the street, Junior showed his parents a glimpse of the Empire State Building.

"We were right over there!" he pointed out. "Man, I'm tellin' you, it's so beautiful there!"

Fort Foote was an improvement from Brooke's Rowe. The environment was friendlier, including the cops who patrolled that beat. They smiled and waved as they drove by, leaving Senior baffled as his mouth hung open.

"What the fuck?" he said, slowly waving back. "What is this place?"

"It's a world far from the ghetto we *all* know, but one we don't get to see often," said Casey. "When I was a little girl growing up in Jersey, I never knew places like this existed."

Before beginning their tour, Casey spoke into Junior's ear to assure her support. "Like I said to you before back at Medgar," she told him. "We're family now. You're my little brother, J., and I'm gonna look out for you always. Hell or high water. New York or Philly. It's all blood now between us."

Smiling back at her, Junior smiled. "My big sissy."

I have no words for your love.
You love me unconditionally
under one condition,
that you love me with all your heart through all of me.
And I am forever so grateful to have you.

LEONARD G. ROBINSON JR.

I know a place
colder than a Mars night
where hearts are broken
and running minds never tire.
There's a place called Brooke's Rowe.
Where black can crack
I bet you couldn't picture that.

—LEONARD G. ROBINSON JR.

Twelve

As the New Year arrived at the Robinsons' doorstep, Junior celebrated the night looking out over the city from his bedroom window. For once, his future was bright. When word got around that Junior was transferring from Medgar, his peers throughout his school and Brooke's Rowe slurred him. They ribbed Junior, calling him a sell-out and telling him he was too soft for Brooke's Rowe. When his classmates heard he was headed to Langston Hughes in Fort Foote, New York, the boys called him snooty and referred to him as an Uncle Tom. On his first week back to Brother Gay's class into the new year, a classmate heckled Junior to death over allegations that he and Casey Haughton were sleeping together. The kid claimed that Junior would birth an ugly, white baby – like Casey. As the day continued, the jokes became colder. On his way back from lunch, Junior's rage boiled over.

"Casey is so ugly, you gotta fuck the bitch with a paper bag over her head," the boy said.

Wham! Down he went. It took Brother Gay all of thirty seconds to scrape Junior off the kid. Though he'd pay for it with detention that afternoon, the blow was euphoric to him and it was the last insult any student would ever make about Casey Haughton in front of Junior.

"You have to learn to control your anger," Brother Gay said to him. "Otherwise, people are gonna take you off a cliff with them, Junior. They'll use your anger to manipulate you. You've got a great opportunity awaiting you at Langston in New York. Don't let it slip away."

Around the neighborhood, the jokes continued. The kids called Junior stupid and prophesized that he'd flunk and end up back in Brooke's Rowe. Strangely, Sandy experienced the same treatment down at the post office. The gossip gallery claimed that Sandy Robinson had gone off the deep end after losing Lawrence and that she and Senior were not capable of taking care of Junior. The rumor going around was that the Robinsons needed a white girl with orange hair to save them. On a job in North Philly, Senior got himself arrested for belting a client across the jaw for saying that *his* kid needed a white girl to save him. As Sandy arrived at the precinct to pick him up, he sat by himself inside a steel cage like a manic gorilla.

In the waning weeks, before Junior was scheduled to depart from Brooke's Rowe, Sandy grew anxious over the move. She popped into Junior's bedroom often, asking to watch him write poetry or play video games. At night, Junior would hear his mother still awake and restless downstairs before Senior would try to con her into coming to bed.

"No, really," she'd say to him. "I'm OK. I feel fine. Everything is fine. I feel... good."

Junior's mother was *not* good. She was unusual. She took up smoking again. After school, when she arrived to pick him up, Junior would look at Sandy's face and know she'd been crying on the way to get him. At home, she spent an inordinate amount of time looking at old pictures of him and Lawrence at their old house in Crawford. One night, Junior awoke to see his mother standing at his doorway. Careful not to make her feel ashamed for being there, he pretended to be asleep. The morning after, Junior overheard Sandy tell Senior of a nightmare she had. In a dream, she received a phone call from Casey that Junior had been killed on his way home from school in New York. Senior brushed off his wife's apprehensions as nerves getting the best of her.

"It'll be alright," he comforted her. "That's just that old devil workin' your nerves again."

On the contrary, on the television after dinner that evening, Junior saw his mother jump around the living room over a kid name Clyde McNeal. Like Junior, Clyde was fourteen years old. And, like Junior, he was on his way from school when a boy robbed and killed him. The sighting of

Clyde's sneaker poking beneath a white sheet on Kennedy Street kept Sandy up throughout the night. At 2 a.m., Junior found his mother hunched over the kitchen sink with a cigarette in her hand. Before he could say anything, Sandy gave her affirmation. "I don't care if I go from one pack to six-packs of cigarettes a day," she told him. "You're gettin' the fuck from around here."

Later that same afternoon, Sandy choked through the phone line with Senior over the story of Clyde McNeal. "They showed his foot and everything!" she complained. "I just can't imagine that being *us* again." Doubting her parenting skills, Sandy called herself every name in the book from a bad mother to being inadequate for sending Junior off to New York and failing to protect Lawrence. She whined into the receiver as Senior listened. The stress of her colleagues' insults and letting Junior go had finally broken her.

"It's a good move. Fuck what they think," he told her. "That girl loves that boy, Sandy. What person you know would help pay the boy's tuition up there? You can hardly get a sumbitch to pay back what they owe."

Laughing in agreement, Sandy hung up the phone. Right after, she walked from her office down to the lavatory to freshen up from a thudding headache. In the bathroom mirror, she splashed her face with ice-cold water and adjusted her hair before noticing that her mouth appeared slightly crooked. The top of Sandy's head pounded harder as if someone had struck her with a baseball bat. Her left foot and hand suddenly curled inward. Knowing something was wrong, she attempted to run and fell over onto her face. As her headache worsened and the limbs on her left side tightened harder, she began screaming for help. Soon, her voice changed to a muffled cry as the vocal cords in her neck felt weaker. The lavatory became dark and cold as images of Junior and Lawrence burned through her mind. Her wedding day. The purchase of her first car. Graduation from high school and every other major life event took shape. Near unconsciousness, she felt her world becoming darker and quieter. Thankfully, a co-worker who had lost her keys went looking for them in the bathroom and found Sandy lying face down on the floor of the restroom. The last Sandy remembered, she was on her way to the hospital and overheard a paramedic claiming she'd suffered a stroke. Junior learned about his mother through Brother Gay, who had received a call from Senior via Casey's phone. Strangely, when the hospital entered Sandy's last name into their system to look for an emergency contact, they had two numbers listed. One of those numbers belonged to Casey, who had placed her name as a contact for Junior after he was assaulted on his way home from Medgar. Both Senior and Casey rushed to the hospital to be at Sandy's side.

When Junior got down to the hospital, doctors confirmed that Sandy had suffered an ischemic stroke to her brainstem. Senior was there sitting beside his wife in the ICU next to Casey. Courtney arrived a short time later. Senior asked doctors about a thousand questions while

Junior sat holding his mother's still hand. Unfortunately for Sandy, she had several hereditary risk factors for her stroke, but doctors highlighted the cause was due to stress. Being a black mother in Brooke's Rowe was a major risk for stroke. When Senior told doctors about the incident from last summer, doctors nodded at one another.

"We lost a son recently," he explained. "And we're getting ready to lose another one real soon. He's headed up to New York." Senior wrapped his arm around Junior as his voice began to change. "He's gonna do a great job up there, right son?"

In the parking lot garage, Junior wailed onto Casey, blaming himself for Sandy's illness, Lawrence, and for wanting to leave Brooke's Rowe.

"This is my fault! I knew she was under so much stress already, but I kept on beggin'. If I would've never went to New York, this wouldn't have happened!"

"No, it isn't, J.," said Casey. "It's nobody's fault. It just happened. It's not your fault!"

"Yes, it is! I should've never gone to New York. I shouldn't have said a fuckin' word!"

In the hospital's chapel next to Casey and Courtney, Junior's daddy prayed for Sandy to wake in one piece. It was one of the few times Senior asked God for anything. He favored his own religion, but not on that night. He relied on the Holy Spirit to revive his wife.

Throughout the night, Junior sat beside his mother in a chair while Senior stood outside talking with doctors along with Casey and her sister. The left side of Sandy's face was slanted and the fingers on her hand were stiff. Within that time, relatives had dropped in to visit Sandy, some losing it out in the hallway, while others began their investigation into what had happened to her. As increasing anxiety built over the circumstances leading to Sandy's stroke, Junior decided that evening that New York was a foregone conclusion. He was destined to Brooke's Rowe and would remain there to care for his mother in her time of need.

From what doctors could tell, the stroke had occurred on the right side of Sandy's brainstem which affected her left side. Her left hand was curled into a tight fist as if she was holding a handful of quarters, her foot pulled inward and she had limited vision in her left eye. But the next morning, Junior and his daddy were given some good news. Sandy had survived — and would have a long recovery ahead of her. Doctors said her survival was a miracle and that her road to recovery would be filled with years of therapy. It was a short but delicate win for Junior's family — as well as for Casey, who had been adopted into the family tree. With Sandy now fully dependent, Junior thanked Casey and her sister for supporting him before kindly turning down the opportunity to attend Langston. Brooke's Rowe was his ultimate fate.

"Y'all have been so good to me – to us," he said. "But with mom the way she is now, there's no way I can leave her behind."

Junior attempted to hand Casey back his key to their townhouse in Fort Foote.

"No! You keep that!" she told him. "You're my brother, J. You'll always have a home in New York. No matter what. Take care of your mom."

As they exchanged hugs, Casey and her sister left, and Junior returned to his mother's side.

> *I need a loyalty like the sun in the sky,*
> *shining over me*
> *Brightening my little dark world each day.*
>
> LEONARD G. ROBINSON JR.

Recovery

In the following week, Sandy made small but considerable gains. As her mind succumbed to the reality of what had happened, she lashed out at staff, cussing at doctors and nurses alike. From her crooked mouth, she talked recklessly, worried to hell about her current state. To ease his parents' anxieties, Junior told Senior and Sandy of his plans to remain in Brooke's Rowe.

Rehab was hell for Sandy. Her day began first with breakfast at 7 a.m. followed by occupational, speech, and physical therapy. At 11 a.m., doctors wheeled Sandy back to her room for lunch where Senior would be there waiting for her. Afterward, Sandy headed back to the rehab gym for more training and occupational therapy until 4 p.m. Junior didn't miss a day. He divided his time between school and catching the bus to see Sandy at the hospital. Some days, he was fortunate enough to bum a ride from his teacher, Brother Gay, while taking turns with Senior to stay overnight. Junior spent his nights reading poetry or entertaining his mother by mimicking Senior.

"That sumbitch owe me forty goddamn dollars!" he imitated. "Where's my hammer?!"

With a crooked smile, Sandy would laugh, patting onto her good leg.

Like all patients, Sandy had her good days and bad days. One day, while Junior was there visiting during OT, a young, blonde-haired intern from Boston named Madelyn wheeled Sandy in front of a mirror to re-teach her how to comb her hair. To demonstrate, Madelyn combed her hair with a comb from her pants pocket. Sandy watched as the fine-toothed comb drove through the intern's straight blonde hair without restriction.

"That won't work on my head," said Sandy. "Our hair is different."

Believing she had given up, Madelyn demonstrated again and again on her head then nodded for Sandy to try. Sandy placed the comb in her affected hand and painfully tried to raise her arm high enough to comb. It lodged into her hair.

"Oh, darn!" said Madelyn. "I'll show you again, Mrs. Robinson. Here, watch me."

Junior didn't care for the young, freckled-faced intern and nor did Sandy. She was snobby at times and exuded the aura of a stuck-up brat. On their first day together, Madelyn reported to her supervisor that she believed Sandy was not trying hard enough. Once, when Sandy told the intern that she had to use the bathroom, Madelyn barely helped her. Now, she was trying to tell Junior and his mother that combing white hair was no different than black hair.

"You're doing it wrong again," said Madelyn. "Would you like some help?"

Sandy didn't respond a word to Madelyn. Instead, she went about combing her hair as best as she could. Rather than let up, the intern continued beleaguering Sandy. Irritated, Sandy threw her comb down onto the floor and kicked it with her good foot.

"That's enough," she grumbled. "We'll try again later."

"How do you expect to get better if you give up, Mrs. Robinson?" said Madelyn, reaching down to pick up the comb. "Would you like me to show you again? We'll go much slower this time. Would that help?"

"No, it won't."

"How do you know?"

"Because black hair ain't like white hair, bitch! That's why!"

Later, in the hospital cafeteria, Junior watched as his mother attempted to feed herself with her fork using her affected hand. As mashed potatoes and celery spilled onto her lap, Sandy became angry and used her hand to dig into her plate of food like a Neanderthal. As spectators watched, she became furious, cursing at them as Junior attempted to roll his mother away to keep from embarrassing herself.

With just days left on Casey's lease agreement before she

officially moved to New York, Junior got the nod from Senior to visit with Casey. In her car, out in the hospital lot, she gifted him with a key to her heart, assuring Junior's decision to remain in Philly was the right one.

"I'm not a big religious person, but God is truly gonna bless you, J.," she told him. "You've got a heart of gold, yo. After I get settled in New York, I'll be back down to visit."

Then, after a warm embrace, Junior watched as Casey's car vanished off into the distance. Afterward, Junior took the long walk back inside.

A month passed by with more of the same, Junior watching as Sandy fought to regain her independence and restore what normalcy she had had before her stroke. Her improvement was small but steady. When asked during therapy about her long-term goals, Sandy told her therapist she hoped to be around to see Junior graduate from high school.

"He's so sweet, my precious Junior." She teared up as he sat next to her. "He reads me little poems every night before bed. He's gonna be the first man in our family to graduate high school. I hope I'm around to see it."

Once a week, every Friday for one hour, Junior sat with his mother during therapy.

"Perhaps you ought to stick around," Sandy's therapist whispered to Junior. "You give her a reason to smile, and our sessions go a lot smoother." With each session, Junior noticed an improvement in his mother's behavior. For Junior, it was nullifying to see Sandy able to decompress all her forty-one years of living into one room. Although it ended in mourning, it was encouraging for her to go on. On the subject of her childhood, Sandy would kindly ask Junior to step out. Senior attended the meetings also, but briefly. Between work and caring for both his wife and their crumbling home, he was burdened with twice the load as Junior. He'd show up at the hospital on his night with Sandy and crash beside her in the chair until the next morning.

One Friday after school, Junior was disappointed to learn that Sandy had canceled her therapy appointment. With her affected hand still cupped into a tight fist, she motioned to Junior with her good hand. "Watch this, Junior!" On her own, she then stood up and counted to ten before falling back into her chair, exhausted. It was the first time Junior had seen his mother stand up in nearly a month.

"Yo, that's good!" Junior celebrated. "When'd you start doing that?!"

"Just today." She cheesed. "Anything is possible. I always taught you boys that."

"You taught us a lot of things."

"Yeah," Sandy sighed. "You know…if I could, I'd throw you 'cross my lap and wheel you up there to New York so you could go to that school. I hate having you stuck here with me like this. It's not good for you – or me, Junior."

"You're my mother. I could never leave you. However this goes, I'll be by your side."

"I wouldn't have it any other way." Sandy touched his hand. "Except for this time…"

Stunned by Sandy's sudden epiphany, Junior launched onto his feet as Sandy attempted to speak life into him.

"You've done us proud and given me the world, my first-born son," she explained. "Now, I think it's time for you to begin your mark on our family tree. I want you to go to that school in New York. I want you to do well, and I wanna come to see you graduate."

Junior couldn't believe his mother's strength – that she was willing to overlook her own devastation for her son astounded him. Junior had no words for Sandy that Friday afternoon in her room.

"You got to go on with your life, Junior," said Sandy. "You can't put your life on hold – not even for me. You did it for Lawrence. That's more than enough. I talked to your daddy about it the other day while you were at school. He's onboard."

"How in the world can I go to New York with you down here like this?" he asked.

"I won't force you," she told him. "But I'd at least like you to think it over."

The air became heavy for Junior as he attempted to digest Sandy's wish for him to leave Brooke's Rowe. For fourteen years, Sandy had been his shelter amidst the storm of rejection. In the wake of losing Lawrence, he and Sandy had bonded closer together. Now, she was asking him to build his own shelter. It was a tall order for a teenager who had yet to get his driver's license. Holding Sandy by the hand, Junior asked for the day to think over New York. Sandy gave him the weekend. Unsure of what to make of his mother's wishes, Junior confided in the one person who would help him make such a decision: Brother Gay.

The following Monday, Junior waited until after the bell to consult with his new teacher. He had spent much of the day gazing out into the world, weighing his fate about whether to leave or stay. During his lunch period, Junior spent the afternoon hiding out in room 328, his old secret hideout, unsure of what to make of leaving Philly behind. Contemplating what road to take, his mind veered and wandered. As soon as classes ended, Junior was the first to the front of the room to ask Brother Gay to stay behind.

"I'm here until 7 p.m. every night and no kid has *ever* asked for me to stay after!" he laughed. "So, what is it? Mathematics? History? English? Which one?"

"Geography," said Junior.

It didn't dawn on Brother Gay instantly: geography. Before long, however, he sat on the corner of his desk to indulge his pupil that afternoon. Junior gave his teacher the backstory of his rugged life in Philly. As Junior told his story, Brother Gay stroked his bearded chin. Rewinding his life from the past year, Junior told the story of Lawrence and how his family's world had been devastated since the loss.

"I keep this picture of him in my wallet." He showed his teacher. "Mom said she had a dream for us to graduate from high school. No other Robinson on my tree has done that. The only thing we've ever graduated from is probation."

Looking over Lawrence's cute smile, he handed Junior

back his photo and went back to stroking his beard, gently pulling on it and releasing it. His poker face remained intact.

"If I stay," Junior explained, "I do what's right and that's taking care of mom. If I go, I leave behind what little family I got left. New York will always be there. I've got time."

"You don't got time, Junior," Brother Gay told him. "Time got you. Remember that. Time has got you. Time doesn't wait for us. You don't know what's on time's mind."

Enlightened, Junior leaned in closer to listen. The room was quiet except for the wall fan spinning next to the clock above the room door. Brother Gay's timeless philosophy slowed Junior's thoughts enough for him to absorb the analogy.

"Some of these kids here are fifteen going on fifty," said Brother Gay. "The lives they've had to live is disheartening. They're lost, some of them. They've got criminal records before seventeen. They're out in the streets at night because their parents are strung out on crack. Most of them won't live to see twenty-five. That's a shame."

Junior got straight to the point. "So, what should I do?" he asked. "I'm lost. Help me."

Brother Gay popped onto his feet and walked behind his desk.

"It's an opportunity, Junior," he said to him. "Few folks in the ghetto get a break – that's what I believe your mom is trying to instill in you. Going to Langston would give your mother something to strive for, to see her son graduate. That makes it worth it in my book."

As Junior exhaled in wonder, digesting Brother Gay's advice, his teacher threw on his coat.

"So, how about a ride over to the hospital?" he offered. "It's on the way."

Blossom my child.
Don't cover up too long.
Don't stay hidden for so long
beneath the fabric of doubt.
Open up! Release your vibrancy!

LONNIE "SANDY" ROBINSON

Gratitude

When Junior walked into the hospital Monday after school, he entered his mother's room to find her asleep in bed with the remote still in her hand. Careful not to disturb her, Junior removed his jacket and laid it across the chair. Standing beside her bed, Junior rehearsed inside his head what to say about New York. Despite Brother Gay's advice, he was still unsure if leaving Brooke's Rowe was the right move. He looked down at Sandy's cupped fist. Although her slanted face had restored some, she was a world away from making a full recovery.

As Junior opened his mouth to speak, his words evaporated into thin air. Losing Lawrence back in '94 crossed Junior's mind; by going to New York, would he just be running from his troubles? A second attempt to wake his mother failed miserably. The thought of telling Sandy that he was leaving her behind for New York was overwhelming. Junior wondered what was going on inside his mother's head in regards to Langston. Would attending Langston aid Sandy's recovery by motivating her to see him graduate?

He thought about Senior. Since Lawrence's death, Junior had been the balance between many volatile discussions at home which had ended in broken furniture and holes in the wall. He wondered what his absence would do to his parents' marriage. Finally, with all his courage, he moved his lips to speak. The words rolled from his tongue unscripted and organically.

"If going to New York will help you get better, I'd go tonight."

Sandy's eyes opened immediately. "What's that, dear?" she asked him.

Junior cleared his voice and spoke again. "I said, if going to New York would help you to get better, I'd go tonight if I could."

Her face softened at Junior as she invited him in close for a hug. As the two embraced, Senior appeared at the door with Sandy's dinner from the cafeteria. Nervous about his daddy's reaction to his decision to leave, Junior tripped over his words before Senior set Sandy's tray of food down and looked at him.

"Well, son." Senior reached into his pocket and placed a quarter into Junior's hand. "Always remember: If it's right for you, then it ain't no need for you to explain yourself. We understand. Why don't you make that call while you still can?"

Relieved by their validation, Junior excused himself out into the hallway to make a phone call to Casey. She answered on the first ring, and rather than a drawn-out explanation of how he had changed his mind about Langston, Junior kept it short.

"I'm ready, Casey," he told her.

Early Tuesday morning, Junior wheeled his mother around the hospital's complex to a window overlooking the courtyard. Shortly thereafter, the two ate breakfast and talked up Fort Foote, New York. The transition instituted new guidelines for Junior as he was now under the courtesy of Casey's care.

"The zip code may be different, but the rules are not," she told him. "Don't you disappoint us up there! Make us proud, Junior. As soon as I get well enough, I'll be there to see you walk. And walk you will. Love you, son."

With his heart on the outside of his jacket, Junior knelt next to his mother's wheelchair and kissed her hand. He then placed his mother's hand against his cheek, hoping his warmth would restore what loss of function had occurred after her stroke. Before long, Senior showed up and placed his huge hand across his son's back. He looked up to the sky to where his daddy's head was and stared into his father's grim eyes. Not a tear was shed as neither said a word. Senior then offered his hand for Junior to shake.

"I'll call as soon as I get to New York," Junior promised. "First phone I see. I won't even put my bags down. I'll be back Friday – that's for sure. It'll be like I never left."

As Junior started toward the elevator, his daddy called out to him.

"Junior?" he said. "Fort Foote ain't Brooke's Rowe. Show 'em how we do it down here."

Grinning back, Junior disappeared into the elevator. Waiting for him outside, in her car was Casey Haughton, his big sissy. With his bags packed and loaded in the back seat, Junior took a breath of hometown air and plopped into the front seat.

"All set?" she asked him.

"One more stop," Junior requested.

As Casey parked her car out front of Medgar Evers Secondary School, Junior asked if she could give him ten minutes to say goodbye to Brother Gay. He ascended the staircase and passed by the crumbling mural of the school's namesake and his contemporaries on the wall. The dice shooters who Sandy had tormented six months earlier were still out there. They stared at Junior as he stared back at them, unphased. Six months ago, he'd walked with his head slumped and his hands shoved into his pockets. That day, however, he walked upright.

"Th'fuck you lookin' at, nigga?" one boy said.

"Nothing at all," said Junior as he vanished into Medgar.

It was just after 11 a.m. when Junior entered Mr. Levy's office to inform his old principal that he was withdrawing. In his usual stupor, Mr. Levy leaned on his chair with his arms folded across his fat chest.

"You can't," he said. "Only a parent or guardian has the authority to withdraw a student."

"My dad will bring the paperwork over this week."

Mr. Levy looked him up and down. "You'll be back. Sure enough. Just like everybody else."

In mocking audacity, he then extended his hand out for Junior to shake. Junior paused, thinking of the perfect get-back at Mr. Levy's attempt to doom his future. He referred to the quote inscribed beneath the mural of Medgar Evers out in front of the school.

"You can kill a man but you can't kill an idea, Mr. Levy," he told his principal.

He shook his head at Mr. Levy and left.

For his last stop, Junior appeared at the door of room 454. The moment his old teacher saw him standing there, Brother Gay interrupted himself at the board.

"So, you out?" he asked.

"It was too good to pass up," Junior said, shrugging. "You were right."

Impressed, Brother Gay nodded his head at Junior. Flabbergasted, his classmates stood in awe of him as he stood near the door, refusing to take his seat.

"Don't be a stranger, Junior," said Brother Gay.

"I won't, sir. Thanks for everything."

Upon leaving the building, Junior descended the stairs to where Casey was waiting for him outside in the lot. He took one last look around at Medgar and breathed in the February cold. He felt like a wrongfully convicted man on death row who had finally been afforded justice. A small smile appeared on his handsome face as he opened the car door. Junior threw on his seatbelt and exhaled again.

"Ready? Casey asked him.

"Yeah," he said. "I'm ready."

The ride into New York was filled with reflection. Along the way, Casey's car passed by Hyatt Park where Lawrence was buried. Junior thought of his brother's last words to him. In his heart, he asked Lawrence to forgive him for leaving him behind.

From the interstate, he stared into the eyeball of Philly from his rearview mirror, watching as his hometown slowly faded from view. Guilt washed over him during the ride as Junior imagined Sandy's slanted face missing him with each passing mile. He wondered how Senior would fare without him there during the week. A bittersweet tear left his eye the moment Casey's car reached the New York line. For Junior, New York was more than poetry. It was paving the way for giving him a new life, bigger and greater than the one he had grown to know. It was about perseverance after navigating through a tough life which many failed to escape, including his parents.

At his new home, located on the outskirts of New York City in a small township called Fort Foote, Junior fished out his key and opened the door. The second his nostrils reached the foyer, he smelled his favorite scent – Domino's Pizza. Posted on the walls of their colonial-style living room were pictures of Casey from her teenage years along with Courtney. With his bags hooked over his shoulders, he lugged his stuff up the wooden staircase and into his bedroom at the end of the hall.

As he turned the light on in his bedroom, the ceiling fan hummed to a gentle spin. He spotted a poster of the Philadelphia Eagles' quarterback, Randall Cunningham, posted on the wall next to a picture of Whitney Houston. Next to his celebrity crush was a framed, polaroid image of the mural of Medgar Evers from his old school. Written below on the white was the same quote he had used to disarm Mr. Levy earlier: "You can kill a man, but you can't kill an idea." Next to his freshly made bed was a work desk along with a new journal wrapped in a pretty bow sitting on top. Also on the desk was a framed photo of Junior and Lawrence taken during the summer of '93. It was the exact photo on his nightstand in Brooke's Rowe. Standing behind Junior at his bedroom door was Casey, waiting to welcome him.

"Hope you like it?" she asked. "Your mom helped out with some of the ideas. I wanted it to feel special, Junior. Like home, you know?"

Junior placed his bags onto his bed and walked over to Casey.

"This *is* special," said Junior. "And so are you. Casey… Yo, I just…I don't have any words for all that you've done for me. I don't know *how* in the world I can repay you, but one day I will."

"You don't owe me anything except a high school diploma, and the promise that you'll make this journey worth it for all of us."

"I promise." Junior grabbed her by the hand. "Thank you."

As the two toured throughout the room, Casey walked

Junior over to his bedroom window to show him a nightly view of the Empire State Building lurking in the city's backdrop. The feeling of being in New York was euphoric to Junior. With Casey's help, he opened his new bedroom window to catch a glimpse of the February moon sitting atop his adopted hometown. Beside him on his nightstand, the sound of a pager sliding across the wooden furniture sounded like city construction.

"Just in case we need to reach you," laughed Casey. "I wanted to get you a phone with a few minutes on it, but your dad said, no. *'Boy barely keeps his room clean. I ain't buying no goddamn phone',*" she mocked as they both shared a harmonious laugh. "I'm really glad you've decided to come live with us, Junior. You're gonna do well at Langston."

Junior looked at the number on his pager and noticed it was from a Philadelphia area code. He grabbed the portable phone next to his bed and dialed the number back. Sandy answered on the first ring. It was the phone from inside her room.

"Junior?! Junior?!" Sandy hollered. "You won't believe what I just did. I just called you with my bad hand! Can you believe that?! The doctor says I can start outpatient therapy in another couple of weeks! That means I can go home!"

Delighted by the great news, Junior looked over at Casey and beamed as she smiled back. Before leaving him to talk, Casey whispered into his other ear.

"Don't stay up too late, J.," she said. "We register at Langston tomorrow!"

The End

School fools with kindness.
Bless worry with wisdom.
Burn yearns for chaos.
That is my religion.

—LEONARD G. ROBINSON JR.

Epilogue

GRADUATION 1999

Buried behind a pile of library books at a back table inside Langston's library in Fort Foote, New York, Junior found himself intoxicated by the sanctity of his latest poem. Lost in his works, the headset to his portable Walkman blared as he took a break from completing his valedictorian speech for his high school graduation scheduled that Saturday. With six days to go, Junior had decided to spend his eighteenth birthday preparing for the unfathomable: finding a few words to describe his experiences over the passing years. He reached into his backpack for his latest hip-hop CD entitled *Things*

Fall Apart, by The Roots. Bobbing his head to his favorite track, Junior failed to notice the group of knuckleheaded troublemakers entering the library. Obnoxious and oblivious to their peers around them, the agitators – two boys, and a girl – made their way to the back of Langston's library to where Junior was preparing for the speech of his life. Upon finding him stuffed inside of his journal, the group decided to confront him. Meanwhile, Junior was unmindful of the danger ahead of him. To bedevil him, the group decided to approach him from behind.

While multitasking on his speech and a manuscript for his first-ever poetry book, he felt the sensation of a warm tongue slide across the back of his neck. Alarmed, Junior's pencil skidded across the page of his journal as he shot onto his feet, slamming his knee into the table. Removing his Walkman, Junior turned to find his girlfriend, Vanessa, along with his two friends, Melvin and Eugene. As the hairs on the back of Junior's neck stood erect from Vanessa's perfect kiss, Junior slumped down into his chair and balked at his graduating class members as they teased him.

"Y'all are fucked up!" He violently erased his page. "What if that was the speech?!"

"Did you really think we'd let you work all day?" Vanessa asked him. "It's your birthday. C'mon. Everyone is waiting back at the house, Junior."

"Ten more minutes."

As Junior attempted to reach for his Walkman, Melvin ripped the headphones from his Sony CD player and Eugene took Junior's journal. Scowling, mad, Junior glared at his buddy Eugene.

"Yo, Gene! Quit playin'," he fussed. "Do you remember what I told you about the last kid to mess with my journal? That's what's gonna happen if you keep on!"

"Junior, listen to your girl, man," said Melvin. "It's your birthday. Your parents came all the way up here from Philly to see you. You still got six days – you can take *one* of those days off, bruh. I promise. Tomorrow, we'll all help. Casey got your favorite: Domino's pizza!"

Domino's had always been the magic word since Junior was young. Conceding to his insatiable hunger, Junior began to pack up his books as both Melvin and Eugene ran down to book the next shuttle to Junior's New York neighborhood. Frustrated by the interruption, Junior stuffed his books inside of his bag as Vanessa placed her hand over his, stopping him.

"Don't be upset with the homies." She wrapped Junior in her arms before caressing the sprinkle of adolescent fuzz around his soft face. "Meet us on the shuttle?"

As Junior went to roll his eyes, Vanessa kissed him again.

"Love you, too." He kissed her back. "Let me get up all this stuff, and I'll be down."

Caught up in the moment, Junior took a glance around Langston's library at the mound of underclassmen working, some buried behind their IBM computers.

Nearly four years earlier, Junior had entered Langston's doors as a shy and quiet kid afraid of his own shadow. Now, he was leaving Langston as a young man, prepared to take on the challenges awaiting him in the everyday world. As he zipped up his loaded backpack, he thought about his long road beginning on Joseph Boulevard in North Philly before his unfortunate detour to Brooke's Rowe on the southside of town. He then closed his eyes and thought of his younger brother, Lawrence, who in Junior's mind had sacrificed his life for Junior to discover writing as an outlet. Overwhelmed with bittersweet joy and pain, he stood beside the window and stared out into the bushy landscape of Langston's campus.

Down below, Junior watched as Vanessa, his lover, stood next to an awaiting shuttle bus. The two had found each other going into their sophomore year when a mutual friend, Melvin, had introduced the two at a play. Initially, Vanessa wanted no part of the joyless boy from Brooke's Rowe who filled blank journals he bought down at the drug store. But after seeing him perform a live read at a school event in July of '97, Vanessa had taken an interest in Junior and pursued him. "You're nothin' like any of these boys here I've ever met." She wrote down her home telephone number inside his hand. "Shall we get ice cream?" It went from ice cream to the movies, and then to Junior's first kiss. Vanessa was nothing like any girl Junior had met before either. At 5'2, she wore a nose ring, and had hazelnut eyes, kinky hair and came from a well-to-do family unlike Junior.

As the two lovebirds noticed each other, she blew Junior a kiss, pointed at her watch, playfully threw up her arms, and smiled at him. Vanessa was right, it *was* time to celebrate.

Shortly thereafter, Junior exited Langston's library and boarded the bus with Vanessa, Melvin, and Gene for the ride back to his Fort Foote townhouse.

For Junior, the ride home was quiet as he chose to partake in a flow of nostalgic thoughts on his eighteen years. In less than a moment, he would be surrounded by a living room filled with precious supporters who had made his journey possible. Holding Vanessa by the hand, Junior leaned down to kiss the back of his lover's hand.

"What was that for?" she asked him.

"Just 'cause," he said. "If only you knew."

Near the front of their shuttle were Junior's two best friends, Melvin and Eugene. Since Junior had started at Langston as a freshman in March of '96, they'd taken him under their wing, introducing him to the New York way of life while respecting his Philadelphian roots. As Junior's eyes wandered throughout the passing trees on the cobble-stoned roadway, he nodded to Melvin sitting near the front of the bus. Melvin, not the mushy type, mouthed the words "fuck you" back at him. Unlike the boys at Medgar, however, Melvin's 'fuck you's' were full of love.

As their shuttle arrived on Ellis Street in Fort Foote, Junior stepped off, took in the spring air, and looked to his left and right. Parked in front of the townhouse was his mother's unstable Buick along with a host of other cars he hadn't seen in some time. Lost between nerves and grate-fulness, he shooed Melvin and Gene away, as he felt the spirit of his emotions coming onto him. As ordered, the boys ascended the staircase as Junior and Vanessa took a short walk up the street.

"Lawrence should be here, man." He shook his head. "It seems like yesterday that I was just living in Crawford with him. Sometimes, I feel like I don't deserve any of this, Vanessa."

"What happened to Lawrence wasn't your fault, Junior," she told him. "OK? It's not your fault. It was just...life, you know? And we both know life sucks sometimes. But we gotta make the best of it while we can, right?" She kissed him. "C'mon babe, everybody's waitin'." She held his face. "Your parents. Casey, and her sister, Courtney, Brother Gay from your old school. Melvin. Gene. Me...Lawrence, too."

Junior placed his hand onto Vanessa's face and kept it there.

"You're right," sighed Junior.

With her hand at the small of his back, Vanessa led him up the stairway. Reaching into his pocket, Junior removed the house key Casey had once given to him and placed it in the lock. As the door pushed open, the filled living room erupted at his grandiose arrival. Before Junior could remove his backpack, Sandy wobbled across the living room on her cane. Her face was still groggy from the stroke she had sustained three and a half years earlier. She rushed to the door with motherly kisses.

"I'm *so* proud of you," Sandy told him. "Valedictorian *and* a scholarship to Steny College?"

As Sandy pecked Junior's face with more kisses, Senior rose from the sofa to greet Junior. His menacing scowl – which had terrified Junior once upon a time – was replaced with a charming grin before opening to the widest smile Junior had ever seen from his daddy. With his bag still looped onto his arm, Junior placed his hand in Senior's wide hand.

"I second that. You did damn good, son." Senior patted him on the shoulder. "Come Saturday, you'll be the first man in our family to graduate from high school. That's a helluva lot to be thankful for. And I'm proud of you."

"Thanks, dad." Junior cheesed.

Across the living room, Brother Gay toasted Courtney Haughton with a glass of champagne before acknowledging Junior encircled by his family and Vanessa. Removing his glasses, he strolled over to Junior and placed a hand on his former pupil's shoulder. Surprised by his appearance, Junior gave his ex-teacher a fist bump.

"Yo, Brother Gay!" he chuckled. "When'd you get in?"

"About an hour ago, Junior," he said. "Came straight in from Cleveland. Had to check on Mom. Wouldn't miss a chance to see you again, though. It's been over three years."

For Junior, three years felt like a lifetime. Between departing from Brooke's Rowe to Fort Foote, his life had changed drastically since the days of Mrs. Hawkins, Mr. Levy, and the perils of hardship he'd experience at Medgar. According to Brother Gay, Junior's old school was under serious reconstruction after the superintendent fired his old principal. Medgar would experience wholesale changes with Brother Gay leading the pack. Junior's ex-teacher from room 454 had promoted up the ranks.

"I made Vice Principal." Brother Gay lit up. "Gonna do the best I can to see that the right changes happen at Medgar.

Who knows when the next 'Junior' might come along?"

As the two laughed, Casey, walked out of the kitchen wearing an apron, playing hostess to their guests. Casey, now thirty-two, and with gray streaks throughout her orange hair, lit up like Christmas in New York when she laid eyes on Junior. Junior's young heart became tunnel-visioned as his eyes met Casey's. Excusing himself, he traveled across the room and held her as his supporters gestured appropriately.

"I love you," he said to her.

"Not like I love you, Junior," she said back.

A tear left Junior's eye as he then turned around to acknowledge a group of his cherished supporters. Moved by their encouragement, he struggled to find the words.

"Y'all are just..." His voice fractured. "Y'all are just too much." He shook his head. "I never thought I'd see the day where little old me could fill a room. Thanks for being here."

Melvin, known for his quintessential "fuck you's", found himself lost in the moment of Junior's humility and graciousness.

"No doubt, Junior," he told him. "We got you, homie."

Brushing through the crowd, Vanessa showed up to kiss Junior as the room oohed with amazement before Sandy rushed in to cockblock their romance. "No babies!" she yelled with a joking-but-dead-serious tone to the amusement of the room. The room clapped in awe of Junior. Casey began dishing out slices of Junior's favorite snack: Domino's pizza with pepperoni, sausage, and extra cheese.

Holding hands, the room gathered in prayer as Junior led

the chorus of thanks for his eighteen years. With his eyes tightly sealed, he paused as he reflected on the day Lawrence was killed. Somewhere in his heart, he felt his brother's winsome smile encouraging him to go on. As he exhaled, he cracked his eyes to steal a peep around the room at his supporters, fulfillment painted on their faces. Before saying "Amen", Junior closed with a poem he'd written in Langston's library less than an hour early.

> *Whatever you do*
> *or wherever you go,*
> *you're never too far*
> *from the place you'll always know.*
> *Thank you, Crawford.*
> *Thank you, Brooke's Rowe.*
> *For making me into the man,*
> *this great family has come to know.*
>
> LEONARD G. ROBINSON JR.

Junior's words tapped into the hearts of friends and family there. He had persevered beyond his poetry, one line at a time.

Acknowledgments

Thank you for reading *Beyond Poetry*. The creation of this delicate work would not be possible without an outpouring of support from family, friends, and of course, my many fans who saddled beside me throughout this literary journey. I would like to take this time to fully acknowledge my supporters and to thank them for their encouragement.

First and foremost, I would like to take this moment to thank God for giving me the strength and discipline needed to write. The resiliency required to complete this novel took an indelible commitment. It was a labor of love. To God be the glory for this gift.

To my wife, Tiffani. Sweetheart, thank you for putting up with me these past two years. Thank you for allowing me space and time needed to write *Beyond Poetry*. Some of those days, I spent more time in front of my computer than beside you which is where I should've been. You stuck it out with me anyway, seeing my vision by allowing me the opportunity to endeavor in my dreams uninterrupted. Thank you for believing in me.

To my mother, Diane, for your sustained love and investment in my education early on. As a youth, my mother instilled the affectionate principles that with upstanding character, hard work, and dedication, you can go far in this world. Thank you for investing in my dream to write by harvesting this seed so that I may sprout.

To the Blackwell and Williams family, thank you for your love, kindness, and for allowing me a place on your family tree.

To my dear friend and brother, Pastor Eugene Pearson, and his congregation at Mount Pleasant Baptist Church. Thank you for lifting my wife and me during our darkest hour and for visiting us at the hospital with words of love and well-wishes.

Speaking of hospitals, I would like to extend a special thanks to the staff at the Virginia Hospital Center's Stroke Recovery Unit. Your professionalism and support of our family have left a genuine impression on us for the need of front-line workers fighting the good fight every day to keep families safe and warm.

To Megan McDonough, a writer with the *Washington Post*, thank you for your lovely feature article about my wife and me.

To my therapist, Mrs. Denyse Fritz-Joefield, thank you for the healing words during the 2020 pandemic and your support.

To actor and director, Bill Duke, thank you for being an influencer in my life and your dedication to teaching young artists the fundamentals of striving for what you believe in with dignity and integrity.

To my editor, Katie, and my friends at Darling Axe. I am forever grateful for the incomparable services provided to this delicate novel. Thank you for helping to paint this story into a reality, and thank you for your professional commitment to *Beyond Poetry*.

To the great city of Cheverly, thank you for showing me what it is to live in a close-knit community, to develop lasting relationships, and to harbor the insatiable nostalgia I get each time I return to visit. Many of my great friends from yesteryear have since moved on, but their memories still live within me. Remember to live in the present. Enjoy the moment. Before you know it, this short life will all be over.

To my family and friends whose names I've forgotten, forgive me. You all are in my heart.

Beyond Poetry is dedicated to the memory of my father, Roosevelt, and brother, Jerrard.

Rest in paradise.

Beyond Poetry Glossary

There were a host of meaningful poems used throughout *Beyond Poetry*. As a gift, I present to you, the reader, a collection of poems used in the book. I've also added a few extras. At the time of writing, I compiled about four journals, front and back, to use for my project. These assorted works are owned exclusively by the book's author, Nathan Jarelle. Enjoy!

Chapter One

Don't get so lost looking up that you forget to look down.
A stumble will make you humble."

As Streams run and rivers rush,
lakes remain on hold like phone calls
from oceans that don't call back from the shoreline.

Chapter Two

I break my own heart. And sometimes you do it for me.

Sadly,
there's a comfort in hurt called familiarity.
Nobody wants new pain.
An old, achy broken heart is better than a new one.

Chapter Three

Pain is in all things. Can you see it?
There is misfortune to being fortunate.
Sickness to being lovesick
And misery to wealth.
No road is perfect. Not even close.

Reside in Heart
And not on some secluded island
inside the fortress of your mind.
Live for others.
Drink harmony. Smoke tranquility.
Become a fertile soul capable of birthing peace, prosperity,
and positivity.

I am free but not dom.

Fathers, let your world revolve around the son.

Can I drink from your fountain?
Your waters are nourishing and fulfilling.
I can feel myself heal at a taste of your eloquence.

"Why do I need permission to be black?"
asked the boy whose black parents told him to behave when it
came to racism.

They enslaved us for 400 years.
Gave us new names.
Raped our mothers.
Raped our fathers.
Whipped us for running. Whipped us for dreaming.
Whipped us for reading.
Then sold us away.
Whipped us for running. Whipped us for dreaming.
Whipped us for reading.
Stole our dreams. Stole our opportunities. Stole our future.
And then called us ignorant niggers.

I no a lot of people so that I won't know a lot of people.

Chapter Four

Plant a seed, water it and birth a tree.
But some young seeds
don't get the nutrients they need.
Instead, they get forgotten by other forgotten seeds.

Black is the skin I reside in.
Love is the language I speak.
Poetry is my air. God is my sun.
Music is my Holy Water.
I am who I am. That's just how it be.
Let the rest just hate on me.

Foolishly, I fell in love with a silhouette and waited for its
owner to show.

You look nothing like what you've been through.

Chapter Five

I don't know yet if it's love I feel,
But when I think of you,
you're the sun that lights my little dark world.

It's your own fault. You hurt you.

People treat love like a winter coat.
Put you on one season. Take you off for this or that reason.
Pack you inside a box. Shove you in the back of a closet
until they need you again.
I'm not a coat or a jacket that you zip and unzip.
My love is year-round.

Now that you're gone.
they stop by to visit.
They line up one-by-one, weeping while you're asleep.
Not a phone call or a Christmas card.
Not a call last year or the year before that.
But on the day of service,
they show up carrying their lakes & their rivers.
I will drown every day for the rest of my days, brother.
Love you,
Junior.

Chapter Six

Love is like a Ferris wheel.
Go up high. Go down low.
Hang somewhere in the middle for a while.
Get off. Get on.
See the top of the world.
Then back on the ground again.
Stop. Hop off.

Start at the end of the line.
Pay for a new ticket and do it all over again.

The latitude of my gratitude
is ocean-wide.
Atlantic. Indian. Artic. You name it.
But to be Pacific.
I wish for my words
to reach every corner of the world.
Touch every heart of every walking soul.
That is my goal.

Chapter Seven

Life is difficult to explain.
How can something so remarkably beautiful
be so cruel and unfair to us all?

It feels good to have a friend in you.
To go through it all, in you.
To experience the world, in you.
To talk, laugh, cry and share things in you,
Thank you
for the friend in you.

Everyone is not your friend.
Your enemies will dress in disguise
right before your very eyes
if you don't soon realize.
Everyone is not your friend.

Don't want your money or what isn't mine.
But if you don't mind,
I would like a little more of your time.
Don't care what's on the outside
because that'll eventually fade away.
And I pray,
our souls become as inseparable
as your sun is to my day.

I breed forgiveness,
though I remain savvy with my heart,
unaware of the direction
to which sinister winds might blow.

Chapter Eight

Don't get misinformed by the uninformed.
Miseducated fools swim together
Like a school of dumb fish
waiting to get eaten by the sharks of their oppressors.

309

The world is not my oyster.
Things do not happen for a reason.
Practice does not make perfect.
Nice guys will not finish last.
Lies given to me by my ancestors shall be abolished,
like rusted chains given to slaves.
You must take what's yours while you still can.
I've decided to take what's mine
and whomever else is weak enough to let me take theirs.

Some prefer the lake while others prefer the ocean.
I prefer the motions of a body of water to cleanse my soul.
Let the rain pour down soon
with streams that run into my wildest dreams.
Lakes & Oceans.
What waters must I swim?

Chapter Nine

I'm a story with no ending.
I am a poem with debatable clarity.
I am asleep but conscious behind my own wheel.
I am dead to everyone, including myself.
I am a loss for words.
I am speechless.
I am beyond repair.
I am a life taken for granted.

You and I,
we're beyond poetry.
Beyond words.
Beyond blood.
Beyond Brooke's Rowe or any part of Philly.
We're two souls
brought together in tragic harmony.

Proudly free to be me.
Free to think. Free to dream.
Free in my heart. Free to cry.
Free not to care what others think.
Free to be me – the only way to be.

Dear Junior,
You're the moon that balances my waters.
The sun that lights up my sky.
The blood that runs through me.
You're the sail in my winds.
The strength to keep me going.
You're the brightest star I'd ever seen skip across the galaxy.
You and me?
We're beyond poetry.

Plant a seed, water it and birth a tree.
But some young seeds don't get the water they need.
Instead, they get forgotten by other forgotten seeds.

Chapter Ten

True love hurts sometimes like new shoes out of a box.
Some shoes fit just right. Some shoes don't fit at all.
Some shoes last a lifetime, and some shoes only a nighttime.
Yearn a love that feels good to stand and walk in
with warm cushy soles that escort you to your dreams.

Remove every cloud from the sky.
Give me the sun.
Let it shine bright over me,
shadowing my every move,
illuminating my awakened soul
from the horrendous cold night.

From the shoreline, I sea waves that gladly wave back at me.
I am ready to sail the world.

Chapter Eleven

Don't drown in your miseries. Paddle your fears.
Kick your legs. Tread the bayous of your subconscious.
Survive the wave and float to ~~shore~~ sure.

You can fix broken. But you can't fix done.

I was once blind, now my eyes can see,
this wondrous world, and all that was waiting for me.
My heart was jaded. I'd fallen asleep.
For days I would weep.
Now, I know where I must be.

We are the night.
Black.
Inherently feared
due to others' paranoia of the dark.

I have no words for your love.
You love me unconditionally
under one condition,
that you love me with all your heart through all of me.
And I am forever so grateful to have you.

Chapter Twelve

I know a place
colder than a Mars night
where hearts are broken
and running minds never tire.
There's a place called Brooke's Rowe.
Where black can crack
I bet you couldn't picture that.

313

I need a loyalty like the sun in the sky,
shining over me
Brightening my little dark world each day.

Blossom my child.
Don't cover up too long.
Don't stay hidden for so long
beneath the fabric of doubt.
Open up! Release your vibrancy!

Epilogue

School fools with kindness.
Bless worry with wisdom.
Burn yearns for chaos.
That is my religion.

Whatever you do
or wherever you go,
you're never too far
from the place you'll always know.
Thank you, Crawford.
Thank you, Brooke's Rowe.
For making me into the man,
This great family has come to know.

Every house, regardless of its grandeur,
has a place there where excess is stored.
Every heart, regardless of its four walls,
has a place there where pain is stored.
Let go of your secondhand goods.
Let go of your backdoor fears.
Let go of it all.

Love is a motherfucker.
Love is hard.
Some love hard.
Others are hard to love.
I used to love Love
as if love was a person
that you fall in love with.
That was until I learned
Not to be in love with Love.
Love loves nobody back, not even love itself.

What is your labor of love?
What would you do for free
or minimal guarantee?
Are you an artist by trade
or a public figure on display?
A musician? Teacher? A healer of wounds?
What is your 24/7 after your 9-to-5?

Nathan Jarelle

"Bye" and "Goodbye" are different.
Bye means see you later,
Goodbye means I can do without you.

When a heart breaks
it shatters into a thousand pieces of you
and you go flying everywhere.

Nothing in this world compares to "No Matter What" love.
No Matter What love is better than regular love.
Imagine being loved no matter what.
No state or province too far.
Regardless of who you think you are.
So, if ever you choose to love in this lifetime,
love no matter what.

The peace in my lake
Can fill an ocean.
But the pieces in your ocean
Can't fill my lake

Most are everyday
Some are once in a while.
Few are often.
But only one
is ever once in a lifetime.

Lord save me.
I'm a sea of lost dreams
Swept away by the waves of time.
Guide me along unassured sands.
Crack my sealed glass bottle.
Free the charred scroll inside of me
so that I can locate the "X" to the treasure
awaiting me in heaven.

Love is being your best self
for somebody else.
Not being your best self
for only yourself.
Love is selfless and unfair.

About the author

Nathan Jarelle is an author, poet, and first responder from the Washington, D.C. metro region. He attended Fairmont Heights High School in Prince George's County, Maryland which was once built as an all-black school during the 1950s. It was beyond Fairmont's walls where Jarelle first developed his taste for drama and literature. Upon graduation in 2001, he studied information technology at Lincoln Technical Institute in Columbia, Maryland. Right after, he returned to literature and graduated from the University of Maryland University College where he majored in English. He went on to earn a spot on the Dean's List. Jarelle's favorite literary work of all-time is Langston Hughes' "The Negro Artist and the Racial Mountain." In 2005, Jarelle began his career as a freelance author, publishing for various internet websites as a sport's columnist. In 2009, he began his career as a first responder.

Along the way, he published several underground eBooks, one of which galvanized the attention of the Washington Post and television show *Good Morning D.C.* In April of 2016, his short eBook, *Stroke of Luck*, a timeless love story providing stroke awareness in young adults, went viral. In 2019, his debut novel, *Beyond Poetry,* first broke ground. "Stop waiting to be discovered. Discover yourself," he explained in a recent interview. "The time to start is today. The future is right now."

To keep up with Nathan Jarelle, please visit his website at www.natejayreads.com. For business inquiries, questions, comments or testimonials send an email to nathjarelle@gmail. com or at P.O. Box 3004, 14605 Elm Street, Upper Marlboro, Maryland 20772.